SWEAT EQUITY

What Reviewers Say About
Aurora Rey's Work

Greener Pastures

"I was hooked on this from the very first moment and enjoyed it so much I couldn't put it down. It had everything I want from a romance and everything I have come to know and love in Aurora Rey stories. Definitely recommend this amazing story and for romance readers, it's another must read!"—*LESBIreviewed*

You Again

"*You Again* is a wonderful, feel good, low angst read with beautiful and intelligent characters that will melt your heart, and an enchanting second-chance love story."—*Rainbow Reflections*

Twice Shy

"[A] tender, foodie romance about a pair of middle aged lesbians who find partners in each other and rediscover themselves along the way. ...Rey's cute, occasionally steamy, romance reminds readers of the giddy intensity falling in love brings at any age, even as the characters negotiate the particular complexities of dating in midlife—meeting the children, dealing with exes, and revealing emotional scars. This queer love story is as sweet and light as one of Bake My Day's famous cream puffs."—*Publishers Weekly*

"This book is all the reasons why I love Aurora Rey's writing. It's delicious with a good helping of sexy. It was a nice change to read a book where the women were not in their late 20s–30s..."
—*Les Rêveur*

The Last Place You Look

"This book is the perfect book to kick your feet up, relax with a glass of wine and enjoy. I'm a big Aurora Rey fan because her deliciously engaging books feature strong women who fall for sweet butch women. It's a winning recipe."—*Les Rêveur*

"The romance is satisfying and full-bodied, with each character learning how to achieve her own goals and still be part of a couple. A heartwarming story of two lovers learning to move past their fears and commit to a shared future."—*Kirkus Reviews*

"[A] sex-positive, body-positive love story. With its warm atmosphere and sweet characters, *The Last Place You Look* is a fluffy LGBTQ+ romance about finding a second chance at love where you least expect it."—*Foreword Reviews*

"If you enjoy stories that portray two gorgeous women who slowly fall in love in the quirkiest way ever coupled with nosy and well-meaning neighbors and family members, then this is definitely the story for you!"—*Lesbian Review*

"I caught myself smiling while I was reading this book. Always a good sign. This book is a second chance of sorts since Taylor has been attracted to Julia for years but the focus is on their butch-femme relationship, a dynamic Aurora Rey writes with confidence. Taylor is so well drawn. Rey understands the fragile ego of a butch, the uncertainty behind the bravado. Her books are a pleasure to read."—*Late Night Lesbian Reads*

Ice on Wheels—*Novella in* Hot Ice

"I liked how Brooke was so attracted to Riley despite the massive grudge she had. No matter how nice or charming Riley was, Brooke was dead set on hating her. A cute enemies to lovers story."—*Bookvark*

The Inn at Netherfield Green

"I really enjoyed this book but that's not surprising because it came from the pen of Aurora Rey. This is the kind of book you read while sitting by a warm fire with a Rosemary Gin and snuggly blanket." —*Les Rêveur*

"Aurora Rey has created another striking and romantic setting with the village of Netherfield Green. With her vivid descriptions of the inn, the pub, and the surrounding village, I ended up wanting to live there myself. She also did a fantastic job creating two very different characters in Lauren and Cam."—*Rainbow Reflections*

"[Aurora Rey] constantly delivers a well-written romance that has just the right blend of humour, engaging characters, chemistry and romance."—*C-Spot Reviews*

Lead Counsel—*Novella in* **The Boss of Her**

"*Lead Counsel* by Aurora Rey is a short and sweet second chance romance. Not only was this story paced well and a delight to sink into, but there's A++ good swearing in it and has lines like this that made me all swoony because of how beautifully they're crafted." —*Lesbian Review*

Recipe for Love

"*Recipe for Love* by Aurora Rey is a gorgeous romance that's sure to delight any of the foodies out there. Be sure to keep snacks on hand when you're reading it, though, because this book will make you want to nibble on something!"—*Lesbian Review*

"So here's a few things that always get me excited when Aurora Rey publishes a new book. ...Firstly, I am guaranteed a hot butch with a sensitive side, this alone is a massive tick. Secondly, I am guaranteed to throw any diet out the window because the books always have the most delectable descriptions of food that I immediately go on the hunt for—this time it was a BLT with a difference. And lastly, hot sex scenes that personally have added to my fantasy list throughout the years! This book did not disappoint in any of those areas."—*Les Rêveur*

Autumn's Light—*Lambda Literary Award Finalist*

"This is a beautiful romance. I loved the flow of the story, loved the characters including the secondary ones, and especially loved the setting of Provincetown, Massachusetts."—*Rainbow Reflections*

"[*Autumn's Light*] was another fun addition to a great series." —Danielle Kimerer, Librarian (Nevins Memorial Library, Massachusetts)

"Aurora Rey has shown a mastery of evoking setting and this is especially evident in her Cape End romances set in Provincetown. I have loved this entire series…"—*Kitty Kat's Book Review Blog*

Spring's Wake

"[A] feel-good romance that would make a perfect beach read. The Provincetown B&B setting is richly painted, feeling both indulgent and cozy."—*RT Book Reviews*

"*Spring's Wake* has shot to number one in my age-gap romance favorites shelf."—*Les Rêveur*

"*Spring's Wake* by Aurora Rey is charming. This is the third story in Aurora Rey's Cape End romance series and every book gets better. Her stories are never the same twice and yet each one has a uniquely *her* flavour. The character work is strong and I find it exciting to see what she comes up with next."—*Lesbian Review*

Summer's Cove

"As expected in a small-town romance, *Summer's Cove* evokes a sunny, light-hearted atmosphere that matches its beach setting. …Emerson's shy pursuit of Darcy is sure to endear readers to her, though some may be put off during the moments Darcy winds tightly to the point of rigidity. Darcy desires romance yet is unwilling to disrupt her son's life to have it, and you feel for Emerson when she endeavors to show how there's room in her heart for a family."
—*RT Book Reviews*

"From the moment the characters met I was gripped and couldn't wait for the moment that it all made sense to them both and they would finally go for it. Once again, Aurora Rey writes some of the steamiest sex scenes I have read whilst being able to keep the romance going. I really think this could be one of my favorite series and can't wait to see what comes next. Keep 'em coming, Aurora."—*Les Rêveur*

Crescent City Confidential—*Lambda Literary Award Finalist*

"This book blew my socks off… [*Crescent City Confidential*] ticks all the boxes I've started to expect from Aurora Rey. It is written very well and the characters are extremely well developed; I felt like I was getting to know new friends and my excitement grew with every finished chapter."—*Les Rêveur*

"*Crescent City Confidential* is a sweet romance with a hint of thriller thrown in for good measure."—*Lesbian Review*

Built to Last

"I adored every minute of this story and it left me feeling all warm and fuzzy, even when the drama hit because these characters gave me so much hope for happiness. A great read, very enjoyable, and highly recommended."—*LESBIreviewed*

Winter's Harbor

"Winter's Harbor is a charming story. It is a sweet, gentle romance with just enough angst to keep you turning the pages. ...I adore Rey's characters and the picture she paints of Provincetown was lovely."—*Lesbian Review*

SWEAT EQUITY

by
Aurora Rey

2023

Credits
Editors: Ashley Tillman and Cindy Cresap
Production Design: Susan Ramundo
Cover Design By Ink Spiral Design

Acknowledgments

The only story I love writing more than a foodie romance is a DIY romance. Or maybe I love them equally. This one is a bit of both, and I'm profoundly grateful to all the readers who indulge— and identify with—these obsessions. Thank you for going on another adventure with me!

Huge thanks to Val and everyone at Lively Run Dairy for the personal tour and cheesemaking lesson. I learned so much and had an absolute blast. Pick up some of their cheese if you get the chance, and you won't be disappointed.

Thanks also to the Bold Strokes team, especially Ash and Cindy, who make me better and make me laugh. And thank you to my cheerleaders, beta readers, and accountability buddies: Leigh, Jaime, and Angie. You make me better and make me laugh, too, and I love you.

Dedication

For everyone who's bitten off a little
more than they could chew

CHAPTER ONE

I can't believe she bought a house without even looking at it. Who does that?" Maddie Barrow paced the length of the milking room, thrusting her hands to the side for added effect.

Clover, Maddie's best friend for enough years to be neither surprised nor bothered by her strong opinions on such things, stood from where she'd finished attaching the milker to Delilah. "It's close to the farm and she needed something fast. And cheap."

Maddie shook her head. "You know why it was cheap, right?"

Clover, still unfazed, stopped Maddie in her tracks, placing a hand on each shoulder. "That's why she has you."

Maddie prided herself on working with clients to get the most out of their home renovations with the budgets they had. But someone who'd buy a dump without even seeing it? That screamed arrogant or stupid, and she didn't do well with either. "Well, it's not going to be cheap to make it livable, that's for sure."

Clover didn't release her shoulders. "You're going to take care of her, right? I need her to stick around for a while."

Maddie huffed out a sigh and grumbled a bit on principle. "I'll do what I can."

Clover yanked her into a hug. "I'd expect nothing less."

"For the record, I don't think she's demonstrated much in the way of sound judgment so far. I'd be careful how much latitude you give her."

Clover waved her off. "She's a brilliant cheese maker who trained in France. She is hands down the best and most qualified person I interviewed."

"And?" She knew the rest of the story.

"And I got her really, really cheap." Clover winked.

Maddie shook her head. Again.

"Cheap by cheese maker standards. It's a very generous salary for the area," Clover said.

By area, Clover meant their town of about six thousand in the foothills of the Green Mountains. Too far from both Bennington and Brattleboro to be a bedroom community of either, it basically fell into the category of small town in rural Vermont—big on charm but not much else. Maddie loved it, but it didn't manage to attract much in the way of newcomers. That Clover managed to coax anyone to relocate counted as a feat. Someone who'd worked in California and trained in France? A veritable triumph.

"You're thinking about how much of that salary you're going to put in your pocket, aren't you?" Clover regarded her with knowing amusement.

"I'm thinking that I hope she doesn't take one look at the money pit she bought and hightail it out of here."

"You're such a pessimist," Clover said.

"I'm a realist. Practical." Maddie glanced at her watch. "And she's officially late."

Clover rolled her eyes. "She's driving across the country. Cut the woman a little slack."

Maddie wasn't actually bothered by the lateness. Or offended or whatever. It was just that this whole arrangement left her with a bad feeling. For Clover's sake, she wanted Sy Travino's arrival in Bedlington to go off without a hitch. But for as much as she didn't want it to be a disaster, she didn't have a lot of confidence it would go well.

At the sound of tires on gravel outside, Clover tipped her head. It might have been her own moment of triumph, but Maddie couldn't help but feel like maybe it was Sy, cosmically sensing the precise moment to prove Maddie wrong. If that idea hadn't already set her on edge, the sight of a lime green hatchback would have. "You know that's not going to get her through winter, right?"

Clover waved her off. "Stop being fussy and come meet her."

Maddie trailed a couple of steps behind, dubious about meeting someone she already felt inclined to dislike. Not dislike. That was such a strong word. Sy might turn out to be a perfectly pleasant sort of person, clueless but eager to make a go of living and working here.

The engine cut and the door opened. She watched Sy extricate herself from the driver's side, and pleasant quickly became the absolute last word in Maddie's mind. Perfect remained, but with an entirely new meaning. Long limbs and a broad-shouldered torso, black hair cut short and styled in a way that had Maddie's fingers itching to touch—the stuff of butch fantasies. Specifically, her butch fantasies. Even Sy's face, with its bronze skin and strong jaw, radiated the sort of masc confidence that would snag Maddie's attention across a crowded room.

"You made it." Clover's buoyant greeting cut through the haze of Maddie's instant and inconvenient attraction.

"I thought Ohio might do me in, but yes. At your service." Sy gave a slight bow, then turned her attention to Maddie. "Hi. Sy Travino. I'm here to make the cheese."

Maddie shook the hand Sy extended but struggled to do much more than nod.

"This is Maddie Barrow. My best friend, but also the best general contractor in Vermont." Clover elbowed her. "Aren't you, Maddie?"

She cleared her throat, now annoyed with herself as much as Sy. "Not sure about being the best, but we do good work. We're also the only contractors in town."

Sy seemed to take her awkward self-description in stride. "From what Clover has told me, I think you're being modest. Either way, I appreciate your willingness to take the job. I've been told I need a new roof."

A new roof wasn't the half of it, but at least it meant Sy had a clue about the state of things. "Clover thought you might want to check things out straight away so we could work up an estimate and get started before the weather turns."

Sy laughed. "Sounds ominous."

Maddie laughed in spite of herself. "Well, you're going to want to be sealed up tight before we find ourselves with a couple feet of snow on the ground."

Sy's expression turned serious. "Yes. Do that, please."

Clover laughed, then. "Have you even seen snow?"

"Once. I went skiing with some of my friends in culinary school." Sy shrugged. "Never made it off the bunny slope and that was that."

Clover had mentioned Sy was from New Mexico, and Sy's short black hair and golden skin hinted that she was Latinx. But it had never occurred to her that Sy might be clueless about winter on top of everything else. Parts of New Mexico got snow, right? Even if much of the state was desert. Her initial suspicion swelled into full-fledged concern that Clover's new hire wouldn't last a season. Which, of course, kicked her protective instincts into high gear. "We'll make sure you're winter ready."

Sy bowed again, this time at Maddie. "Then I'm at your service, too."

They'd see about that. Maddie made a sweeping gesture with her hand. "Do you want to see things here before we go?"

Sy looked genuinely eager at the prospect. "You wouldn't mind?"

"Not at all." Since Clover practically vibrated with enthusiasm, it seemed like the least she could do. Besides, the cheese room was slated for some upgrades as well. They wouldn't be hashing through those plans for a couple of weeks still, but the sooner Sy got a feel for the space, the better she'd be able to guide the decisions.

"Do you want to come?" Clover asked, already knowing the answer.

"I've got a couple of calls to make, so I'll let you two have at it. Sy, I assume you have the address. Shall I meet you there in half an hour or so?"

"That sounds great. Thanks." Sy smiled and it sent Maddie's thoughts to places they had no business going.

"Of course." She offered a parting wave. "I'll text you later, Clo."

Clover returned the wave, but her attention was already on Sy. And the prospect of talking cheese. Maddie took that as her cue to get out of there. Because she actually did have calls to make. But also, if she was being honest, because she could use a minute to herself. Because for all that Clover had raved about her new cheese maker, she'd neglected to mention that said cheese maker was distractingly, disarmingly hot.

❖

Sy made the five-minute drive to her new house, still riding the high of seeing the space where she'd have full domain to craft, experiment, and produce cheese exactly the way she wanted. Clover had promised as much, but only after seeing the setup firsthand did reality sink in. It might be a small operation, but it would be hers.

Sort of like this house. She'd never owned a house before. Even as a kid, she and her mom had rented. Apartments had given way to houses, but they'd always belonged to someone else. In truth, she hadn't minded. They never lived anywhere fancy, but the places had been nice enough. She'd been able to decorate her room how she wanted and anytime something had gone wrong, there'd been someone to call.

That option didn't really exist in Bedlington. Sure, there was an odd room to rent here and there, but she'd promised herself no more roommates. The closest apartment she'd been able to find was two towns over and, given the hours she intended to work, that was a dealbreaker. So, here she was. Homeowner.

Since Maddie had parked in the street out front, Sy pulled into the driveway and took the spot in front of the tiny garage. The maple trees in the front yard were aflame with vibrant reds and yellows that she'd only seen in pictures. She wasn't prone to finding things charming, but that was the word that came to mind. Especially with a gorgeous redhead in snug jeans and work boots standing in the confetti of leaves that had already fallen.

The charm lasted all of thirty seconds. She got out of the car and joined Maddie, who stood with her arms folded and a scowl on her face. "What's wrong?"

Maddie pointed to the roof. "You see that dip there? That's not good."

She breathed an internal sigh of relief, glad Maddie was irritated with the house and not with her. "We already knew the roof was shot, didn't we?"

"Yeah, but there's shot and there's actively leaking. That? That says leak."

"Not the end of the world, right? Replacing the roof will fix that?" She wasn't an expert or anything, but that felt pretty basic.

Maddie shook her head, and Sy was pretty sure an eye roll accompanied it. "It won't fix any water damage that's happened in the meantime."

Oh. "I guess we should take a look."

"Yeah. Let's start in the attic and work our way down."

Seemed logical enough. "You're the boss."

They headed up the crumbling front walk, but both stopped short of the door. "You have the key, right?" Maddie asked.

"Right. Sorry." Sy laughed and fished out the keys she'd stuffed in her pocket.

Inside, dust seemed to envelop them. Which was a weird way to describe it since there was no furniture and therefore no obvious surfaces for it to settle on. It hung in the air, though. Like cobwebs that couldn't quite organize themselves. She flipped a switch, but nothing happened. "Huh. I called the power company. It's supposed to be on."

Maddie pointed to the ceiling. "No bulb."

"Ah." A relief, even if it made her feel a bit foolish.

Although she mostly wanted to get a look at the kitchen, Sy led the way upstairs, then up the much narrower staircase to the attic. More than a crawl space, but not by much. Again, no light bulb, but between the tiny window at the far end and the flashlight Maddie seemed to pull out of thin air, they were able to get a decent enough view of the roof joists and rafters, along with some insulation that had seen better days.

"This is all going to have to go." Maddie gestured to the dark patch that lined up with the sagging spot they'd seen from the outside.

"Define all." What she really wanted to say was "tell me how much it's going to cost," but that seemed like a bad way to start off.

"These rafters and all the roof decking here." Maddie gestured to about a quarter of the roof.

"Okay." Even without an answer to her unspoken question, dollar signs flitted through her mind.

"The insulation will need to be replaced, too, but it doesn't look like much water has gotten all the way through."

She liked the sound of that.

"I'll work up an estimate on the work that has to be done to make things structurally sound. Then we can get into the more cosmetic stuff."

She'd sort of hoped the roof would be the only thing in that first category, but again, it didn't seem like the thing to say. "All right."

"Let's check out the bedrooms and bath on the second floor, then we can do the main level and basement."

It struck her that, even though only two of the floors held living spaces, she technically owned a four-story structure. A far cry from the ranches she'd grown up in. "I'll follow you."

Unfortunately, things only got worse as they made their way down. The leak from the roof had made its way through, leaving a sagging ceiling in the main bedroom. And the bathroom didn't technically need to be gutted, but it might as well have. The fixtures weren't just ugly; they were cracked and, in the case of the sink, coming off the wall.

She resisted the urge to cuss or complain, more out of pride than propriety. Something told her Maddie already didn't think very highly of her. No need to exacerbate the situation.

By the time they made it back downstairs and detoured to scope out the basement, her fantasies of a six-burner stove and quartz countertops had vanished in a cloud of, as Maddie started calling them, the must-dos. The saving grace was a serviceable furnace, a water heater that hopefully had a few good years left in it, and some wood floors that could be beautifully refinished but didn't have to be. The electrical panel was another story.

They ended in the kitchen, a lovely large space marred by some late eighties cabinetry and mismatched appliances that had seen better days. Sy tried not to think about the debt she'd go into for just the essentials, but she struggled to keep doom and gloom at bay.

"Are you okay? You look a little shell-shocked." Maddie regarded her with what appeared to be equal parts pity and judgment.

"Just trying to take it all in. I've never done any of this before."

"Reno, you mean?"

She blew out a breath. "All of it. Owning a house. Being the one responsible for the must-dos. Paying for the must-dos."

"Oh." Maddie let the word hang, and that single syllable said so much.

"Yeah."

"There's this thing called a home inspection. I know it's not helpful now, but, well, there's a reason for them."

Sy laughed because what else was there to do? "Now she tells me."

"All joking aside, it really is a thing. They don't feel cheap in the moment, but they're a hell of a lot cheaper than the kind of surprises you could find after the fact. Especially in an old house. I don't know who your Realtor was, but if they didn't explain it to you, I'd seriously question their ethics."

It was hard to tell if Maddie was on a roll in general, or if she found particular satisfaction in scolding Sy. Though, really, did it matter? "He may have mentioned it."

Maddie's disapproving look packed even more punch than her words.

"I needed to move quickly, and the owner had already disclosed the worst of it. Or what I assumed was the worst of it." She resisted cringing at her own defensiveness.

Maddie opened her mouth, then closed it. She closed her eyes for a moment and took a deep breath. Sy couldn't decide whether she was trying for calm or gearing up for a full-blown tirade about all the good assuming did.

"I promised Clover I'd be here. I wasn't going to make that happen if I didn't have a place to live."

Playing the Clover card proved to be the right move. Maddie looked her in the eye and gave a decisive nod. "We're going to make it work. It's going to be okay."

"I appreciate the vote of confidence, even if you're lying." Not something she made a habit of saying to beautiful women who had the power to cost her a shit-ton of money.

"It's not going to be cheap, but I've saved worse. And your being here is really important to Clover, which means it's important to me." Maddie gave another brisk nod, as though she needed to say that last part for herself as much as for Sy.

"I appreciate that, too. So, what next? You work up some numbers and I sign over my firstborn?"

Maddie laughed then. "Don't worry. I don't take offspring as collateral."

"Oh, good. Especially since I have no intention of birthing any babies anytime soon."

"Noted." Maddie's smile became more of a smirk and Sy had a flash of wondering what it would be like to kiss her.

She shoved the thought aside as quickly as it came. She had no business developing the hots for her contractor. Or her new boss's best friend. Even if Maddie's green eyes danced with humor and the dusting of freckles on her alabaster skin made Sy think of the Strawberry Shortcake doll she had as a kid. "So, you'll be in touch?"

"I'll work up an initial estimate and as long as you're ready to sign off, we can start the roof work next week."

"Really?" It was pressing for her, obviously, but she hadn't expected the feeling to be mutual.

"I knew the situation was dire, so I took the liberty of penciling you in."

Since she couldn't tell if that should be a point of pride or shame, she went for a smile. "Thanks. I think."

"Where are you staying in the meantime?" Maddie asked.

Clover had offered her spare room, but just the thought gave her flashbacks of bunking with fellow culinary school grads trying to hustle their way into a decent living in California. "Here."

Maddie blinked one of those waiting-for-the-punchline blinks.

"I know it's not ideal, but I've got an air mattress and I'm used to roughing it," Sy said.

Maddie's lips pursed this way and that, like she was debating how much to argue. "I'd suggest camping out down here, then, at least until the roof is on and we've dealt with any mold. And we'll have to discuss things when the water needs to be shut off."

Sy lifted both hands, channeling a level of easy-going she didn't entirely feel. "It's all good. I'm flexible."

"Okay. Well, then. I guess I'll leave you to unpack. I'll have an initial bid for the roof for you tomorrow."

"Yeah?"

"You'll need to make lots of decisions along the way, but that one is pretty basic." Maddie shrugged. "As in, pick your shingle color."

"I feel like I should say 'surprise me.'" She considered the comment at least as funny as the one about her first born, but Maddie didn't even crack a smile.

"I'll bring you samples. You'll be at the farm?"

Sy cleared her throat. "Yeah. But I can meet you if that's easier."

Maddie waved her off. "I'll stop by."

With that settled, Maddie headed for the front door. Despite the hiccup in the banter they had going, Sy was almost reluctant to see her go. Silly, really. She had plenty to do. Including hunting down some groceries and heavy duty cleaning supplies. "I'll see you sometime tomorrow, then."

Maddie opened the door but hesitated. After a second of seeming indecision, she smiled. "Good luck with your air mattress."

CHAPTER TWO

Maddie dropped into the chair behind her desk at the Barrow Brothers Construction main office. Main office, only office. Same difference. The space was empty except for her baby sister, Logan, typing away with all the attention of a woman on a mission. She respected that about Logan, even when the tenacity occasionally got on her nerves. "Well, that was an adventure."

Logan looked up from her computer, blinking in surprise like she'd only just noticed Maddie was there. "What was an adventure?"

Despite being close to seven years her junior, Logan was all about the serious. Girl had been born serious, and her biggest struggle in life thus far was being the baby of the family and therefore not taken as seriously as she'd like. "Clover's new cheese maker. Bought an old house based on some pictures and proximity to the farm, and I'm pretty sure she's regretting her life choices."

Logan came over to her desk, brow furrowed and frown firmly in place. "Is she being difficult about it?"

"No, no. Nothing like that. Clueless, mostly. About houses and owning them. And I'm pretty sure about New England and winter and a whole lot else."

Logan's frown intensified. Clover might be Maddie's best friend, but they were all practically family. "Is she clueless about cheese?"

Maddie shrugged. "Clover said she apprenticed with one of the best cheese makers in France."

"That's nothing to sneeze at."

"And she's a trained chef who spent a few years in fancy restaurants in LA before that." It struck her as an odd trajectory, but what did she know? "Clover thinks it gives her depth."

Logan snorted at the last bit, and Maddie couldn't blame her. Clover had a habit of giving everyone the benefit of the doubt, whether or not they deserved it. Which, of course, Clover argued was exactly the point. "Do you think she's going to stick around?" Logan asked.

"Hard to say. But she's prepared to sign a contract for a new roof and wants a bid for a whole mess of other work on the house, so she must think she is."

"Hopefully she won't head for the hills at the first sign of snow."

"Or back to the desert." Though saying that made her wonder what made Sy flee the desert in the first place. It didn't appeal to her, but for Sy it was home. And home was a language Maddie spoke fluently.

"Or France." Logan stuck out both hands. "Why would anyone move to France and then leave?"

Yet another thing to wonder. Maybe Sy had family she wanted to be closer to. But was Vermont all that much closer to New Mexico than France? Obviously, yes. And easier to get to, even if Bedlington felt out of the way to just about everything. "I guess we'll find out soon enough. About her sticking around at least. The rest is none of our business."

"Mm-hmm." Logan returned to her desk, but not before dropping a totally judgmental eye roll.

"Don't even with that," Maddie said. Logan teased her about being a busybody, but all she really did was take a professionally appropriate personal interest in her clients. A trait that made her better equipped to give those clients exactly what they wanted. Not to mention more likely to refer their friends and family to Barrow Brothers, which maybe hadn't been a big deal a decade ago but mattered now more than ever.

"I'm just saying, she sounds like a puzzle, and I know how you love those."

"I like puzzles I can solve," Maddie grumbled. Something told her Sy would not be that. "Anyway. What are you working on?"

Logan's whole face lit up. "Jack finished the estimate for the electrical work at the library and there's some room left in the budget based on the grant they got, so I'm working up a couple of options for them to consider."

"Nice." They didn't do a lot of projects outside of residential, but they also didn't turn down business. The library job would barely cover expenses, but it would make for fantastic PR. They might not have a lot of competition for business, but in a town their size, getting people to think about home improvements in the first place counted as a win. "What do you have so far?"

"A redesigned circulation desk and a first floor layout flip that would give them a fully accessible meeting room."

"I hope they pick the meeting room." It would serve the community better. It would also tick another box in the good PR column.

"If I play my cards right, they can have both."

"Yeah?" Logan pinched pennies like nobody's business but still. Her artistic vision often got the better of her.

"If I throw in a few hours off the clock," Logan said.

And there it was. "Define few."

"More than ten, less than a hundred?"

For as serious as Logan could be, she could also be the biggest freaking bleeding heart. "How about less than twenty?"

"Forty, but twenty of them are on my own time."

"Thirty and I'll give you ten," Maddie said. Because Logan wasn't the only one with a bleeding heart. Even if she made a point of keeping hers more to herself.

"Deal." For all her frowning before, Logan shot a grin across the room that made her look about sixteen.

Maddie laughed because, at the end of the day, they'd all pitch in. It was the library, after all. Who didn't love the library?

With that settled, she booted her computer and got to work, sending her roofers a note that they were just waiting on a final sign-off and materials selection. Then she tackled a more thorough estimate and scope of work for Sy. She got about twenty line items in before her phone buzzed with a string of texts from Clover.

How did it go?

You didn't scare her off, did you?

How bad is the house?

I really need her to stay.

I know you know this. Sorry.

Where are you?

Maddie chewed her lip for a second, debating how much to share, before dashing off a reply. *It's fine. The house isn't but it will be. Assuming she can afford it.*

When Clover didn't answer, she dove back into the work estimate. So much would depend on Sy's choice of materials and finishes, but at least she could give a ballpark for the guts of the work so Sy could make an informed decision. Hopefully Sy wouldn't be one of those clients who watched all the home design shows and wanted the high end finishes even if they didn't match the style of the house. Or wishy-washy types who changed their mind a thousand times.

Something told her wishy-washy was the last word in the world that would describe Sy. No, Sy struck her as a confident, decisive sort, at least when it came to things in her wheelhouse. Would she get to see that side of Sy? Did she want to?

No. Yes. Maybe.

She wanted Sy to succeed for Clover's sake. That mattered. The rest? The rest would be nothing more than another job on the Barrow Brothers docket.

She'd do the work and bring a sad old house back to life, cash her paycheck and go about her life as normal. She wouldn't waste a second thinking about the way Sy's hand felt strong and sure in hers, the way her skin had rough patches in all the right spots. Or about those onyx eyes a girl could oh so easily get lost in. The way that glossy black hair might feel sliding through her fingers or the way her body might feel pressing Maddie's against a wall.

Maddie huffed out a breath. Fine. She wouldn't waste another second thinking about those things.

❖

After unloading her car and ensuring the fridge was in working order, Sy ventured to Bedlington's one and only grocery store. Nothing to write home about, but it stocked the essentials, including local jellies and maple syrup. Notably absent was any selection of Grumpy Old Goat chèvre, which she'd have to ask Clover about. After getting home and unpacking again, she calculated she'd just catch the second half of her mom's lunch hour and decided to try calling her sooner rather than later.

"Well, if it isn't my world traveler."

Sy closed her eyes for a moment, shutting out the chaos of boxes and buckets and brooms that surrounded her and basking in the familiarity of her mother's voice. When nothing else in the world made sense, she could count on that voice. "Hi, Mama."

"Hi, mija. Did you make it to Vermont?"

"I did. A few hours ago, actually. I stopped by the farm, and now I'm standing in the middle of my new living room."

"World traveler and home owner. Have I told you lately how proud of you I am?"

Only every other time they spoke. "I think so. I also think I might be more of a money pit owner."

"Oh, no. Is it very bad?"

She had no intention of dumping her looming money woes on the woman who'd singlehandedly raised her and put her through culinary school, but they were close enough that she'd never outright lie. "More than I bargained for, but Clover's best friend is a contractor, so I know I'll be working with someone I can trust."

"It's all blessings and curses, isn't it?"

Sy chuckled at the phrase, one her mother had used as far back as she could remember. "Something like that."

"What else?"

"I might need a new wardrobe, too." She shivered at the idea of winter in New England more than the chill in the house.

"For making cheese?" Mama asked.

"For snow." She'd picked up what she thought was a decent coat and it barely held up to the blustery fall day. And she had a sinking feeling Maddie's reference to two feet of snow was not exaggeration.

"I can send you some money."

She thought of her dwindling savings and the bills from Maddie that were about to start rolling in. "You will do no such thing."

Mama huffed. "It's a mother's prerogative to take care of her child, even after they've grown up."

She longed for the day she could take care of her mother for a change. It had fueled her move to LA, where the restaurant scene had the potential to catapult careers. Only instead of launching, she'd crashed and burned. Hopefully, this new chapter would be different and that day wouldn't be too far off. "Save your pennies and come visit me. That's what I really want."

That got her a chuckle. "Fine. I always wanted to see New England."

"Give me a couple of months. I'll be able to play tour guide and put a roof over your head." Literally.

"I can't wait. Now, tell me some good things."

Another of her mother's signature phrases, it reminded Sy there was always room to look on the bright side. "My space at the farm is fantastic. It has the basics already, so I can get started right away. But Clover has plans to add and upgrade the equipment to branch into hard cheeses and wants my input on it."

"That's very exciting. And since I know you'll practically live at work, the house stuff won't feel so stressful."

That was one way of looking at it. "Exactly."

"What else?" Mama asked.

As she wandered among the boxes, the trees in the front yard came into view. "It's fall here and all that carrying on people do about the foliage is legit. My lawn needs to be mowed, but the view out my front windows is a postcard."

"Yard needs to be mowed." Mama tutted.

"I know, right?" Even when they'd upgraded to places with yards, it was all native plants and hardscaping to conserve water.

"You'll have to send me pictures."

She conjured a few angles that wouldn't put the worst of the work to be done on display. "I will."

"The farm, too. I like to see where you spend your days."

"I promise." That would be the easy part. It might not be as picturesque as the dairy in the Loire Valley where she'd spend the last year, but it was pretty damn idyllic. Big red barn with a crumbling stone wall that had helped give Falling Barn Farm its name back in the sixties when it had been purchased by a bunch of hippies who set it up as a co-op. Grazing goats that, in the true manner of goats, leapt into the air for no reason beyond the inspiration of the moment.

"You sound tired," Mama said.

"I am, but it's from all the driving. It's good. I'm good."

Mama tutted again, more mother hen than amusement this time.

"What about you? What's good?" Sy looked for a place to sit before remembering she didn't own any furniture. She settled on the floor instead, kicking her legs out in front of her and wondering if there were any thrift stores nearby.

Meanwhile, Mama filled her in on Nina, the neighbor getting a good riddance divorce, and Gigi, the cocker spaniel they'd adopted when Sy was in high school, whose arthritis seemed to be improving on the new medication the vet had prescribed. She filed away the details but mostly enjoyed listening to the sounds of home. By the time they hung up, her mom's lunch hour was more than done, and Sy's motivation for cleaning had waned.

She swept the downstairs bedroom, got the air mattress set up, and called it good enough. A quick internet search revealed no thrift stores in Bedlington, but two in the next town over. She'd check them out over the weekend. It would do her good to explore. And if she managed to pick up a chair or two—or maybe a dresser—in the process, bonus.

CHAPTER THREE

"Sixteen thousand dollars?" Sy looked from the sheet of paper outlining the cost to Maddie. "For a roof?"

Maddie managed to neither sigh nor swear. Though she cringed internally at the totals on the pieces of paper she'd yet to pull out, the ones outlining the cost for the rest of the renovation. "It's a competitive price, especially with the amount of structural repair that needs to be done."

Sy cringed and there was nothing internal about it. "I believe you. It's just way more than I bargained for."

She could sympathize, in theory at least. She made a point of doing her homework before the first exchange with anyone she intended to hire or buy from. But biting off more than she could chew? Been there, done that. "The supply chain hasn't helped matters. Lumber is still running twenty-five percent more than it did a couple of years ago."

Sy nodded, more defeat than disbelief. "I mean doing it in the first place, not the price. Obviously, the cost is non-negotiable. And I trust you're giving me a fair price."

She appreciated the distinction, even if it had more to do with their mutual connection to Clover than anything Sy might know or believe about her. "I hate to say this, but I feel like we should discuss the full scope of work before moving forward."

"Make sure I don't freak out and do a big never mind?" Sy asked.

Maddie chuckled. "Something like that."

"Okay. Lay it on me."

She handed over the document. "You'll see a lot of ranges, especially in the kitchen and bathroom. That will depend on the materials you go with. I started with builder's grade and went up to nice without being ostentatious in a house this size and age."

"Okay." Sy scanned the first page before flipping to the next. She didn't linger though, thumbing instead to the end. "Whoa."

"Yeah." She'd never apologize for the cost of the work she did, but she could acknowledge it went beyond the means of a lot of people.

Sy looked at her, a low-grade panic in her eyes. "I can't afford this."

"You can pick and choose some things to do now, others to do later if at all. I did draw up a remediation plan in case you wanted to look at that, too."

"Remediation plan?" Sy made a face. "That sounds ominous."

"Not ominous, just bare bones. The work that would make the house livable in the eyes of a lender in case you decided to sell." She didn't love the language, but she did embrace apples-to-apples industry standards.

"But I'm not looking to sell," Sy said.

"Right. Sorry. I didn't mean to imply that. It just means the house is considered safe to live in."

Sy's face fell. "And it's not that now."

"Well, you got a mortgage, I assume, so it's not utterly dire. There are some federal lending programs with higher standards," Maddie said.

At that, Sy scrubbed both hands over her face. "What am I going to do?"

A little homework before you drop close to a hundred grand on something? Since saying that would be both snarky and unhelpful, she whipped out the option she really hoped she wouldn't have to. "You could do some of the work yourself."

Sy perked up at the mere existence of another option, but her eyes remained wary. "I don't know anything about houses."

She smiled, in part to be encouraging and in part because it was nice to have Sy admit it rather than bluster over her ignorance. "So you've said. I'd coach you and it would be mostly grunt work. If you're willing to put in the sweat, you can turn it into equity."

"Huh." Sy seemed to mull the offer, like she couldn't decide if it was legit or a pity move.

Since it was technically both, Maddie opted not to elaborate on her motivations. "It's actually called sweat equity."

That got a smirk out of Sy. And damn it all if it wasn't a dangerously good look on her. "You know, I've heard the phrase."

The playful callout made Maddie blush. Clover had literally made the same offer to Sy. A modest salary with stake in the business. Standard entrepreneurial fare and Clover's plan to grow the company faster than her existing capital would allow. "Right."

"Do you offer that to all your clients?"

"Absolutely not." She hadn't been going for emphatic, but that's what came out.

Again with the smirk. "Why are you making an exception for me?"

She really shouldn't but indulged in giving Sy a long, slow once-over. "You seem able-bodied."

Sy opened her mouth but closed it again without speaking.

"Kidding." Or at least she knew better than to admit to meaning it. "You being here is important to Clover, and Clover is important to me. Besides, I like pulling cool old houses back from the brink instead of seeing them fall into complete disrepair."

Sy nodded, but Maddie would swear a trace of color rose in her cheeks. "Totally. That makes sense." She coughed. "And for what it's worth, working with Clover and making something happen here is important to me."

"So, we have something in common." Which wasn't a terrible place to start.

"We do." Sy grinned. If the smirk was dangerous, that grin was lethal.

"Okay. I know you have work, obviously, so maybe we can plan to meet up on the weekends to go over the stuff you'll be doing?"

For the first time since Maddie handed over the estimates, Sy seemed confident. "I can shift my schedule at the farm, too. I plan to put in more than forty hours a week, but since I'm mostly working solo, it doesn't matter when or how those shake out."

"I'm sure we'll figure it out." Lord knew she wasn't the queen of keeping regular hours, either.

"What do you need from me now?"

"A deposit for the roof, so I can get those guys working. That's not something either of us will touch. And a signature on the remediation bid. That'll get the ball rolling, and you can decide what to add in based on how much work you're ultimately able to do." It would be a start. And hopefully something neither of them would regret in the end.

"Excellent. Let me grab a pen." Sy went over to a box with OFFICE scrawled across the side. She returned with both a pen and a checkbook.

Maddie handed her the contract first and Sy signed it without further examination. While she wrote the check, Maddie studied the scribble. "Is Sy a nickname?"

Sy tore the check from the book and handed it over. "Yeah. I was named after my grandma."

Maddie glanced at the top right corner and barely resisted a laugh. "Sylvia."

"Not even my mother calls me that anymore. I've been Sy since kindergarten."

She smiled at the emphatic response, and at having one more thing in common. "I'm named after my grandmother, too."

"Madeleine?"

"You'd think. Marigold, actually. But we already had a Mary in the family." She shrugged. "And yes, it's all very WASPy."

Sy laughed. "I wasn't gonna say it."

"Can't pick family, right?" Though she wouldn't pick another for the world.

Sy's features softened. "No."

"Are you close with yours?" She hadn't meant to stray into personal territory, but Sy was turning out to be almost too easy to talk to.

"My mom, yes. She raised me by herself. And a bunch of aunts and uncles and cousins and stuff. You?"

"Barrow Brothers is the family business. Fourth generation. My dad and uncle run it. My sister, brother, and I all work there. We'll take over some day." Not that anyone seemed in any hurry to retire.

Sy's eyes went wide. "Wow."

"We get on each other's nerves now and then, but it's mostly great." Better now that they were dragging the whole operation into the twenty-first century.

"Will I get to meet the whole fam during the project?"

She smiled. "Probably. My brother, Jack, is the electrician of the group and my sister, Logan, does design on top of being part of the crew."

"That's really cool."

She resisted a cheeky reply, if for no other reason than she'd already been more casual with Sy than she would a new client under normal circumstances. And while the personal connection with Clover made these circumstances not exactly normal, some reasonable boundaries would do her some good. Especially if she was signing on for the kind of one-on-one time her project proposal would entail. "Okay, so, um, demo will be first. I'll text you to set up some times. Oh, and to let you know what day to expect the roofers. They tend to show up at dawn, so it's good to know when that's going to happen."

Sy laughed and, much like the smirk and the smile, it had the potential to get Maddie into trouble. "Thanks."

"Okay. I'll, um, let you go then." If for no other reason than she needed to stop saying "okay" and "um."

"Sounds good. Thank you for being willing to work with me. Like, truly thank you. I obviously got in over my head, and I need a place to live."

She offered another decisive nod and her good-byes. In her truck, she checked her email and replied to texts from Logan and her father. Then she took a deep breath and headed over to the kitchen reno job she had going on the other side of town. She rolled down the window and let the brisk fall air fill her lungs. And despite her best intentions to leave all thoughts of Sy behind, that look of gratitude Sy gave her in the end lingered in her mind.

❖

Until the condenser and shelving came in for the aging room, Sy was limited in how much she could experiment with new cheeses, including the brie and hard styles she'd discussed with Clover during her interview. Still, she had the cooler space to try her hand at a couple of blues and there was a whole world of flavor profiles she wanted to add to the existing Grumpy Old Goat chèvre.

The latter was on her docket for the day. She didn't know how it would go over in Vermont, but she'd ordered some dried ancho chiles that she wanted to pair with smoked salt. And because she had promised Clover a couple of nods to New England—ones that would fit right in on a traditional Thanksgiving table—she wanted to play with a fennel and orange zest combo and something TBD with cranberries. Many cheese makers considered those sorts of add-ins beneath them, but the chef in her found it a perfect way to keep her culinary muscles flexed.

She prepped the pasteurizer and filled it with the milk that had come in the day before, both from Clover's herd and the farm where she sourced the additional milk needed to keep up with production. If all went well, that volume would have to double within the year. But first things first.

She set the milk to heat and opened the logbook to track the details of the day's batch—time, temperature, the precise amount of culture used to acidify the milk and set the curd. It was the work she'd done the first three months of her apprenticeship and the foundational process for all cheese making. The repetition could get boring, but Sy never ceased to marvel at the ways science and art danced together to make magic.

"How's my fromager this morning?" Clover called the greeting from the door.

"Fantastic, thank you. And hard at work on a fresh batch to play with. You'll need to suit up if you want to come in."

Clover disappeared momentarily, returning in a hairnet and a pair of bright blue booties over her work boots. "You have to tell me when you're going to play. I don't want to be left out."

Sy laughed. "I was going to call you in before the fun started."

"Damn right you were." Clover elbowed her in the ribs. "What's today's fun?"

"Well, since we're still waiting on the new press and stuff for the aging room, I thought I'd start a batch of chèvre we can use to sort out the seasonal flavors."

Clover clapped her hands together and rubbed them with the delight of a cartoon villain. "Excellent."

Sy checked her watch and did some mental math. "This batch won't be ready for cutting until tomorrow, obviously, but I've got some I made yesterday and held back from packaging. I thought we could use that to narrow down the basic profiles we want, then I'll use this to nail down the nuance."

"Is it wrong that I'm a little turned on when you talk like that?" Clover asked.

They hadn't worked together long, but she knew Clover well enough to know the comment had nothing to do with her and everything to do with the cheese. "I'd be disappointed if you weren't."

"Speaking of turned on, how was your meeting with Maddie?"

Heat rose in Sy's cheeks at the thought of the gorgeous contractor she'd met with that morning. "I'm sorry?"

"Maddie. The contractor. My best friend. The one who's working on your house?"

Sy nodded and scrambled for something remotely appropriate to say.

"She's always joking about how sexy lumber and power tools are. You should definitely tease her about that if the opportunity comes up," Clover said.

"Ah." Sy continued to blush, only now it was because she felt like an idiot as opposed to feeling like she'd been found out for having the hots for her boss's best friend.

Clover frowned. "It went okay, right? Your meeting?"

"Oh, yeah. Totally." Her nodding kicked into high gear. "I mean, the house needs way more work than I can afford, but Maddie said she'd help me sort out some of the unskilled labor I can do on my own."

"I'm sorry it needs a lot. I feel bad you had to buy it without being able to see it first."

Sy lifted a hand. "My own decision. I didn't want to rent far away and not be able to work the hours I want to work."

Clover made a tsking sound. "So now you'll be close but won't be able to work because you're drowning in DIY projects."

Her other hand came up. "I swear it won't impact my work. I've got evenings and weekends, and honestly, not much of a life."

"Whoa, whoa, whoa. Slow down there, cowboy." Clover gripped her shoulder. "I was kidding."

Sy blew out a breath, feeling foolish for an entirely different reason. "Sorry."

"Those restaurants really fucked you up, didn't they?"

She didn't like griping about past employers, but she didn't lie, either. "Yeah."

"Well, none of that here. I trust you to do good work and I'll tell you if it feels like something isn't working. I trust you to do the same. Deal?"

Sy nodded. "Yeah. Totally."

"Good." Clover grinned, clearly happy to be done with serious talk. "Now, tell me all about how Maddie is going to make you get your hands dirty."

She did, at least to the extent she understood what Maddie had attempted to explain. Much of it was beyond her, but she figured Maddie would give clear directions and not let her mess anything up too badly. Clover listened, offered little snippets of advice from her own attempts at sprucing up her house. Under the watchful eye of Maddie, of course.

"As long as my roof doesn't leak and I have a kitchen I can use, the rest is gravy. Oh, and a shower. I do feel strongly about being able to take showers."

Clover gave a knowing smile. "Don't forget heat. You don't want to find yourself without that around here."

"Right. That, too." Maddie had said the furnace was in good working order, and it seemed to be doing fine so far. After Maddie gave it a trial run, Sy hadn't turned it off. It might still be fall by Vermont standards, but night temperatures were already dipping into the upper thirties and that counted as cold in her book. She had the fireplace, too—a total novelty for a kid from the southwest. She'd have to get her hands on some wood and give that puppy a try. Because not even she needed a contractor to teach her how to make a fire.

CHAPTER FOUR

When Sy didn't answer her text, Maddie took a chance and headed over to the farm. Sure enough, Sy's hatchback already sat parked next to Clover's old pickup. It wasn't any of her business, but she liked that Sy seemed to be an up and at 'em sort of morning person. Or at least she hoped that's what Sy's presence meant. And hopefully Sy wouldn't be so focused on work that she'd mind sparing a few minutes to discuss her house.

She found Sy in the barn with Clover and the goats, in for their morning milking. Only Lulubelle looked up from her breakfast to bleat a greeting. But it was enough to get the attention of Sy and Clover, who both looked happy to see her. "Good morning," she said.

"Good morning," Sy and Clover said in unison, which was rather adorable.

"You never visit me in the morning," Clover said.

"I confess I'm here to see her." Maddie tipped her head at Sy.

Sy seemed surprised by that declaration. "I'm not in trouble, am I? My check didn't bounce?"

Since Sy was smiling, Maddie didn't take the question seriously. "Not that I'm aware of."

"Oh, good. Talk about making a bad impression."

It sort of felt like banter, but Maddie's need for efficiency won out. Well, efficiency and not quite knowing how to banter with Sy without being flirty about it. "Before you get to work, I want you to take a look at some samples so I can get things ordered."

Clover stood and gave Lulubelle's rump a pat. "Fun."

"Sure thing," Sy said with markedly less enthusiasm.

Maddie rested the box on her hip. "Normally, Logan would do this, but she's busy onsite at the local library, so you're stuck with me. I'm not the true designer, but I have a decent eye."

Sy smiled. "I don't mind being stuck with you."

Something in Sy's tone sent a shiver up Maddie's spine. The kind of shiver that came with the innuendo of flirting, not some innocent back and forth with a client. Not even close to where her brain should be. She cleared her throat. "I'm hoping we can get everything sorted for the bathroom."

"Don't do it here," Clover said. "I can't be tempted."

Sy laughed. "All right. Let's go into the packing area. The table is clear."

She followed Sy out of the animal barn and into the one that held the cheese operation and set the box of samples on the stainless steel surface. "Okay, we've got a couple of vanity options, then tiles for the shower and floor."

Sy watched her set each item out the way a tennis fan might watch the volley of the ball. "That's a lot."

She smiled. "I promise it's not."

Sy didn't look convinced.

Maddie pointed to the square of plastic sheeting and the rectangle of tile. "You can go with the surround for your shower, but it'll definitely look slapped on in a house as old as yours. Tile is more expensive, but if you go with a basic subway and let me show you how to lay it yourself, it's a nominal difference."

"Uh-huh." Sy nodded noncommittally.

"Subway isn't far from the original style-wise and would look great with pretty much anything you pick for the floor." She started pulling out the flooring options. "Now, again, you could go with a vinyl, but the square footage is small enough that you'll get a lot of bang for your buck going with something porcelain."

"Okay." Sy seemed even less impressed with that than she had with the shower tiles.

"Did you have something in mind or are you open to suggestion?"

Sy angled her head. "Oh, I'm open."

"That's going to work in your favor." Maddie rubbed her hands together, excitement building. "I got a whole mess of these mosaics when they went on clearance at one of the big box stores in Albany, so you could do that cheap. I've got this one with the blue and green and one with black and gray. And there's the faux marble. Always classic. Oh, and the black and white hex are actually overage from a project I did a couple of months ago. I think we'd have just enough to do your space and I could give them to you at cost."

She waited a beat, then another. Sy simply stared.

"Do you not like any of them? It's okay, you won't hurt my feelings."

"They're fine." Sy's curled lip implied otherwise.

Not the word she wanted to hear. "Well, you're going to be the one living with it, so you should probably think it's a little better than fine."

Sy sighed. "Look, I don't mean to be a jerk, but I don't really care."

"How can you not care?" In her experience, people said that when they didn't want to make a decision. But when push came to shove, they had plenty of opinions, especially after the fact and with things they didn't like.

Sy shrugged. "I know it's your bread and butter, but it's all kind of the same to me."

She bristled, taking it more personally than maybe she should have. "Really? And if I said I'd no sooner eat your cheese as a Kraft single?"

Sy's shoulders dropped and her expression turned stony. "That seems uncalled for."

Not so blasé when the tables are turned, huh? "It's absolutely called for. My work is no less a craft than yours."

Sy scratched the back of her head. "I didn't mean it like that."

"Didn't you?" She couldn't see another way to take it.

"I just don't pay attention to that stuff, you know? If the water's hot and I don't feel like someone is lurking on the other side of the curtain waiting to murder me, I'm good." Sy shrugged. "It doesn't mean I don't respect the person who put it all together."

She wanted to find fault with that argument but had a hard time. Because when push came to shove, she bought her blocks of cheddar from the grocery store like everyone else and only had the fancy stuff when Clover brought it to her. Still. She hated giving in when it was something she cared about. "Even if you don't make it a priority, you can notice the details. Appreciate them."

"I'll appreciate it being done." Sy sounded dismissive rather than defensive which, for Maddie, turned out to be worse.

It would be easy enough to say fine, to make the choices herself based on whatever she liked or would cost the least. Only, she didn't want to. She wanted to be right. "Will you humor me for a minute?"

Whether Sy felt sheepish about inadvertently insulting her or something else, Maddie couldn't say. But whatever the reason, Sy nodded. "All right."

"Close your eyes."

That got her a flash of suspicion, but Sy complied.

Maddie took Sy's hand and laid it over the patterned tile. "Okay, imagine your bare feet on that." After a moment, she moved it to the ultra-smooth faux marble, then finally the small hex. "You can open them."

Sy grinned and pointed to the hex. "Those."

"Because?" She didn't even pretend not to be smug.

"Because they feel the best."

She should have known texture would be the angle to work with someone like Sy. "See? You do care."

Sy's eyes narrowed slightly, but she didn't argue.

"And they'll pair great with subway tile." Which Sy hadn't technically agreed to yet. She lifted her chin. "Assuming you're not afraid of a little mortar and grout."

Sy seemed to take the comment as a challenge, which was exactly what Maddie wanted. "I'm not scared."

A pithy comeback leapt to the tip of her tongue, but she swallowed it. If for no other reason than Clover might be in earshot. "Thank you."

"I'm pretty sure I should be thanking you." Sy circled her finger over the samples. "That was very clever."

"I just needed to figure out what part would speak to you." And I didn't want to deal with you griping about it after the fact.

"I see."

She quirked a brow. "Taste and smell weren't really an option."

"Both very important, but yes. Touch is definitely the way to go."

It seemed perhaps like they were talking about more than tile. More than cheese making, too. Maybe it was simply her overactive imagination. It had been taking field trips the last few days, going places it absolutely should not. It bugged her that arguing had done little, if anything, to quash that. "Well, congratulations. You've decided on your bathroom. Oh, except for the vanity, the plumbing fixtures, the lighting, and the paint color."

Sy went from possibly flirty to slightly horrified in under a second. "You're serious, aren't you?"

She pulled out the spec sheets she'd printed. "I narrowed it down for you based on cost and what's in stock now."

"I'm supposed to thank you for that, aren't I?"

Sy's tone—more playful than snarky—left Maddie even more off balance than if Sy had simply been difficult. "Yep."

For all her not caring one way or the other, Sy managed to have some opinions: dark wood over light, chrome fixtures over gold. It didn't take long to check everything off the list. When they'd finished, Sy made a show of being exhausted. "Are you going to make me do that for every room?"

"The rest will be paint colors and light fixtures mostly. I think you'll survive."

"Thank God."

She smirked in spite of herself. "Aside from the kitchen, of course."

"Oh, well." Sy lifted one shoulder, then the other, gesturing back and forth with both hands. "The kitchen is different."

"Is it?" She expected nothing less from a chef but didn't need to let on.

"I know I won't be able to afford what I really want, but I have thoughts."

The gleam in Sy's eye gave Maddie thoughts, too. Only they weren't about the kitchen. "Let's get the space cleared and we'll see what we can come up with."

Sy clapped her hands together, rubbing them back and forth with exaggerated vigor. "Can't wait."

"Are we still good to start tomorrow?" Though the prospect of working in close quarters, without a crew milling around, felt like less and less of a good idea.

"I absolutely am. Are you sure you don't mind working on a Saturday?"

She often worked weekends, mostly because she liked the quiet of working alone and the ability to see the forest for the trees. Working with Sy wouldn't be that by a long shot. But between how booked she was and the desperate circumstance of Sy's house, she didn't see many other options. "It was my idea, remember?"

"I know." Sy seemed to waver for a second. "I guess I don't want you to feel obligated."

Funny word, that. "It's an obligation I don't mind having. How's that?"

Sy considered, and Maddie imagined her coming to the conclusion that she didn't have much of a choice. "I hope you'll let me find a way to repay the favor."

"You do right by Clover, and we'll call it even."

Sy's smile had a knowing quality about it, leaving Maddie with an uncomfortable sense of being seen. "I understand. But I hope you'll let me do something for you, too."

"I'm sure you'll come up with something." Which wouldn't be her normal response, but agreeing would hopefully satisfy Sy and chase away the feeling of being exposed. "Besides, however much we get done will come off the hours the crew needs for demo next week."

As if sensing Maddie's desire to shift gears, Sy gave a brisk nod. "My piggy bank appreciates that."

Maddie scooped up the samples and hefted the box. "I'll see you in the morning, then."

"I'll see you then."

❖

Sy had barely finished her first cup of coffee when the sound of tires in the driveway caught her attention. Girl doesn't waste time, does she? She set her mug to the side of the sink rather than in it, hoping she could talk Maddie into a cup before wielding sledgehammers.

She greeted Maddie at the door, channeling all the get-up-and-go she could muster at quarter after seven in the morning. Maddie didn't seem to suffer even a trace of the slow-to-starts. It made Sy think of the phrase she'd never quite understood: bright-eyed and bushy-tailed. Like a cartoon woodland creature. But also hot?

It still caught her off guard how feminine Maddie could look in a pair of faded jeans and a flannel shirt—practically identical to what she'd pulled on herself from the jumble of clothes still wanting for a dresser to call home. Maybe it was the tank top underneath that didn't show cleavage exactly, but hinted at it. Or that flame of hair, tamed into a tidy French braid that had Sy's fingers itching to muss it up.

"What's wrong?" Maddie regarded her with a mixture of suspicion and concern.

"I'm trying to decide whether my outfit is butch enough." Silly and true enough not to be a flat-out lie, yet somehow easier to say than what she'd actually been thinking.

Maddie looked her up and down, making Sy wonder if maybe she was getting herself into more trouble rather than less. "You'll do."

It killed her that Maddie managed to give nothing away. One second, Sy would swear they were in full flirting territory. The next, Maddie seemed to be weighing whether to even take Sy seriously. It was ridiculous. And exasperating. And hot. "I'm used to getting my hands dirty, for the record."

Maddie smiled then. A reluctant smile, maybe, but a smile. "No doubt."

She stepped back so Maddie could come in out of the chilly morning air. "Did you, uh, want coffee before we get started? I made a whole pot."

"I'm good." Maddie lifted the travel mug she'd been holding in plain sight. "But I'll take you up on a refill before the morning is done."

"Yeah. Of course."

Maddie lifted her chin. "You ready to work?"

An innocent enough question, but Sy would swear it came with a trace of challenge. For better or worse, she could work with that. "Oh, I'm ready."

Maddie's serious look became more of a smirk. "I'm really glad you didn't say 'I was born ready.'"

Sy coughed, grateful she didn't have a mouthful of coffee to send spewing every which way. "I promise I'll never say that."

"Same." Maddie stuck out her hand like they were closing a business deal.

She shook it, enjoying the brush of Maddie's palm against hers. "So, where do we start?"

"Upstairs for sure. Getting that ceiling down before there's a whole mess of roof debris to rain down on us is the way to go. Then whatever falls will fall through and you can clear it easily."

"Makes sense."

Maddie angled her head toward the door. "Let's go grab tools."

She spared a single longing thought for the second cup of coffee that would have to wait before opening the door. Maddie headed to her truck without waiting for Sy to concur.

Sy followed, perfectly content to let Maddie take the lead. In this scenario, at least, where Maddie was the clear expert.

"The dumpster should be here later today. I'm going to leave filling it for you to do on your own."

"Of course." Sy accepted a sledgehammer and what appeared to be a cross between a rake and a pitchfork from Maddie. "Unskilled labor at your service. Or my service, I guess."

Maddie unhooked a ladder from the side of her truck and frowned. "We'll make sure you have a little bit of skill. It's demo, but you can still do a lot of damage."

She opened her mouth, but swallowed the insistence she took this whole process seriously. Because Maddie seemed irritated all of a sudden and Sy couldn't figure out why. And because actions would speak louder than words anyway.

Back in the house, they spent a few minutes in one of the bedrooms. Maddie showed her how to use the sledgehammer and pointy thing—that turned out to be a demolition fork—to pry drywall from the ceiling joists and wall studs. She scrawled a large X on each of the walls she deemed beyond repair, going out of her way to point out the price to replace any decent drywall Sy damaged by being careless. Even with Maddie's admonitions, it seemed to fall squarely in the realm of things she could do unsupervised.

The bathroom proved a different matter. Since she couldn't turn off the main water supply without cutting water to the whole house, they had to demo carefully to each fixture's cutoff and work around the plumbing that would remain. After doing that, Maddie charged her with lugging the sink and toilet down the stairs and out to the front porch. Both turned out to be even heavier than they looked, though she'd be dead before admitting as much—in general but especially to the slightly judgmental version of Maddie currently overseeing her efforts.

With both gone, the bathroom had enough space for them to stand side-by-side without their shoulders brushing. Better for working, probably, but Sy kind of preferred the close proximity. Even with Maddie's grumpy attitude. Maddie handed her the sledgehammer. "Are you ready to work out some of your rage?"

She folded her arms. "What makes you think I have rage?"

Maddie mimicked the gesture. "Who doesn't?"

Sy chuckled. "Fair point."

Maddie sighed. "But if you're not feeling it today, it's okay to swing the hammer in good spirits. I'm not one of those people who believes in forcing it."

Was that a concession? A warning? Sy got the sense Maddie wasn't talking about rage exclusively. Though, given how things were going, Maddie might be speaking in truisms more than flirtisms. Sy wanted to read flirtation into whatever Maddie happened to be dishing out, but the reality was that Maddie ran more hot and cold than the dated faucet taps they just pulled out.

Maddie pointed to the avocado-green tile surrounding the tub. "You don't have to tell me one way or the other. Just take a few swings and don't be shy about it."

They'd already discussed needing a delicate approach to the wall with the faucet, so she went for the one opposite. She picked up the sledgehammer and slipped her safety glasses into place. Maddie stepped out of her way, and Sy had at it. Well, sort of. The first couple of hits landed the way a stone might hit a windshield—a single divot with a web of hairline cracks emanating from the center. "Am I doing it wrong?"

Maddie leaned in to assess the damage. "You're doing it perfectly. The mortar is starting to give way. Keep going."

Sy took another swing and a massive chunk of tiles fell from the wall and into the tub. She yelped, but the sound came out as a squeak.

"Sorry. I should have warned you that could happen," Maddie said, though she didn't seem entirely sorry.

"No, no. If I'm going to die of a heart attack, I want it to be at the age of thirty-four in the ugliest bathroom I've ever seen."

Maddie laughed. "Cute. You're cute."

What was that about hot and cold? But once again, Sy wanted to read more into the comment than perhaps was there. "I prefer rugged."

"Then maybe don't squeal like a little girl while doing demo."

She deserved that. And since a teasing Maddie was a hell of a lot more fun than put-upon Maddie, she'd take it. "Noted."

"Do you want me to take over, or are you good?"

Now that she knew what to expect, it was kind of fun. Not to mention a socially acceptable way to show off a little muscle. "I'm good. I might even be tapping into my rage."

Maddie smirked. "That's the spirit."

CHAPTER FIVE

With the Winterson project finally back on schedule, Maddie left the crew working on drywall and headed to Sy's for the afternoon. With the upstairs demo done and roofers starting the next day, she wanted to turn their attention to picking materials for the kitchen and getting Sy started on the exterior work before the weather really turned.

She walked in through the side door, as she'd taken to doing, with a cursory knock. No sign of Sy, but smoke billowed from the living room. The sight of it assaulted her first, though the smell wasn't far behind. She coughed reflexively and narrowed her eyes against the stinging sensation. "Sy? Are you here? Are you okay?"

Sy appeared in the cloud, like something out of a movie. Only instead of a hero's stride or a survivor's limp, her arms flailed with comical intensity. "I'm here. I'm fine. Everything's fine."

Fine certainly wasn't the word she'd use, but since Sy seemed neither hurt nor in serious danger, she took the answer with a grain of salt and shimmied open the nearest window. "Should I ask?"

"I picked up some firewood at the gas station. I thought I'd take the fireplace for a spin." Sy stopped flapping her arms and her shoulders fell. "The chimney must be clogged."

There were so many things wrong with that statement, she hardly knew where to begin. "Probably. The flue might be closed, too."

Sy cringed. "The flue closes. Son of—"

"I don't mean to insult your intelligence, but maybe ask me before trying house stuff? At least if it's stuff you haven't done before." Because it wouldn't do either of them any good if Sy burned the place to the ground.

Sy grumbled but didn't argue.

"Hey, I'd never try to coax a vat of milk into a nice chèvre without enlisting help from the experts." She scooted around Sy and opened two of the living room windows, and the smoke began to dissipate.

"For the record, I was about to do that when you interrupted me." Sy pointed to the windows and let out a sigh, but it turned into a cough. She sighed again. "I don't like feeling clueless."

Admitting that probably didn't come easy. The fact that Sy did gave Maddie a pang of empathy. "I get that. You'll learn." She cleared her throat. "You're already learning."

"Thank you." Sy offered a wry grin. "Now please stop before I have to admit you're patronizing me."

"I'm not." Though it certainly could have slipped into that had Sy not called her out.

Sy gave her a look that said she figured as much.

"Okay, maybe I was a little, but I take it back. How could you have known?" Besides asking her, obviously, or doing a basic internet search.

"You know, I've been known to use the Google," Sy said.

Maddie snorted, as much at Sy's deadpan delivery as the answer that tracked so close to her own snarky thoughts. "Sorry."

Sy lifted a hand. "It's fine. I deserved it."

"Maybe. But you don't deserve a house full of smoke. Do you want me to take a look?"

Sy's stance shifted back to her usual confident ease. "I'm not a big enough idiot to turn down help when I clearly need it. But first tell me what brings you by. Do we have a meeting I blocked out?"

She'd been so caught up in the hubbub, she'd forgotten why she came over in the first place. "I—wait. Do you make a habit of blocking out our meetings?"

Sy smirked. "Only the ones where you make me make decisions about materials."

"Seriously? We've done that one time. And you were kind of a baby about it." She hadn't planned to tease Sy about that, but seriously, Sy had been a total baby.

"I prefer obstinate and ornery," Sy said without missing a beat.

"Noted." It felt like bantering more than bickering, which made her more uneasy rather than less.

"Anyway. I take it I didn't miss a meeting. So, why are you here?"

"Oh, right." She blushed at her own distractibility, then chided herself for blushing. "I wanted to drop off a few tools for you. Things that'll make your jobs easier but you don't need to own."

"Like what?" Sy asked.

"Like an extra wide scraper for you to go to town on that popcorn ceiling in the living room."

Sy clapped her hands together. "Goody."

"And some more contractor grade trash bags because I can get them way cheaper than you can."

"You really know how to charm a girl, don't you?"

"Well, I do need you to make some decisions, too." Which didn't technically require a face-to-face, but would go quicker with one than without. At least that's what she'd said when Logan asked where she was going.

"You did that on purpose, didn't you?" Sy shook her head and gave a tsk of disapproval.

"Did what?"

"Plied me with presents so I'd look like a jerk if I complained about choosing between things that are basically the same."

It irked her that Sy refused to meet her halfway. "We've been over this. You might think they're the same, but they aren't. And I'm not going to have you changing your mind after the fact. Or complaining that you don't like something after it's been installed."

Sy's bland look confirmed she found the insinuation dubious, if not downright offensive.

"I could also remind you that it's your responsibility to make these decisions. You're paying me to be your contractor, not your interior designer."

Sy look slightly cowed. "You're right."

Maddie took the win and let the rest of her jumbled reactions to Sy and this whole situation go. "Besides, this is about the kitchen. I know you have opinions."

"I do. Even if I can't afford any of the things I really want." Sy didn't pout, but it was close.

"Maybe we can get you a few of those things." More of a concession than she'd intended, but whatever.

Sy grinned. "I'm all ears."

"Okay." She rolled out the plans she'd spent far too long fiddling with. "With this galley setup, we really can't put in an island."

"I know. I've resigned myself to that."

"But we can do a rolling cart that lives in that weird little nook. You can pull it out when you're cooking for extra prep space." She'd done something similar the year before, so it wasn't a concept she'd come up with just for Sy.

"Oh, that's cool," Sy said, seeming to mean it.

"I can probably get a stone remnant pretty cheap if you want to do that for the top. I thought maybe butcher block for the rest." Practically the same price as laminate these days, and so much better for people who actually used their kitchens.

"See, you really are a sweet talker."

"You're okay with that?" She'd expected grousing about not getting granite and had her form over function lecture ready.

"This may surprise you, but I'm more interested in function than beauty."

She laughed because that was easier than admitting Sy had read her mind. Though she continued to wonder if a temperamental artist lurked under the easygoing surface. "I'm learning. And you mentioned new appliances. You want to splurge on that and paint the existing cabinets, right?"

Sy nodded. "Yes. Well, splurge in getting new ones, at least, and in having a gas line run for the stove."

"Not a splurge by chef standards?" She was teasing now, but they'd drifted into that territory when she wasn't looking.

"Not by any stretch of those standards." Sy winked and somehow made Maddie think about a very different sort of indulgent standards.

"Right." What was wrong with her? "So, that leaves flooring, faucets, the sink, and the cabinet hardware."

Sy groaned. "Sorry, I had to. I do know I want a stainless sink. Big. Single basin."

She scribbled that in her notes. "Look at you."

"And something vinyl on the floor. Easy to clean, won't immediately break anything that touches it."

"Have you seen the planks that look like wood? They've come a long way and would fit the age and character of the house." She'd resisted liking them at first, but they were too damn versatile—not to mention cost effective—not to. Kind of like Sy? No. Not going there.

"Sold."

"I should warn you, they come in literally dozens of colors."

Another groan.

It should be getting on her nerves, but Sy had to be so damn good-natured about it. "I'll narrow it down to what's readily available and won't clash with the finish you have on the rest of the floors since that's going to stick around for a while."

Sy put her hands together and bowed. "Bless you."

It felt like pressing her luck at this point, but she was on a roll. "What about the cabinets?"

Sy shrugged and winced slightly. "A color?"

Maddie sighed. She should have known that was too much to ask. "Yes, they do need to be a color, one way or the other."

"No, I meant color, color. Like a pop of color."

She tipped her head, delighted and not even pretending to hide it. "Like what?"

"Dark teal maybe? Or dark green?"

She could work with that. "I'll bring over some samples."

"Great." Sy smiled. "Thank you for making that as painless as possible."

Maddie smiled and it wasn't even forced. "Thank you for keeping your whining to a minimum."

"I try."

It could have been a line, but it wasn't. Or, if it was, it came from a place of authenticity. She liked that. Liked Sy. Even if she'd been dead set on not.

"Why are you laughing? Are you making fun of me? I don't mind if you are, I just want to know in case I should be laughing at myself, too," Sy said.

See? How could she not like someone so willing to poke fun at themselves? "I'm just pleasantly surprised that went so well."

Sy didn't appear to believe her but seemed to know better than to press.

"Oh, while I'm here, I thought I'd get the shutters off. There's no rush on them, but it's going to be warm this weekend and if you have time to get them scraped and painted, I can hang them before the snow comes and they'll make the front of the house look good as new."

"I will do exactly as I'm told." Sy offered a playful salute.

"Be careful with that. I might be tempted to take advantage."

"I'll keep that in mind."

She hadn't meant it as suggestive as it came out—hadn't meant it suggestive at all—but the look on Sy's face told her that was exactly the way Sy took it. Though, to be honest, Sy didn't seem bothered. Maddie cleared her throat. She could get herself into trouble if she wasn't careful. Good thing for her, careful came second nature. Especially when it came to good-looking newcomers unlikely to stick around for long.

❖

Sy hoisted the garage door and set up the sawhorses Maddie had brought over the week before, insisting Sy would need them more than she did. Before Sy had the last one in place, Maddie carried in the first of the shutters. "How do you do that so fast?"

Maddie lifted her chin. "Practice."

"You know how badly I want to say, 'that's what she said,' right?"

Maddie shook her head but pressed her lips together in a way that made it clear she wanted to laugh. "If I compliment your restraint, will it make you less likely to do so in the future?"

She quirked a brow. "Less likely to say it or to practice restraint?"

That got her an eye roll. "You're a handful."

Sy gave her a bland look, then simply mouthed, "That's what she said."

Maddie groaned. "I'd be annoyed with you, but I so walked into that."

"You did." And while she wasn't in the habit of making inappropriate comments in professional settings, things with Maddie finally seemed to be straying into friendly territory. And it was only a little inappropriate, really.

"There are worse things, I suppose," Maddie said, like admitting so was a genuine concession.

Indeed there were. "Will you show me what to do before you go get more? I might as well start on them now since I'm home."

"Of course." Maddie rooted around in the box of supplies she'd brought, pulling out a pair of masks and a tool of some sort. A scraper? She handed one of the masks to Sy. "I'm not going to bother testing this for lead since you don't have kids, but we're going to assume it does."

She could get behind that. "Safety first."

Maddie nodded, all business again. "Safety first." After getting their masks in place, Maddie ran the tool—a scraper—over a small patch of the wood. Some of the paint flaked away, but not all.

"Please tell me I don't have to strip these down to bare wood."

"You don't."

"I can't tell if you mean that, or if you're just saying it because I asked nicely."

That got her a smirk. "I wouldn't lie to you."

They were joking, but she got the feeling Maddie meant it. At least when it came to her work. "I appreciate that."

"Really, though. You only have to get the loose stuff off. We'll give it a light sand and that'll be enough for fresh paint to stick. Not quite good as new, but close enough."

She could get on board with close enough, maybe not with everything but certainly when it came to her house. "I'll take it."

"Okay, you have at it and I'll be right back."

Maddie turned to go, but Sy grabbed her wrist. "Did you hear that?"

Maddie angled her head, clearly amused by the exaggerated whisper. "Hear what?"

"That squeaking noise. Is it a bird? A mouse?" It came again and Sy took a step in the direction it seemed to be coming from. Only she hadn't let go of Maddie, so she ended up pulling her along.

"Okay. I heard it that time." Maddie frowned. "Definitely an animal."

Sy let go and picked her way to the far wall of the garage. In addition to the boxes she'd started to break down for recycling, it's where she'd piled all the crap left by the previous owners—gnarly looking cans of paint with rusted rims, some drop cloths that had seen better days, and the remnants of a particleboard foosball table. "It's coming from back here, I think." She started shuffling things around, half afraid a rat or a squirrel would leap out and run up her pant leg or, worse, land across her face.

As if sharing her concern, Maddie came up behind her. "Careful."

"I am, I am," she said with more confidence than she felt.

"You don't want to scare whatever it is. Things bite when they're scared."

She looked over her shoulder. "Not helping."

"Sorry."

Sy picked up one of the drop cloths, and the owner of the squeak came into view. Not a rat or a squirrel, but a tiny ball of gray and white fluff with a pink nose. She gripped Maddie's arm. "It's a kitten."

"It most certainly is." Maddie bent right down and scooped it up.

"Is it okay to pick it up?" She didn't want to admit kittens were one more thing she knew absolutely nothing about, but she didn't see much choice.

"Well, I wouldn't pull one away from its mama, but this little guy is all alone." Maddie touched her nose to his. "And he's cold."

Maddie tucked the kitten into the crook of her arm and he began meowing in earnest. Sy's brain kicked into overdrive. "Where is his family? Do you think he's been abandoned? What should we do?"

"I'm guessing he wandered off or accidentally got left behind. Maybe mama was relocating them and got spooked by a predator."

Maddie spoke matter-of-factly, and the rational part of Sy's brain agreed with the assessment. The rest of her, however, promptly melted into a puddle. "He's so small. And probably hungry. We have to help him."

Maddie shot her a look of exasperation. "You say that like I'd just leave him."

Sy laughed in spite of herself. "Sorry. I don't mean to overreact, but I hit my daily max on things I've never dealt with when I almost burned my house down."

Maddie laughed and the kitten mewed again, though it was hard to tell whether in agreement or protest. "He can come home with me, at least for the night. My cat doesn't make friends well, but he can hunker in the bathroom."

"Alone?"

Maddie laughed again, but it was more the spluttering sort of sound that came with encountering the disarmingly absurd. "Don't take this the wrong way, but you're kind of adorable right now."

Sy didn't want to be adorable, but she'd take it over ridiculous. "What if I kept him?"

"Would you?"

She'd never taken care of a kitten before. Never had a cat, even. Just dogs, and they tended to be loping things that didn't ask for much beyond dinner and belly scratches. "Um, yes. Yes. Absolutely."

Maddie grinned. "I feel like I should warn you that one night is sometimes all it takes."

"All what takes?"

"For a kitten to convince you that you can't live without it." Maddie held the puffball out and he mewed, definitely in agreement.

Sy took him with both hands though, really, he would have fit easily in one. "How do you feel about giving me yet another crash course?"

"I'll do you one better," Maddie said.

"Yeah?"

"Yeah." Maddie gave the kitten a gentle scratch between the ears then bumped her shoulder to Sy's. "I'll take you shopping for supplies."

CHAPTER SIX

Maddie checked the final item off her office to-do list and shut down her computer, silently wishing it good riddance. For the rest of the day if nothing else. "I'm going to be out of the office this afternoon."

Logan and Jack looked up from their respective computers. As did their mother. Jack, always the one to say what everyone was thinking, asked, "Are you ever in the office in the afternoon?"

Not if she could help it. Some desk time was required, obviously, but she did her best to get it out of the way on cold, damp mornings and leave the rest of her day for working on one site or another. "I meant office in the broader sense. I'm going to be out."

"Out?" Logan planted an elbow on her desk and propped her chin on her fist. "What kind of out?"

Not like she could have dropped off the radar unnoticed, even for an afternoon, but she regretted bringing it up. Especially with this much of an audience. "I'm going to Bennington."

"For…" Logan made a circular motion with her head for added effect.

"I need to pick up a few things and I told Sy Travino I'd show her how to pick out a legit winter coat." Maybe she could have gotten away with just the first part, but not likely. She hated shopping even more than she hated being on the computer.

Logan rolled her chair from behind her desk. "Let me make sure I understand. You're helping her DIY some of her reno, you got her set up to take care of her newly adopted stray kitten, and now you're taking her shopping for a winter coat?"

Maddie let out a huff. "Stop trying to make it sound weird."

"Oh, it's not weird," Logan said.

"Thank you."

"If you're dating," Logan continued.

"Not helpful." She made a simpering face. "Or funny."

Jack lifted a hand. "Wait. It's also not weird if it's your kid."

Maddie huffed. "Okay, you're both being assholes."

Logan shrugged. "Tell me we're wrong."

"You're wrong," she said, more out of habit than conviction. She'd offered without really thinking, then chalked it up to trying to be nice for Clover's sake. But the truth was, if the tables were turned and it was Jack or Logan in this situation, she'd be giving them a hard time, too.

Logan jutted her chin. "Tell me I'm wrong and mean it."

Maddie opened her mouth but closed it without speaking.

"That's what I thought."

She looked to her mom, who could usually be relied upon to be the voice of reason. Mom made a cringy, apologetic face. "Sorry, honey. It does sound rather...familiar."

Jack snorted. "Familiar. Is that what the kids are calling it these days?"

Logan let out a cough that barely covered a laugh.

Maddie shot him a pointed glare. "You are no help."

Jack, on a roll and with a captive audience, kept going. "If you're having fun and getting along and you think she's hot, why don't you go out with her already? Or at least go to bed with her?"

"Maybe I will," Maddie said.

That did the trick. Jack opened his mouth and closed it again.

"For real?" Logan asked.

Maddie smirked. "No, but it shut this one up."

Logan let out a whistle and Jack angled his body so he could flip her off out of sight of their mother.

It was too late to back out now. And just because her siblings considered insinuation a pastime didn't mean it had to amount to anything. Sy wasn't her type, plain and simple. At least not when it came to the things that mattered. She grabbed her bag and jacket and headed for the door. "See you jerks tomorrow."

Since it was more Sy's errand than hers, and since her car got better gas mileage than Maddie's truck, she offered to drive. Maddie climbed in and resisted asking if Sy had considered investing in snow tires. It wasn't her business. Though maybe she'd mention it to Clover. Because a Sy who skidded off the road into a tree wouldn't be much good for making cheese. Or working on her house.

Despite starting off stiff, Sy's ease with conversation smoothed things over and let Maddie set aside her second thoughts about spending the day together. Between talk about the house and asking what Sy had gotten up to in the cheese room, it was easy enough to pass the time. Sy had questions, too, mostly about Maddie's cat.

"Why is her name Kira?" Sy asked.

Maddie coughed. "It's short for Shakira. And before you ask, she came with that name and answered to it, so I didn't feel right changing it."

Sy pressed her lips together, like she was suppressing a laugh. "Mm-hmm."

Maddie rolled her eyes. "Because Henry is such a great name for a cat."

"Henry is a fantastic name for a cat. And it's for Henry David Thoreau since I basically moved to Walden Pond. Minus the pond."

Maddie laughed in earnest, amused but more than that. Charmed. She hadn't expected to find herself charmed by Sy, but that's exactly what she was. Even if she'd be dead before saying as much to Logan and Jack. "I don't suppose I can argue with that."

A debate about pet names more broadly ensued, and Sy won the nonexistent contest for most absurd with the dachshund mutt she'd helped her mom pick out when she left for culinary school: Andouille. She made a show of bowing to the victor, as much as the passenger seat would allow. Then they fell into a surprisingly easy silence.

The only downside, of course, was that the quiet gave the little voices in her head room to play. "Do you think it's weird that I offered to take you coat shopping?"

Sy took her eyes off the road long enough to glance at Maddie. "Do you think it's weird?"

"I didn't, but…"

"But?" Sy seemed genuinely curious.

"But Jack and Logan were giving me a hard time about it and I let them get under my skin." And now saying so out loud made her feel silly.

"Do they often get under your skin?"

Maddie laughed. "They try to."

"You know, I always wanted siblings. I never thought about that part."

"We goad each other. It comes with the territory. But we have each other's backs, too. It's more than a fair trade."

Sy's features softened. "It's nice to know my longing was for something worthwhile."

"For sure."

"But they're giving you a hard time about helping a poor desert girl brace for her first New England winter." Sy shook her head. "That's harsh."

"They think I'm babying you." Which felt easier to admit than the implied girlfriend commentary.

"You should tell them I find that very offensive. Though I imagine I'll meet them at some point. I'll tell them myself."

Normally, the prospect of someone giving her siblings an earful would be a source of entertainment. But in this instance, she knew without a doubt it would come back to bite her in the ass. "I set them both straight, I promise."

Sy looked dubious. "But it's still bugging you."

"No." She frowned. "No."

"Are you asking me or telling me?"

This was dumb. Why was she letting this get to her? She was now the one making it weird. "It's not bugging me. I explained how Clover had to take care of her mom unexpectedly and that you and I were, you know, friendly. And I offered to go with you because I needed to go to Bennington anyway. And I could use a coat that isn't for work."

Sy nodded slowly, leaving Maddie to wonder whether she'd made matters better or worse. Eventually, she angled her head. "Friendly?"

"Friends. But also still sort of becoming friends. No?" More than she'd bargained for when they met, inconvenient attraction to Sy notwithstanding.

"Absolutely," Sy said with just the right level of conviction.

Still, Jack and Logan's assertions danced through her mind. That hitting it off with someone you also found hot wasn't coincidence, or something to be ignored. That chemistry was chemistry, and it needed a place to go or, like a chemistry experiment gone wrong, it could blow up when you least expected it.

"Was that the wrong thing to say? I didn't mean to poke fun." Sy paused, seeming to hesitate. Then she added, "I'm glad we're becoming friends."

See? There it was. Chemistry or not, when push came to shove, they were on the same page. That's what mattered and what she needed to remember. Especially when the desire to kiss Sy crept up on her.

❖

"Are you sure it's going to be warm enough?" Sy patted her chest through the suspiciously thin jacket. "I expected something…"

"Something what?" Maddie regarded her with amusement.

"Puffy."

Maddie snickered. "You're cute."

"Wait. Do you mean naive cute or charming cute?" Because, really, it could go either way.

"The second." Maddie looked her up and down in a way that implied a third kind of cute. The I-want-to-kiss-you kind.

Sy stretched her arms in front of her to test the length of the sleeves. "Well, as long as it's that."

Maddie put her hand on one of those arms. "It isn't your fault you don't have any experience with the cold. It wouldn't be fair to make fun."

"Aw, thanks."

"That said, I do plan on laughing when you realize you have to shovel your driveway."

It took a second for the combination of words to register meaning, but then she groaned.

"We'll make sure you get one of those. And a brush for your car."

She wondered how many times between now and spring she'd regret moving to one of the snowiest parts of the country. For the moment, though, she had no complaints about a gorgeous local helping her prepare. Even if it came with a healthy dose of teasing.

By the time they were done, she settled on the jacket, a couple of thermal shirts she could layer, four pairs of wool socks, and a puffer vest—which Maddie insisted was perfect for the in-between seasons. "I have about as much faith in this to keep me warm as I do that jacket having a comfort rating to zero degrees."

"Comfort is relative." Maddie shrugged. "I'm telling you, I have that exact coat in green and it's better than the old school kind so puffy you can't even put your arms down."

Sy laughed because that's what she'd been expecting. "And you said you wanted to get something, too?"

"Yeah, but I need to go to the girls' department." Maddie's lip curled.

She'd gotten a tomboy femme vibe from Maddie, but maybe she'd been wrong. "If you don't like girly clothes, why are you buying it?"

"Oh, I like it just fine," Maddie said. "But it's invariably more expensive and less well made than what I get in the men's department. I find that personally offensive."

"That's the argument I made to my mom when I wanted boy's clothes in high school."

Maddie stopped her purposeful stride across the store and turned. "Did she buy it?"

"No, but she pretended to. She might have wanted a girly girl sometimes, but she wanted me to be happy more than anything."

"That's really sweet." Maddie let out a happy little sigh, then resumed her march to the women's department.

Now that Sy was old enough to understand things—like the happiness her mother wasn't allowed at the same age—she appreciated it all the more. "She's the best."

"My poor mother didn't stand a chance. I liked girly things, but couldn't keep them clean to save my life. My middle sibling realized he was trans pretty much in kindergarten, and my baby sister is about as butch as they come."

"Wow. Three queer kids. I would have loved growing up with that. I mean, siblings in general, but queer ones? That sounds amazing." She had her share of cousins, but it wasn't the same.

"My parents had their hands full, but they took it in stride. And we've all gone into the family business, so there's that."

As close as she and her mom were, it was different from a big, nuclear family sort of thing. She'd longed for it as a kid, spent a chunk of her teens resenting the father who wasn't around, and mostly settled into being grateful for what she had.

"What do you think?" Maddie held up a charcoal gray peacoat.

"I like the buttons and the cut. I think you could pull off a color, but if you want to go subtle, then yeah, it's great."

Maddie returned the coat to the rack, folded her arms, and frowned.

"What?" Sy asked. Did she have any idea how often she did that? The arm folding, not the frown.

"You just had more opinions about a random wool coat than you did your entire bathroom."

Should she own the fact that she was more inclined to notice the way a woman looked in a well-fitting article of clothing than she was the color of the tiles in her shower? Probably not. She shrugged instead.

Maddie seemed to take that as a sufficient answer. She circled the racks with all the efficiency Sy would expect from her, settling on a double-breasted style in dark plum. Sy nodded her approval, not that Maddie needed it. She slipped it on, did a quick back-and-forth turn in front of one of the mirrors dotting the space, and called it done.

They checked out and loaded their bags into the back of Sy's car. For as much as she didn't love shopping, she wasn't ready for the afternoon to end. "Can I buy you dinner?"

Maddie raised a brow.

"As a thank you. For today. For your infinite winter wisdom." And because I like you and want to spend more time with you and maybe—probably, definitely—want to kiss you.

That got her a chuckle. "You don't have to do that."

"But I want to. I'd like to, I mean. If you'd like that." She resisted a facepalm, if for no other reason than it would highlight the shroud of awkward she'd draped over herself like a bad ghost costume.

"Why do I feel like we're having the consent talk?"

Since the ship of playing it cool had not only sailed but disappeared into the horizon, she pressed the heel of her hand to her forehead.

"Kidding." Maddie smirked, clearly enjoying herself.

Did she own how much she'd like to have the consent talk with Maddie? Or, rather, how much she'd like to do all the stuff that came after. "Sorry. You must have broken by brain with all that talk of twenty below."

"Ah."

Surely that was better than admitting she very much wanted dinner to be a date. Or that she wanted that date to lead to kissing. And the kissing to lead to all that other stuff. "Anyway. Thank-you dinner."

Maddie nodded slowly, as though catching glimpses of those inner thoughts. "That would be nice."

"I confess I have ulterior motives, though." Ones she was willing to admit, even.

"And what are those?" Maddie asked.

"I'm starving and, if you recall, I have no kitchen in my house."

Disappointment might have flashed in Maddie's eyes, or maybe Sy simply imagined it. Either way, it was gone in a second and replaced with a laugh. "Right. Well, then. Let's eat."

Maddie steered them to a cozy little pub with dark wood, dim lighting, and a roaring fire. They'd spent the better part of the day talking, but it didn't dampen conversation over dinner. She talked about growing up in the southwest, her decision to go to culinary school. Maddie told her about breaking her arm falling from the tree house she'd insisted on helping her father build, and starting her first official job in the family business at sixteen.

When the food came, they traded bites of Guinness stew and chicken pot pie. Maddie asked about her favorite dishes from home, as well as from France. She prodded Maddie about where she might like to travel, about whether she'd ever want to live somewhere besides Vermont. Maddie's adamant declaration that she'd never live anywhere else caught her off guard, but given Maddie's personal and professional roots, it really shouldn't have.

By the time they left the restaurant, the sky had gone dark, and the temperature had fallen a good ten degrees. "Good thing we got you that coat when we did," Maddie said.

"Between that and the amount of stick-to-your-ribs food I'm going to eat, I might just make it."

They got to the car, but Maddie turned. Like at the store but more slowly. And with a suggestive look in her eye. "There are all sorts of ways to keep warm. You just need practice."

Maddie didn't wait for an answer, sliding into the passenger seat and busying herself with her seat belt. Good thing, really, since it took Sy a second to remember to breathe and shove away the alarmingly vivid images of how she and Maddie might generate heat.

On the drive home, Maddie chatted casually. But Sy would swear there was a flirty edge to it. And when she stole glimpses across the center console, Maddie would do the same. It left her with the giddy buzz that came with a first date and lingering questions about whether Maddie felt it, too.

The hour passed way too fast for Sy's taste, and she was almost sad to pull into her driveway next to Maddie's truck. "Do you want to come in and see Henry? He's a terror in the best possible way."

Maddie hesitated. "I do, but it's late. And I'll be at your house tomorrow to check on the roofers. Could I come in for a minute then?"

"You're welcome anytime, and I won't even put you to work."

"Okay, great. Thank you."

Was that a blush creeping into Maddie's cheeks or wishful thinking? "Pretty sure I'm supposed to be the one thanking you," Sy said.

Maddie lifted a shoulder. "No reason it can't be mutual."

Much like the phantom blush, Maddie's words seemed to hint at meaning beyond the surface. Probably not the best time to tell Maddie she was thinking about all sorts of things beneath the surface, too. Like what her lips would taste like if Sy kissed her. Or where besides her cheeks she might have freckles.

Chapter Seven

"How was your date?" Jack asked, before Maddie had so much as taken off her coat.

"What date?" Logan asked, before Maddie could open her mouth to argue it wasn't.

"You had a date?" Mom, who could usually be relied on to check the sibling harassment, seemed more interested in the answer than the fact that it was none of their business.

"There was no date. If you recall, Jack decided that, barring some weird maternalistic urge, taking Sy shopping for a coat must equal a date." Which it definitely felt like, if she was being honest, between the cozy dinner and conversation that rivaled her last few actual dates. Despite all her intentions to keep any time with Sy squarely out of that category.

"Ah. That." Mom nodded and smiled, drumming her fingers on the stack of invoices and receipts in front of her. "It did sound rather like a date."

"It wasn't a date," she said, even as the phrase "protesteth too much" flashed in her mind.

"So, how was the thing we're not calling a date?" Jack smiled extra sweetly, the way he always did when stirring up trouble.

"It was great. I'm no longer concerned that one of my clients is going to die of hypothermia, and I got this great dark purple peacoat I can wear when I go on actual dates." No need to mention dinner. Or the comments about doing things to keep warm. Or how many times she caught herself staring at Sy's lips and imagining what it would feel like to have them sliding over hers. Because even if she indulged her attraction to Sy in the privacy of her own thoughts, that was the extent of it. Sy wasn't the sort of person to stick around a place like Bedlington. She had no delusions about that. And since Sy wasn't sticking around, there was no point in thinking it could be anything more.

"Oh, I love it when you buy yourself something nice," Mom said.

She barely caught it, between her flitting thoughts and Logan's pithy, "Because you go on so many of those."

Maddie made a show of looking at their mother. "I'll bring it in tomorrow, so you can see it."

Dad walked in, effectively sparing her any further commentary from Jack and Logan about her love life or lack thereof. But better than that was seeing Dad in the office at all. He hadn't been in since his fall from a ladder that had left him out of commission for close to two months. Since she hadn't even sat down yet, she hurried over to be the first to give him a hug. "I didn't know you were coming in."

He hugged her back, almost as tightly as before the accident. "I told your mother if I had to be cooped up in the house one more day, I'd throw myself off a ladder just to have a change of scenery."

Serious or not, she gave him a stern look. "Let's maybe not joke about that."

He laughed, the sound rich and full and almost as reassuring as his presence in the office. "Gotta make sure things are running smoothly over here."

"You worried we're going to botch a job?" She folded her arms and stuck out her hip, feigning offense.

"Of course not." He waved a finger. "You three are the future of this company and I have every confidence in you."

They'd had plenty of conversations about it—even before getting hurt left him thinking seriously about retirement—but hearing him say it never failed to make her chest swell with pride.

He slung an arm around her shoulders. "But I have less confidence you and your uncle won't come to blows over something or other before that happens."

She laughed, along with Logan and Jack, because it was funny but also true. Uncle Rich liked to call himself the brains of the operation, but really he was the mouth. He could talk up a potato and close a deal better than a used car salesman on steroids. He drummed up plenty of business but managed to get on everyone's nerves in the process.

For better or worse, Rich's two kids had zero interest in the business. A good thing as far as Maddie and her siblings were concerned, though it did mean they'd probably want to cash out their shares when Rich retired. Hopefully, she and Jack and Logan would be positioned well enough to buy them out when the time came. Not something to think about today, fortunately.

Today was for working and building and making things new. "As much as I'd love to spend the day hanging with you guys, I'm heading over to the farm. Clover's new cheese making equipment is coming in, and I promised I'd be on hand to help get it situated."

Logan's eyes lit up. "Are you working on the cave while you're there?"

"Probably. I have the first half of the shelves, and I think Sy will want to start filling it with stuff sooner rather than later."

"I can come help, if you want. I can't wait to see it all done."

They'd designed it together, turning the hundred-year-old cellar of Clover's barn into a climate-controlled cave that would provide the perfect environment for aging cheese—not completely out of their wheelhouse, but definitely a stretch. The end result should be the perfect alchemy of old and new, art and science. "If you have time, that would be great."

"Yeah, I'm hitting a wall on the Nicholson design. I'll help you at the barn, then take that home to ponder over a glass of wine." Logan tipped her head in the direction of her laptop. "I just need to send a few emails."

"Okay, come over whenever." She imagined Sy would be around and willing to help, but an extra pair of competent hands would make quick work of it.

Logan offered a playful salute. Maddie grabbed her things, gave both her parents a hug, and headed to her truck. On the drive over, an almost giddy feeling bubbled up in her chest. She told herself it had to do with seeing Clover's dream one step closer to completion.

In the privacy of her own thoughts, though, she could admit it had at least as much to do with seeing Sy. She stood by what she'd said to Logan. Shopping for coats and having dinner together had absolutely not been a date. But that didn't mean she couldn't imagine what it might be like to go on an actual date. Or indulge in thoughts of what might happen after said date. They were her own private thoughts, after all. Nobody's business but hers.

❖

Sy studied the computer-generated layout of the room, then the room itself. "How big of an ass am I if I ask to change things?"

Maddie, who'd bent over to free the new press from the straps that held it to the shipping pallet, stood. She blew at a wisp of hair that had escaped her ponytail before narrowing her eyes at Sy. "What kind of changes?"

"Just a flip-flop of those two things." She pointed at the packing table and vacuum sealer. "Okay, technically three."

"Since it doesn't require moving plumbing or electric, I'll allow it." Maddie smirked in a way that told Sy she was sort of joking, but not.

They shifted things around, and Sy nodded her approval. This would create better flow for the days she and Clover worked together and make space for the assistant she hoped to be able to hire in the next few months.

"Wow, it looks legit in here."

Sy turned. She didn't recognize the voice or who it belonged to, but one look told her it had to be one of Maddie's siblings.

Maddie lifted her chin. "Nice of you to show up, right when the heavy lifting is over."

"I got caught up." The newcomer held up a bag. "But I brought sustenance."

"Please say it's cider donuts." Clover crossed the room and gave her a hug. "Hi, by the way."

When Clover let go, Maddie stepped forward. "Sy, this is my sister, Logan. Logan, Sy Travino."

"Great to meet you." Logan stuck out a hand.

Sy accepted the handshake. "Same."

Logan grinned. "Though, I feel like I practically know you. I've heard so much about you."

Sy glanced at Maddie just in time to catch the tail end of a death glare. She coughed to chase away the laugh that bubbled up. "Again, same."

"Oh, really? All good things, I hope." Logan spoke to Sy, but her gaze went to Maddie.

"Of course." In truth, there hadn't been much, good or bad. But even in the case of friendly sibling sparring, she wanted to establish herself as squarely Team Maddie.

"I'm going to go put on a pot of coffee to go with these." Clover held up the bag she'd taken from Logan.

Maddie jumped in. "How about we unload the wood from my truck while she does that so we can get to building as soon as we're done?"

Logan looked to Sy. "Is she this bossy with you, too?"

Sy shrugged. "Only when she knows what she's talking about and I don't. In which case I'm happy to take direction."

Maddie looked genuinely surprised that Sy would accede so quickly but recovered quickly. "See? Some people appreciate direction from someone with more knowledge and experience."

Logan rolled her eyes, but it seemed good-natured. "Okay, boss. Let's get this wood unloaded."

Between the three of them—and the fact that only half the shelves were ready courtesy of her request for oak over pine—it didn't take long, and they were done before Clover returned with coffee. When she did, they took a donut break, then got to work installing. Since Maddie had already put in the framing to Sy's specifications, getting the shelves in place didn't take long, either.

Sy fiddled with the thermometer and humidity gauges she'd bought while Maddie and Logan got the compressor hooked up and running. The room instantly started to cool. Not quite the ambiance of the stone-lined cheese caves of France, but the conditions would be right and they'd get the job done. Technically, with more precision and consistency than those stone-lined caves.

"You're thinking about all these shelves lined with wheels of this and that, aren't you?" Maddie asked.

"Yep." No point pretending otherwise. Even at half capacity, it would be a sight to behold.

Clover clapped her hands together. "I am, too, for what it's worth."

"I'm thinking about cheese on a plate with some crackers that I can eat." Logan lifted her chin at Sy. "How long till that happens?"

"We should have the first brie styles in five or six weeks. The blues and harder ones will take a few months."

Logan shook her head. "I'm sure they'll be worth it, but damn."

"I have the chèvre varieties we're playing with for the holidays. I'll send you home with some if you fill out the rating sheet I made up." Because it would be helpful to have more than Clover and her weigh in.

Maddie folded her arms. "Why wasn't I offered samples and a rating sheet?"

"You're being offered them right now?" Sy played sheepish, but the conversation felt more like a game than a dress down.

"Acceptable."

Sy wrapped and labeled some samples for each of them. Logan headed out to work on her design plans and Clover went to see to the afternoon milking, leaving Maddie and Sy standing in the cheese room. "Thank you for your help today."

Maddie lifted a shoulder. "I'm happy to see Clover's vision coming together. She's wanted this for so long."

"I'm glad I get to be a part of it." So different than the path she'd imagined taking, but one she could see more and more clearly each day she spent here. It might not be her final destination, but the direction felt right.

"Are you going to head out soon or stay and putter?"

She considered her options. "Probably stay. The frozen burrito and air mattress waiting at home aren't really calling to me."

Maddie frowned.

Sy raised a hand. "I'm not complaining. I know you're moving as fast as you can. And I'm the one who hasn't gone out to buy a bed yet."

"Still. It's got to suck not having a functional kitchen. Especially if you're a chef."

"I mean, yes. I miss cooking almost as much as I miss eating real food. But I'll deal." It wasn't the first time in her life she'd roughed it.

"You should come cook at my house."

Not what Sy was expecting. And if the look on Maddie's face was anything to go on, it caught her by surprise, too. "I don't want to impose."

She could practically see Maddie catch herself, then shift gears. "You wouldn't be. Especially if you shared whatever you made."

The offer appealed, though she'd be hard-pressed to say whether it had more to do with cooking in a real kitchen or having an excuse to hang out with Maddie again. "Of course I'd share."

"Sweet. What time do you want to come over?" Maddie asked.

Was it as easy as that? When it came to Maddie, she could never be sure.

"Wait," Maddie said.

Apparently not. "Changing your mind already?"

"No, but I forgot I have this thing."

Sounded like a mind change to her, gracious coverup or not. "A thing."

Maddie pouted, and Sy had to chastise herself for finding it adorable. "It's a networking event sponsored by the Chamber of Commerce. I promised my dad I'd go and be the face of the company while my uncle is out of town."

What part of that to unpack first? "Bedlington has a Chamber of Commerce?"

"Well, the county. The event is over in Greenwich, at the Moose Lodge."

Of course it was. "Ah, well, then. Wouldn't want to miss that."

Maddie narrowed her gaze and looked every part the put-upon teenager. "It might not be LA, but it's how businesses in a small town network with one another."

She cringed. "Yeah, totally. I didn't mean to make fun."

Maddie huffed out a sigh. "Besides, it's a big deal to my dad. He's the real brains of the company, but my uncle is the front man. Only my uncle is in Florida at some convention put on by one of the tool companies."

"Sure, sure," Sy said, nodding like it was the most logical explanation possible, and her mind tripped over just how comically small-town it all was.

Maddie's expression went from slightly exasperated to legit offended. "Wait. You think I'm making it up."

Sy laughed. "No, no. I believe you. It's too random to be a lie."

That seemed to snap whatever weird tension she'd created, and Maddie rolled her eyes. "Seriously."

At the risk of overplaying her hand, Sy went for one of Maddie's signature arm folds. "So, if your dad is the brains, and your uncle is the face, what are you?"

That got her a smirk. "I'm both."

"And humble, too. Total package right there." Not to mention smokin' hot.

"Ha ha. Really, though. Logan and I both meet with clients, though she's more design and I'm more construction."

That division of labor made sense, especially from what she'd seen of Maddie and her sister thus far. Even if Logan was the butch foil to Maddie's more feminine energy. "Isn't there a brother, too? What does he do?"

"Jack's the master electrician who prefers interacting with as few people as possible."

"Right, right." Maddie had mentioned that on their shopping trip. "I can respect that."

Maddie folded her arms. "Is that because it's your preference, too?"

"Eh, I like a good schmooze as much as the next person. Especially when there's good food involved." She imagined some of the hobnobbing she got to do in France and the seemingly endless cheese that came with it.

"There's food, but I'm not sure it quite makes the leap to the realm of good."

Sy shrugged. "You'd be surprised how much your standards drop when you don't have a working kitchen."

"Do you want to come?" Maddie asked.

For all that she poked fun, she probably should, in general if not tonight. "I'm not sure I can make myself presentable in time, but rain check? Assuming these things happen on the regular."

"They do, so I'll hold you to that. And what about dinner at my place?" Maddie's expectant look had Sy thinking about more than just dinner.

"If you really mean it, I'd love that." She figured Maddie had glommed onto the distraction for a reason.

"I absolutely mean it. I'll even buy groceries." Another smirk. "Unless you're picky about that sort of thing."

She was but didn't need to admit it. Especially with a dinner invite on the table. "Bringing the groceries is the least I can do."

"Tomorrow?"

Well, that was easy. "Tomorrow."

CHAPTER EIGHT

At the sound of a muffled knock, Maddie hurried to the back door. She found Sy, as expected, wearing her new puffer vest and looking far too kissable for her own good. Less expected was the massive haul of groceries literally spilling over the top of the bags Sy clutched in each arm. Maddie instinctively reached for one. "You know it's just the two of us, right?"

Sy shrugged, her sheepish smile only intensifying the kissable quotient. "I may have gotten carried away. I promise I'll take home whatever's left over that you won't eat."

Maddie carried the bag to the kitchen and set it on the counter, motioning for Sy to do the same. "What if I would eat whatever's left?"

"Then I'll happily leave it for you."

"Maybe we could share." She had a not unpleasant flash of taking little containers of Sy's creations to work, warming them in the microwave at the office or eating them cold from the container on a job site. Hot on the heels of that flash came the teasing she'd endure from Jack and Logan about the perks of having a girlfriend who cooks. Sure, she could poke fun at Logan's propensity for peanut butter and jelly and Jack's bad habit of skipping meals, but that would do nothing to counter the girlfriend part. Sy was one hundred percent not her girlfriend, and she needed to keep it that way.

"I like the way you think." Sy winked, sending Maddie's thoughts skipping away from leftovers and back to kissing.

Maddie cleared her throat. No kissing. No thinking about kissing. This was a friendly dinner, nothing more. "What can I do to help?"

"Honestly?" Sy sort of cringed as she asked.

"Honestly." As long as "honestly" didn't turn out to be code for "please stop staring at my mouth because it's freaking me out."

"Stay out of my way." Sy lifted a hand. "But not too far away since I don't know where anything is."

Maddie laughed, relief mixing with genuine delight at the diva-like contradiction. "How about I pour myself a glass of wine and sit right there?" She pointed to one of the stools at the breakfast bar.

"Perfect, assuming you're pouring me a glass of wine, too."

She went to the fridge, glad Sy hadn't been there to see her fretting over her rather meager wine collection. "I put a Chardonnay in the fridge, but I have a Pinot Noir, too."

Sy started pulling produce from one of the bags—red onions, garlic, cilantro, and at least four different kinds of citrus. "The Chardonnay would be great. I brought a Tempranillo to go with dinner, but it's a little loud on its own."

"Loud?" She enjoyed wine but had never taken the time to learn much beyond a few likes and dislikes.

"Bold, full-bodied. You know?"

She nodded, at least vaguely familiar with the terms.

"I'm not saying we should drink two bottles of wine with dinner, mind you. I just think it would be a nice starter. And, you know, there are worse things than leftover wine."

Considering she sometimes hesitated to open a bottle for just herself, she could get behind the idea just fine. "For sure."

"Great. Before you pour, would you point me in the direction of a cutting board, a knife, and whatever pots you have on hand?"

Maddie jockeyed around Sy, pulling out the requested items before turning her attention to the wine. By the time she had two glasses poured, Sy had set up right at the bar, facing the stool she'd indicated. Not the most efficient spot but definitely the most intimate one. She handed one glass to Sy and lifted the other. "To friends who cook."

"And friends who share their kitchens."

After the requisite clink and sip, Maddie settled on one of the stools. "I can chop an onion, you know. And garlic."

Sy looked up, but her fingers continued separating the crushed cloves from the skins. "Do you always have a hard time letting people do nice things for you, or is it specific to cooking?"

A pithy question but rhetorical, too. That maybe hit a little close to home. "Offering to help doesn't mean I'm uncomfortable with what you're doing."

"I stand corrected." Sy's words were conciliatory, but mischief danced in her eyes.

"But maybe I am more used to doing than watching." Which was true, and somehow easier to admit than the letting people do nice things for her business.

Sy relented, tasking her with zesting and juicing a lime, an orange, and a grapefruit. "Do you like to cook?" Sy asked.

Maddie folded her arms. "That feels like a trick question coming from a chef."

"I promise it's not. Besides, I quit being a chef."

"Because cheese?" She quirked a brow, kidding but not.

"Cheese offered an escape hatch. Professional kitchens are intense, and more often than not, toxic and misogynistic."

She had a vague sense of that—from TV, from her own experience with an industry known for being a boys' game. "I'm sorry."

Sy shrugged. "I realized it wasn't for me. And without the capital to open my own place, I decided I needed to look at other options."

"I respect that. Even if it boggles my mind that a goat farm in France somehow made it to the top of your list." She'd never be that adventurous, that brave. A fact that had been painfully pointed out to her when her ex set her sights on Boston and wanted Maddie to join her.

"My mom has this saying. Work hard but let the universe give you gifts along the way. Don't let it all be about the hustle, you know?"

"Yeah." Her family didn't do the gifts from the universe thing, but they did believe in balancing work with rest and play and family and whatnot. One of the reasons she held on to that life, even when it cost her. "That's what France was? A gift from the universe?"

"Something like that."

Conversation lulled while Sy rubbed a pork loin with the marinade she'd been building. She let Maddie slice sweet potatoes into half-moons and before long, Sy slid everything into the oven. "Is it possible for it to smell amazing already?" Maddie asked.

"Yes." Sy grinned and held up a bunch of cilantro. "Yes?"

"Oh yes." It sounded way more suggestive than she'd meant, and Sy definitely noticed. A beat passed, then another.

"Thank God." Sy smirked like she'd waited on purpose, then gave it a twist, separating the leaves from the thicker part of the stems and chopping it like nothing had happened.

"I have no idea what we're having, but I'm almost stupidly excited for it," Maddie said. Because dinner. Tonight was about dinner, not baring her soul or food as foreplay.

"I'm pretty excited, too. Bedlington is charming and all, but I got tacos from the little place off Main Street earlier this week and I confess they left me wanting."

Maddie laughed. "Even I think they're bland."

"This won't be that. But it won't be too spicy, either."

Sy was one hundred percent talking about the food, but Maddie's mind went in a dozen other directions. Okay, not a dozen. One direction. One problematic direction that held so many possibilities. But for all the arguments with herself to be cool, she couldn't seem to help herself. "I like spicy."

❖

Sy set one of the plates in front of Maddie. "Bon appétit."

Maddie looked from the food to her and back again. "This might be the most beautiful thing I've ever been served."

"Stop." She slid into the spot Maddie had set for her—adjacent at the little round table rather than across.

"I'm serious. You may not have noticed, but we're not exactly a fine dining mecca around here."

She had noticed, more because it reminded her of the town where she grew up than to pass judgment. She imagined Maddie had been to Boston, though, and New York. But maybe not. Or maybe not to the sort of high-end restaurants where a single meal could cost a person's take-home pay for the better part of a week. "Well, thank you for indulging me. I hope it's not too much. If you don't like it, it's okay. You won't hurt my feelings."

Maddie smiled, clearly knowing that last part was a lie, at least a little. "I'm pretty sure I'm going to love it."

Sy poured them each a fresh glass of wine from the bottle she'd brought to go with the meal. "Dig in."

Maddie went for the pork first. It might have been totally cliché, but Sy held her breath. As Maddie chewed, her eyes drifted closed. "Oh, my God."

"I'm taking that as a vote of approval."

Maddie opened her eyes. "You're kidding, right? This is amazing. Like, stuff the whole thing in my mouth in a really unbecoming way kind of amazing."

"I'm glad you like it." Though she'd be lying if she said that look of pleasure on Maddie's face didn't make her think of other ways she'd like to put it there.

"Like is definitely an understatement." Maddie tried the salad, then the sweet potatoes she'd roasted with adobo and drizzled with cilantro crema. "I'm already calculating the labor I can trade you to do this again."

Sy chuckled. "Until my house is done, all you have to do is let me use your kitchen."

"Be careful or I'm going to have you here every night."

"I can think of worse things." Though, if this chemistry between them didn't settle, she wasn't sure she'd be able to keep pretending it wasn't there. Which could make for awkward dinner conversation.

"Well, maybe not every night. Sometimes all I want is a bowl of cereal at the kitchen sink before a hot shower and bed." Maddie made a circular motion with her hand. "And you probably have a life and stuff."

"Eh?" She'd hung out with Clover a few times, but Clover got up even earlier than she did to take care of the goats, so it was usually limited to a quick bite at Fagan's.

"Is it hard, being in a new place?" Maddie asked.

"It's hard being away from my mom. We're really close. I've moved enough times that I'm used to making new friends, and to having lots of time to myself." She wasn't prepared to admit how often she conversed with Henry. Or the goats.

"Yeah, but here's probably a lot WASPier than you're used to." Maddie tipped her head at the admission, then took a sip of her wine. "Fuck. That's really good, too. Sorry."

Sy smiled at the shift more than the sorry. "No need to apologize. And actually, Bedlington is less white than the town I lived in while doing my apprenticeship in France. Plus they spoke mostly French."

Maddie laughed. "Okay, that sounds worse."

"I had a little cred from being raised Catholic, though. The village ladies loved seeing me at Mass." She winked, hoping to convey she didn't take any of it too seriously.

Maddie nodded, expression serious. "I think I take for granted how easily I've had it."

"What do you mean?"

"I've only ever lived here, and I've always fit in." Maddie went from serious to a full frown.

She hadn't had a rough childhood, at least not by the standards of what she'd seen, but she definitely hadn't had that. "It's not something to feel bad about. But for sure something worth appreciating."

Maddie's nod turned brisk, agreement but also an indication she'd just as soon not delve any deeper. "What about you? Did you move around a lot as a kid, too?"

"I wouldn't say a lot. My mom raised me by herself. We stayed in one town for most of my childhood because her parents were there. But when I was old enough to look after myself after school, she took a better job a few towns over." Then there was the move after Bonita realized the schools on that side of town were pretty awful, but that was a different story.

"It must have been hard, starting over and having to make all new friends."

Sy shrugged. "It's pretty common though. And I was smart enough and athletic enough to do okay."

"Athletic enough, huh? What did you play?"

"Basketball, mostly. It was accessible and cheap and I was tall. You? Did you play any sports?"

"No. I played the clarinet rather badly. But I started working as soon as I was old enough." Maddie chuckled. "All I ever wanted to do was build things."

"I'm sure your dad loved that." She didn't really long for a dad these days, but little pangs still caught her sometimes.

"Both my parents. My mom does the books for the business, so it's a full family affair. They never pressured us, but I think they're thrilled we all wanted to stick around."

"And in really different ways, right? It's cool you all do something different." Truth be told, she'd longed for siblings more than a dad most of the time.

"Yeah, and we're really different personality-wise, too. Jack is quiet and analytical, with an undercurrent of grumpy old man. Logan is outgoing and arty but hates when people don't take her seriously." Maddie's features softened as she described them, highlighting how close they were, even in their differences.

"What are you?" Besides smart and gorgeous and competent.

"I'm the executive. I know it's cliché for the oldest to be the bossy one, but I am and I'm good at it."

She had a flash of Maddie that first day, arms folded and looking at her disaster of a house. "Hey, if it works, why change?"

Maddie took another bite of pork and chewed thoughtfully. "I suppose." She pointed at Sy with her fork. "I'm trying to learn about you, but you keep changing the subject back to me."

A skill she'd developed back in the days of starting at a new school. It served her well then, and then in culinary school and the various kitchens that came after. Most of the time, people liked talking about themselves and didn't even notice. "What can I say? I'm curious."

Maddie smirked. "Me, too. Tell me about France."

She did, and Maddie seemed genuinely interested in the details. They swapped stories about travel and places they'd never been but wanted to see. Maddie asked about her mom; Sy asked about the history of Barrow Brothers and what it was like to be part of a fourth generation anything. Time melted away and the next thing she knew, it was after ten.

They did the dishes together—maybe like friends, maybe like a date. The line hadn't been entirely clear from the get-go. Now, with a couple of glasses of wine in her system and the giddy haze of getting to know Maddie more deeply, Sy found herself way past wanting to kiss Maddie and well on her way to wondering how mutual the feeling might be.

"Thanks again for coming. I should probably let you go. I know you head to the farm pretty early." Maddie tucked her hair behind her ear in what could have been habit or just as easily a tell.

"No earlier than you're hauling ladders and getting your crew going."

"The days are getting so short. Gotta make hay while the sun is shining." Maddie squeezed her eyes closed. "God, I sound just like my grandpa."

"For what it's worth, I think it's cute."

"If Logan was here, she'd tell you not to encourage me." Maddie moved toward the door, so Sy followed.

"Good thing Logan isn't here." Sy snagged her vest from the hook over the bench and slipped it on.

"Yeah." Maddie looked at the ground for a second, then at Sy. "Encourage away."

What was that? An invitation? A suggestion? Come-on? If it was, and she biffed her chance, she'd never forgive herself. But what if it wasn't? An unexpected, unwelcome kiss could make things awkward to like the millionth degree.

Maddie put her hand on the doorknob, but didn't turn it. Sy looked at her hand, then into Maddie's eyes, pausing just long enough at Maddie's mouth for her to notice. Assuming Maddie wanted to notice that sort of thing.

Maddie must have, because she licked her lip and gave Sy one of those little encouraging smiles. Sy leaned in. Maddie did, too.

"Oh!" Maddie lurched back.

Sy fought off a wave of panic. "What? What's wrong?"

"Sorry." Maddie cringed, then rolled her eyes. "I forgot something and I just remembered."

Better than horrified by the prospect of being kissed. "What did you forget?"

"Can I steal you from work Wednesday? I want to take you somewhere, but it has to be Wednesday."

She pretty much set her own hours, so that part wasn't a big deal. But could it possibly be more pressing than what had almost just happened? And if Maddie thought it was, what did that say about her chances of making it happen in the long run? "If I say yes, will you tell me where?"

"No."

She couldn't help but laugh at Maddie's immediate and firm reply. "Will it be scary? I don't like scary."

Maddie made a face. "God, I hope not."

"Are you going to give me any clues?" She didn't hate surprises, but she did like feeling prepared for things.

"Dress comfortably and be ready by nine," Maddie said.

"Not really a clue."

Maddie shrugged. "It's all you're going to get."

She made a show of pouting. "Fine."

"It should be cool."

"Not helping." Though she wasn't genuinely worried.

Maddie shrugged again, playful smile making it clear she didn't plan to budge. Sy smiled in return, because even if she didn't love being surprised, she could enjoy the fact that Maddie wanted to surprise her. Maddie's hand returned to the doorknob. "So, I'll see you then?"

Whatever sizzly, kissy mood might have been there before was gone now. Maybe she'd been rushing things, anyway. Or imagining them altogether. Either way, probably for the best. At least for now. "See you then."

Chapter Nine

W here are we going?" Sy asked the second she climbed into Maddie's truck.

"You'll see." Maddie had scoped the auction ahead of time and knew a couple of stoves would be available, but she had no idea if they were what Sy wanted. Or if they'd fit in the house. Or if they'd go for a price Sy could afford.

"If you're taking me shopping for snow shovels, I beat you to it. I saw the weather report."

They were forecast to get the first real accumulation of the season mid-week. She'd already made a mental note to check on Sy if it materialized. And maybe show up with the old pickup her dad had outfitted with a snowplow for the family residences and various project sites they had going at any given time. "I'm not taking you shovel shopping. I saw the one you picked up and it'll do."

"It'll do?" Sy looked more worried than offended.

"I mean, if it's really bad, I'll come plow you out. After the roads are cleared, though. I'm a friend, not a miracle worker."

The look of alarm escalated to something resembling panic. "This is how I'm going to die, isn't it? Buried alive in a blizzard, only to be found after the spring thaw."

Maddie snickered. Sy was clearly joking, but it was that sort of forced, ha ha isn't this funny, kind of joking that pretended to veil a genuine freakout. "You're not going to die. Unless you go out in it without a coat on and get yourself lost somewhere."

Sy shook her head. "Oh, no. I'm staying put. I've got canned goods and flashlights and everything."

Since her feelings wouldn't be all that different were she bracing for a hurricane, she opted not to tease any harder. "This one is going to be no big deal, I promise. And if we get an actual blizzard at some point this winter, we can hunker together."

Sy's whole body seemed to relax. "You'd do that for me?"

The implication of her offer sank in and the truth of it was she wouldn't mind one bit. Though it might be the final straw for her poor resolve. Terrible idea or not, no way could she spend multiple days cooped up with the likes of Sy and not have sex with her. Assuming Sy wanted her back, of course. "Absolutely."

"That's really sweet. If we were trapped together, I'd totally cook for you."

Yeah, but would you go down on me? She cleared her throat, startled by how close she'd been to saying that out loud. "I would let you."

Sy seemed content with that answer, shifting the conversation back to where they were going and why. Eventually, she caved. Not because she couldn't keep a secret but because she started to worry the trip would be a bust, and she didn't want to build up too much anticipation.

"An auction?" Sy asked.

"Yeah. They might not have anything you want, but it's close by, and I figured it was worth a shot." And also, maybe, a nice excuse to spend the morning together.

"Like, furniture?"

"Like restaurant equipment." She shrugged. "The listing said there would be a couple of commercial stoves."

Sy's eyes lit up. "For real?"

"They might be huge. Or crap. I've never been to one of these before. I just saw it and thought of you."

Sy reached across the bench seat and gave her arm a squeeze. "That's the nicest thing anyone has ever done for me, aside from my mom. Thank you."

Maddie told herself the tingle along her spine had to do with Sy's words, not the moment of physical contact. She didn't believe it, but she told herself anyway. "Don't thank me until we see if there's anything worthwhile."

"Nope. It's really thoughtful no matter what."

"You're welcome, then. But I'm still hoping for a find."

Find turned out to be an understatement. There were two six-burner stoves and one eight. All functional and one practically brand new. Best of all? A meager turnout that meant Sy stood a chance of getting one of them.

The auction started with a pair of convection ovens and a fryer. Sy watched the bidding and Maddie watched Sy. She pointed to the oven. "You want one of those, don't you?"

"I mean, I'm not really a baker and I don't have room for it, but who doesn't?"

Maddie raised her hand but turned to face Sy and kept it close to her chest, wanting to indicate herself without accidentally joining the bidding.

Sy rolled her eyes. "Okay, fair."

"For the record, I like to bake." She waved a hand in the direction of the oven taller than she was. "But not like that."

The eight-burner came up first and went for a fair price. Sy decided not to bid, since it would take up practically half the space in her kitchen. "I hope I don't regret that."

The newer six-burner came up next. Sy raised her little paper paddle and was immediately countered by a bearded guy in flannel who looked more hipster than lumberjack. They went back and forth, creeping over what she would consider a reasonable price. The bidding slowed and she braced herself for disappointment.

But then Sy made one more flick of her wrist and hipster guy shook his head and the auctioneer pointed at Sy and said, "Sold."

Sy turned to her, grinning from ear to hear. "Did I just do that?"

"You did." Maddie cringed. "Are you okay with the price?"

"Are you kidding? That's less than half what they go for new. And not that much more than what I'd pay for a nicer residential model."

She'd seen said models. She'd even put a few in houses. They cost a pretty penny. A whole lot of pretty pennies she wasn't sure Sy would be willing to part with. "I'm reserving all rights to make fun of what you choose to splurge on."

Sy's grin turned smug. Like she was prepared to end any and all teasing with a kiss and dared Maddie to try her. Maddie swallowed and braced herself. Not where she expected their first kiss but whatever. She'd take it whenever, wherever at this point, consequences be damned. Only Sy didn't kiss her. She raised a brow. "Even if that splurge means I cook you dinner again?"

Maddie blinked, certain she looked like an idiot. "Dinner?"

"On the stove? I'll make you dinner again." The smirk faded, a look of confusion in its place. "I mean, I don't have to. You just seemed to enjoy it last time."

"Oh, I did. And I'd love you to cook for me again." But also maybe take me to bed.

"Are you okay?" Sy asked.

Just horny and distractable, apparently. "Totally."

"Okay. Cool. I don't think we can pay until the auction ends. Do you mind if I try to snag one of the lots of utensils and stuff?"

It was the reason they'd come here, after all. "Take your time."

"You're sure you're okay?"

She went for a bright smile, refusing to slosh around in feeling foolish. "Yep."

Sy clicked the mechanism one last time, then tested the tension. "I can't believe you keep ratchet straps in your truck."

Maddie shot her a bland look. "Really?"

"Okay, fine. Of all this, you having the right tools is the least surprising part."

"Thank you."

She joined Maddie at the tailgate just as Maddie slammed it closed. "I can't believe you found a restaurant auction one town over, and that auction had the stove of my dreams. I can't believe I had the winning bid, and that it fits in your truck, and that I get to take it home today."

Maddie smiled. "I'm glad it worked out."

The momentary weirdness from earlier had vanished. In its place, Maddie's usual demeanor—a seemingly incongruous mix of easy and all business. That mix, along with Maddie's infectious smile and the way her body filled out a pair of jeans, had been invading Sy's thoughts more and more. But just when she'd start to think the feeling might be mutual, Maddie would look at her like she'd grown a second head and perhaps a few extra limbs.

It was confusing. Slightly maddening. And it left her totally turned on and utterly at a loss for what to do about it.

"I kind of want to give you a hug right now," Sy said. Not a solution and it might make matters worse in the long run, but she couldn't seem to help herself.

"All right." Maddie opened her arms, but her eyes narrowed with suspicion.

The hug was brief. Slightly awkward. Friendly at best. But it left Sy's skin tingling. More, it gave her brain a more tangible sense of Maddie's body. The shape of her, the softness that her clothes and workhorse energy hid. And best of all—or maybe worst?—it hinted at the way their bodies fit together. Any hope she had of brushing her attraction aside evaporated.

"What?" Maddie took a step back, suspicion now mixed with concern.

"Nothing."

Maddie folded her arms. Sy was getting used to it, though she'd seen that exact stance send grown men on Maddie's crew scurrying to do her bidding. "You look like I punched you instead of hugged you."

"Sorry."

"Don't apologize. Tell me what's going on."

Sy coughed, buying time. "I just realized I haven't hugged anyone since I got here."

Maddie frowned.

Since it wasn't a lie, she decided to stick with it. "It struck me is all."

"I'll hug you anytime."

"It's okay." Because as much as she might like the physical contact, pity hugs were the absolute last thing she wanted from Maddie. "It's just weird. I'm usually around friends or family or a woman I'm dating. At least one of those."

The frown intensified. "Aren't we friends?"

"Of course." She knew better than to admit Maddie was the sort of friend she wanted girlfriend hugs with.

"Well, then. Come here." Maddie opened her arms again.

She couldn't decline without seeming like a jerk. Maybe that first touch was a one-off. Novelty. They embraced again, and Maddie held on a little tighter, a little longer. The tingling gave way to full-on arousal. So much for being a one-off. Sy stepped back and cleared her throat.

"Better?"

Sy nodded.

"Are you lying?"

Yes. "Of course not."

Maddie shook her head, basically sending the signal that she didn't buy it but wouldn't press.

"Let's get this bad boy home." Sy turned both her gaze and her attention back to the stove. "Wait. Girl. She's definitely a girl."

Maddie chuckled. "How do you know?"

"I just do. Is your truck a boy or a girl? Or an enby?"

Maddie studied her truck. "It's a truck."

"You're going to tell me you don't name your vehicles?"

"You're telling me you do?"

Absurd or not, she hopped on the tangent like the last train to anywhere. "No. But I did name my pasteurizer at the farm. And I named the stove at the restaurant where I was a sous chef."

Maddie's eyes narrowed, and she nodded slowly. "Interesting."

"Did you name your first truck?"

"Nope."

"Huh." Sy racked her brain. "Do you name anything?"

"Pets, obviously. And dolls and stuffed animals when I was a kid." Maddie wrinkled her nose. "You think I'm a stick-in-the-mud, don't you?"

"Absolutely not." And even if she did, she sure as hell wouldn't say so. "Do you think I'm fanciful?"

Maddie seemed to consider before saying, "No."

She couldn't help but wonder if Maddie was having her own bout of sure as hell not saying so. "To each her own, right?"

"What did you name the pasteurizer?" Maddie asked.

"It doesn't matter."

"Oh, but it does." Maddie's eyes sparkled with mischief now.

Sy sighed. "Velma."

"Velma?"

"From Scooby Doo. Everyone had the hots for Daphne, but Velma had the brains. I've always been a sucker for a woman with brains." Even if Maddie found the whole thing silly, Sy could at least stand by that.

"Okay. I can get behind that." Maddie hooked a thumb at the stove. "And what will you name her?"

"I don't know yet. I need to see her in action." Which was true, but also saved her having to come up with something clever on the spot. "And you're going to help me get her home so I can."

Maddie took a deep breath and blew it out. "Yes. Home. I think she's secure."

Sy took that as her signal. She reached over the tailgate and gave the oven door a pat. "Travel safe, girl."

They situated themselves in the front seat and Maddie got them on the road. Maddie fell quiet, so Sy followed her lead. Her mind wandered, flitting over the various prized possessions she'd personified through the years.

"Beulah," Maddie said, seemingly out of nowhere.

"Beulah?"

"I'd name my truck Beulah."

Grandmother, maybe? Favorite aunt? "I hope you're going to tell me why."

Maddie glanced over, sly grin in place. "Beulah Louise Henry. This amazing inventor that practically no one knows about. And those who do refer to her as the Lady Edison, which is totally offensive. She deserves to have things named after her."

"Ah. So you have the hots for smart women, too."

Maddie blushed but didn't deny it. It made Sy wonder if Maddie would think of her as smart. She didn't have a traditional college degree. Then again, she didn't know if Maddie did, either. And she might not know a damn thing about DIY or snow, but she'd learned her craft and made something of herself. Two times over, technically.

Of course, that made her wonder if Maddie found her attractive in other ways. If Maddie thought about her when they weren't together, the way she did whether she wanted to or not.

Conversation lulled again and it wasn't long before Maddie pulled into Sy's driveway, artfully turning around so the back of the truck practically touched the garage door. They got the stove unloaded and Sy gave it a loving stare. "Thank you again."

"She really is a beauty." Maddie smirked when Sy looked her way for signs of sarcasm. "If you're into that sort of thing."

"I really, really am," Sy said.

"I'm sorry you can't cook on it—her—right away."

Sy waved off the apology. "I don't always like being patient, but I've gotten quite good at it."

"Have you?" Maddie asked.

"You have to in my line of work." A fact she'd learned the hard way.

"Oh, right."

Was it her, or did Maddie look disappointed? "But patience pays off in some other interesting ways, too."

That earned her a smile. "I know that in theory, but sometimes I struggle in practice," Maddie said.

Okay, they definitely were talking about more than work styles now. They had to be. "You know what they say, right?"

"What's that?" Maddie lifted her chin, all playful defiance.

"Practice makes perfect."

CHAPTER TEN

Clover waved both hands, like a director cutting a scene that had gone sideways. "Wait, wait, wait. Start from the beginning."

Sy rolled her eyes. "I told you. Maddie took me to a restaurant equipment auction and I got the most gorgeous stove for a not obscene amount of money."

Sy might be selling it, but Clover wasn't buying. "In the middle of the day. In the middle of the week."

"That's when it was." Sy shrugged. "She didn't pick the time."

Clover, who'd popped into the cheese room unannounced, dropped onto the stool Sy kept in the corner. "After she took an afternoon off the week before to take you coat shopping and you had dinner together?"

Sy lifted a finger. "Going to dinner was my idea, to thank her for taking me shopping."

Clover pressed her lips together.

"What?"

"I was talking about the dinner you made for her at her house. I forgot there was another dinner." Clover shook her head in what appeared to be a mixture of amusement and disbelief.

"That was about me cooking in general, and not being able to in my own kitchen. Not asking her to eat with me would be pretty damn rude, don't you think?" She projected indignation, but even she had to admit how ridiculous it was starting to sound.

"You could make dinner at my house, you know." Clover folded her arms in a way that channeled Maddie.

"I'd love to. Name the day. And for the record, I'd have made dinner at your house if you'd asked me." Not a lie, if not the entirety of the truth.

"Any night this week and that's not my point."

"What is your point?" The back and forth had felt like a game, but now she wasn't so sure. "Wait. Does it bother you that I'm spending time with Maddie?"

"Of course not," Clover said a little too quickly.

She considered Clover a friend as much as a boss, but maybe the feeling wasn't mutual. Or maybe it was and it weirded Clover out that two of her friends were spending so much time together without her. Or maybe she had feelings for Maddie and this stirred up jealousy or unrequited longing or something else equally awful. "Hey, if it's a problem, I want you to be honest with me."

"It's not a problem. Oh." Clover's eyes got big. "You think I have a problem problem."

"Do you?" She'd back off if that was the case, but it would suck. Not that she and Maddie had officially started dating or anything. Or even kissed.

Clover seemed to genuinely consider the question before giving a decisive, "No."

"Are you sure?" Sy asked.

"Absolutely sure. Unless you go for it and it ends badly and then it's icy and uncomfortable every time you're in the same room together."

She hadn't gotten that far, but she appreciated why it would be at the top of Clover's list. "Yeah."

"Mostly I think it's hilarious that you two are obviously into each other, but you both insist it's NBD." Clover hopped down from the stool. "Not surprising, mind you. Just hilarious."

Being teased felt like a small price to pay for confirmation that Maddie was into her, too. "Has Maddie done that? Talked about me but made it seem like NBD?"

Clover stuck both hands straight out in front of her. "Uh-uh. I am not getting in the middle."

"Sorry." She meant it. She wouldn't want to do that to anyone. Doing it to her boss? Giant red flags.

"You don't have to apologize."

"Still." She didn't want to make anything between them uncomfortable.

"It's all good, I swear." Clover came over and made little circles with her index finger. "Tell me what you're making."

Questions congregated in her mind, but she relegated them to Things to Mull Over When Alone. Because she respected Clover—and her job—enough to focus on the task at hand. And because, without exactly saying so, Clover had dropped some really nice breadcrumbs as to the nature of Maddie's feelings. "I got the cultures in for our gouda style, so I'm just waiting for the curd to set so I can hoop it."

"Wait, didn't you start that this morning?"

"Yes, but hard cheeses get a lot more rennet and set in a matter of minutes rather than hours." One of the reasons they were so fun to work with.

"Ooh."

As if on cue, Sy's timer went off. She donned a glove and gently worked two fingers into the block forming in the vat. She lifted gently and the curd cleaved cleanly. "See?"

"So, you're going to get that into baskets today?"

She'd come in early so she'd be able to start the pressing before calling it a day. "Yep."

Clover grabbed her arm with both hands and gave it a squeeze. "I'm stupid excited for this."

She'd done this exact process probably a thousand times by now. But doing it under her own direction rather than someone else's changed everything. "Same."

"I gotta go feed the herd, but I'll check back later?"

"Absolutely." She loved that Clover checked in and even helped but entrusted her with the planning and decision making.

"Excellent." Clover went to the door but turned. "Oh, and, Sy?"

"Yeah?" She stopped what she was doing just long enough to look up.

"That thing we were talking about earlier?"

"Yeah." She frowned and braced herself for words of warning.

"It's totally mutual." Clover winked and left without waiting for a reply.

Sy opened her mouth, but the only thing that came out was a halting noise that didn't even qualify as a syllable. She snapped it shut and dropped her shoulders. She could feel the grin spread and didn't try to stop it. And since no one was there to poke fun or judge, she let it linger while she went about her work.

❖

Maddie had just sent the last member of her crew home for the night when Sy pulled into the driveway. She stood on the porch, feeling weirdly domestic while Sy parked and made her way over. She resisted making a joke about it because, well, because.

"I wasn't sure I'd see you today." Sy seemed genuinely pleased, which only fueled how much Maddie had been thinking about her throughout the day.

"I had a couple of things I wanted to show you." Even if sticking around had more to do with wanting to see Sy than needing to.

"That sounds promising." Sy hesitated. "Or ominous."

She did her best to ignore the way her body reacted to Sy's proximity as Sy followed her back into the house. "It's good. I swear."

"Good. I like good."

"We got the kitchen gutted. Well, as gutted as it's going to be." She stepped to the side and splayed her arms, game show hostess style.

"Whoa." Sy walked into the kitchen and turned a slow circle.

They'd removed the countertops and the sink, pulled out the old stove that no longer worked, and moved the fridge to the living room. She'd even had time to take off the cabinet doors and put them in the dining room for Sy to paint. "I know it's even less functional than it was, but I hope it feels like progress."

Sy finished her second spin and stopped to look right at her. "It feels like potential."

Potential was a magical thing in home reno. Projects invariably looked worse before they looked better, but even in the mess, people could begin to see what would be over what was. Not everyone got that feeling, though. A few got anxious and depressed and convinced they'd made a terrible mistake. She hadn't expected Sy to fall into that latter category, but the true delight on Sy's face was better than she'd hoped for. "I'm glad it feels like that."

"It's amazing," Sy said.

"Hold onto that feeling because it also means you have a crap ton of painting to do."

"Right." Sy nodded, but her mood didn't appear dampened.

She showed Sy the setup she'd built—a pair of sawhorses and a stack of little cones she could set each door on to dry. "It's too cold to paint in the garage now."

Sy smirked. "For me or the paint?"

"The paint. You're fine in the cold. You just have to get used to it."

"Touché."

"Now." Maddie lifted a finger. "I don't know how you're going to do it, but you're going to have to keep Henry off of them while they dry."

"You don't recommend the paw print look?" Sy feigned confusion.

"It would be a statement," she said.

Sy laughed. "I can manage. If I put him in the bedroom with enough toys, he'll entertain himself."

"Same process as we discussed for doors. Get into all the nooks with a brush, then roll the flat surfaces to cover and blend."

"Yes, boss." Sy offered a playful salute.

"And you'll find this out soon enough, but dark colors are notoriously unforgiving when it comes to blemishes. You'll have to decide how fussy to be." She had a feeling Sy was particular about such things, even if she played the part of anything goes.

"What about the backs? And the insides?"

"What about them?"

"Should I paint them, too?"

What was that about being particular? Usually if people weren't springing for new cabinets, they just wanted them to look good from the outside. "You can."

"I was thinking white, maybe. Is that weird?"

"I mean, some people like to do that in their closets. Makes everything feel fresh and clean."

Sy frowned. "But I want that for my food and dishes more than where I keep my clothes."

Of course she did. "Then you should. It'll be tedious, but it's your time."

"How much are you going to make fun of me for it?"

It was hard to tell if Sy cared about her opinion or not, but she wasn't about to rain on anyone's parade of making their house the tiniest bit closer to their dream home. "Not at all. I might even help."

Sy regarded her with suspicion. "What's the catch?"

"No catch." She could think of plenty of things she wanted from Sy, but none of them were up for barter.

"Hmm."

"Well, not a catch, but we do need to move it along and my help would speed up the process." And would mean more time together, just the two of them. She might not be ready to admit it, but Sy was quickly becoming her favorite pastime.

"Oh." Sy's shoulders fell. "I don't want to hold things up."

"You won't. Let's start this evening. I'll show you how to do it and then you can work on that and the doors when you have time."

"Are you sure?" Sy looked excited, but like she was trying not to show it.

"Absolutely." Because in addition to wanting to spend time with Sy, there wasn't a whole lot waiting for her at home besides Kira and some leftover spaghetti from Sunday dinner at her parents' house.

Sy's enthusiasm bloomed. "Okay, great. Can I use the white we got for the doors and trim or do I need something else?"

"You can use that or keep the same color as the cabinets. I can get more paint mixed in the color you chose."

"What would you do?"

She doubted Sy was this deferential when it came to other things, but it was nice to have her knowledge and experience respected on things house related. "White would look clean and bright, but color would give the sense they're custom. And you wouldn't have to worry about making clean edges anywhere."

"Sold." Sy went to the uppers along the far wall and peered inside. "I have brushes, of course, and, ooh, that tiny roller you brought me. Do we need anything else?"

Maddie laughed, strangely delighted. "Just time and patience. And maybe a hat or a bandana. Painting the insides of things is hard to do without getting it in your hair."

Sy's eyes narrowed. "Worse than ceilings?"

She'd forgotten to warn Sy about that and arrived to find Sy's entire head—face included—flecked with white. "Different. Inadvertent smears."

"Right, right." Sy nodded. "Sounds like my attempts at chocolate work."

It wasn't hard to imagine Sy in a crisp white chef's coat, pouring and shaping and manipulating melted chocolate into perfectly shiny, dazzling shapes. But even as she tried to keep her mind on that pristine visual, Sy's reference had her seeing smears of chocolate across her knuckles. Maybe one along her jaw. And from there, it wasn't a leap to imagining what it would be like to lick and kiss and suck that chocolate away. The taste and texture of Sy's skin mixed in.

"Maddie?"

"Huh?"

Sy stood before her, roller and brushes in hand. "You okay?"

"Oh, yeah. Totally. Sorry. I was remembering something I need to do in the office."

"Do you need to go?" Sy asked.

"No, no. I'm just going to make myself a note." She pulled out her phone and pretended to type a reminder. She actually typed *Get a grip*.

"Okay. Well, if you need to give me some pointers and go, I understand."

Maddie waved the notion away. Since Sy already knew the basics of painting, she prepped a small tray and the handled cup she'd given Sy for edging. She started with one of the lowers since there were fewer shelves to contend with, crawling partway in and propping herself on her side to reach the back. "Getting a perfect finish is less important in here, obviously, but you do have to contort yourself to get into all the corners."

Sy hunched over and peered inside. "Is it wrong to say I'm enjoying watching your contortions?"

It could have been a joke, and it could have been a come-on. Like so many of her interactions with Sy, she couldn't quite tell. Which proved equal parts maddening and arousing. "Don't get too comfortable. You're next."

She finished the edging in that space then scooted out and gestured for Sy to take her place. Sy made a production of it, grunting and groaning and insisting her body wasn't built to bend that way. In the end, she made out just fine, getting paint where it needed to go and only a little in other places.

They made their way around the room, stopping to order pizza just after seven, debating the relative merits of pineapple and agreeing it had its place. Preferable with ham, hot peppers, and a good amount of char. Since Bedlington's sole pizzeria couldn't be trusted with such a tall order, they went for pepperoni and extra cheese. When it arrived, they ate cross-legged on the floor with a bottle of cabernet that Sy poured into coffee mugs. For not the first time, Maddie found herself thinking that, for an evening that was in no way a date, it was turning out a lot more fun—and a lot more like a date—than many actual dates she'd been on.

After polishing off the pizza, they got back to work. She told herself finishing the first coat would put them in a good place. Mostly, though, she simply wasn't ready to leave. They took turns with the brush and roller, crawling into the lowers and perching on a ladder to reach the nooks and crannies of the uppers. Snippets of conversation here and there, but mostly quiet. With moments of surreptitious appreciation of Sy's butt.

Sy stepped off the ladder after finishing the last one with a streak of paint across her cheek. Maddie chuckled and went to wipe it with her thumb. Only Sy's head turned and her lips brushed Maddie's thumb instead. She thought Sy might jerk away, but she didn't. If anything, Sy went almost eerily still.

"Sorry," Sy said, barely above a whisper.

"I'm not." She heard the words more than she intended to say them, but the look in Sy's eyes told her it hadn't been a mistake.

The faintest hint of a smile played across Sy's mouth. "Then I'm not either."

She could take that as a gracious pass, laugh the whole thing off, and move along. Only she didn't want to. She'd been thinking about Sy for weeks now, wanting to kiss her for almost as long. And for whatever lines it blurred between them, whatever teasing would inevitably come from her siblings and Clover, she had no doubt in her mind that Sy wanted that kiss, too. When it came down to it, that's all that really mattered.

Maddie studied Sy's mouth for a second before looking back into Sy's eyes. Then she closed hers and let instinct take over. She brushed her lips over Sy's. No chocolate, but a lingering trace of red wine. Smooth and rich, with an earthy lushness. Warm. Sure.

She might have initiated the kiss, but Sy didn't hesitate to take over. Well, not exactly take over. More like she met Maddie in the middle, a delicious push and pull born of desire and curiosity.

Sy's tongue traced her bottom lip, sucked it gently. After willing her knees not to buckle and send her collapsing into Sy's arms, Maddie began her own exploration of Sy's lips, her mouth. She gripped the front of Sy's shirt, even as Sy held her shoulder. Not possessive, really, but it seemed to convey the same sentiments pulsing through Maddie. The ones that said Sy would happily rip her clothes off given the opportunity.

She was this close to proposing exactly that when Sy broke the kiss. "Wow."

Maddie chuckled. "Understatement."

"You okay? Was that okay?" Sy searched her face, desire still apparent, but concern too.

"Only if your definition of okay is fucking fantastic." Aside from the fact that she already wanted more.

Sy smiled. "I'll take that."

"You?" she asked.

"If we're going with your definition, I'm very okay."

Relief and a whole new wave of desire washed though her. "Glad we're on the same page."

"I should probably walk you out, though, or it's entirely possible I'll ask you to stay."

If her libido was disappointed, the rest of her appreciated the idea of taking things slow. Well, slower than hooking up after a single kiss, at least. "Yeah."

"Don't get me wrong. I really don't want to."

That simple assurance appeased her libido enough to get on board with the plan. "Not to be redundant, but yeah. Same page."

CHAPTER ELEVEN

S ince Sy had taken the day off to work on the house, Maddie hoped to get there early, but a flooring debacle at one of her other job sites had her zigzagging across town twice before eight a.m. and pulling into Sy's driveway at the same time as the rest of the crew. She called out the usual greetings and good mornings, only to repeat them when Sy stepped out onto the porch a moment later.

They filed into the house and congregated in the living room to get the rundown for the day. Since she was serving as both project manager and site supervisor, she doled out tasks and priorities, starting with the plumbing rough-ins for the bathroom and finishing drywall in the rest of the upstairs. Sy made her standing offer of coffee and the crew scattered to their work.

It left Maddie and Sy momentarily alone, which turned out to be a perfect opportunity for each of them to stare at their feet. Fortunately, the guys who'd left a moment before returned, hauling tools and supplies from their trucks to the various rooms where they were needed. Perhaps pouncing on the distraction made her a coward, but she didn't care. "Since you know what you're doing with the cabinets, I, um, thought I should show you spackling today. The seams are tricky, but the holes where the screws are don't take much finesse."

Sy regarded her with what appeared to be amusement. "Are you saying I don't have finesse?"

The question gave her mind license to think about just how much finesse Sy did have. The way Sy made that first tentative brush of lips feel like a matter of consent more than timidity. The seamless slide into a more assertive kiss—not possessive but sure. Sure and exquisitely thorough. Like she'd done a college degree on making out and that kiss was her dissertation. Maddie's lips tingled at the memory and she had to bite her lip to chase away the sensation.

"Should I take that as a yes, but you're too nice to tell me?" Sy asked.

"Huh?"

Sy smirked, clearly enjoying that Maddie had spaced out. "Finesse. We were discussing whether or not I had any."

Since they were practically surrounded by members of her crew, she satisfied herself with giving Sy a brief once-over. "Oh, I think you manage just fine."

"Maybe we should go over it, point by point, so I can really understand my strengths and weaknesses." Sy returned the once-over, lingering in just the right places to hint at a few points she might like to make.

Maddie didn't consider herself bashful, but heat rose in her cheeks. Of course, desire had as much to do with it as embarrassment, if her skittering pulse was anything to go on. And the chance they might be heard by members of the crew. Her team respected her, but they'd worked together long enough and had solid rapport. The teasing would be relentless. "Maybe we should focus on work."

Sy blinked a few times, and the flirty look on her face cooled. "Sure."

Maddie winced. "For now, I mean." She flicked her head at Leon, who'd just come in with a ladder.

Realization dawned and Sy lifted her chin, flipping the flirty back on seamlessly. "Yes, boss."

She leaned in to give Sy a well-deserved elbow to the ribs but didn't get the chance. Leon needed her to go over the electric being added and upgraded in the kitchen, including new can lights. Ange had questions about plumbing and how much of the original pipe could be salvaged. And then the gutter company showed up a day ahead of schedule, which required a bit of wrangling since she hadn't fully cleared the perimeter of the house for them to work.

She eventually found Sy in the dining room, painting cabinet doors. "Sorry. Just a little bit of chaos today."

"You handle it well. Can I say it's fun to watch you work?" Sy's tone was casual, but the look in her eyes was far from it.

She tipped her head back and forth, pretending to consider. "I think so."

"It's really fun to watch you work," Sy said.

"Well, finish that door and meet me upstairs. You're going to get to watch me put you to work." She hadn't meant anything suggestive, but it sounded like a Grade-A double entendre. Sy's smirk confirmed it landed with her the same way.

"Yes, boss."

She at least managed an eye roll before heading upstairs, where she prepped one mud pan and putty knife for Sy and one for herself, then got to work taping the drywall seams.

"Are you ready for me?"

Sy's voice came from mere inches behind Maddie, sending her halfway out of her skin. She spun around, hand pressed to her chest. "Jesus, you scared me."

Sy had the decency to look sheepish. "Sorry."

It didn't help that, in addition to being scared senseless, Sy's particular choice of words sent her addled brain right to thoughts of Sy standing behind her in a completely different context. One that may or may not involve a strap-on. "No, no. I just didn't hear you come in."

"I swear I didn't mean to sneak up on you."

She waved away the addendum to the apology. "It's fine."

"Is this a good time? You ready to put me to work?"

If only she could. "Absolutely. If we move quickly, things will dry enough for a second coat today and you'll be able to paint whenever."

"And then I'll be able to sleep in here." Sy's grin fell into a frown.

"Why do you say it like that?" she asked.

"I really gotta get a bed."

As if her imagination wasn't already having a field day. "You really do."

Sy lifted a hand. "Problem for another day. Today is for whatever you're about to show me how to do."

Maddie demonstrated the basics. Sy had filled nail holes a time or two through the years, so they weren't starting from scratch. She set Sy up along one wall and Maddie finished taping.

They worked quietly for a few minutes, though it was hard to tell whether Sy had been cowed earlier or was especially focused on the task at hand. Maddie kept stealing glances, telling herself it was to make sure Sy was doing it right but knowing full well it wasn't.

Maddie cleared her throat for the third time in as many minutes. Realizing it made her sneak yet another surreptitious glance at Sy, who of course chose that exact moment to look at her.

"Are you okay?" Sy asked.

"Mm-hmm." She took a swig from her water bottle and smiled. "All good."

"Okay." Sy resumed smearing and scraping joint compound over the drywall screws.

Maddie started coating the joint tape that covered the seams. After about a minute, the slap and scrape from Sy's putty knife stopped. Seconds passed. Sy remained quiet. Maddie looked at her again but didn't try to be sneaky about it this time. "Wait. Did you ask so I would ask you? Are you okay?"

"I'm great." Sy lifted a shoulder. "But I feel like we should talk about it."

It. Sy's meaning was obvious, but referring to "it" as "it" made it all seem rather ominous. Or secretive. Or something else in the not good category. "Okay."

"Do you wish we hadn't?"

She remained unconvinced that kissing Sy had been a good idea, but she couldn't bring herself to regret it. If for no other reason than it was a fucking spectacular kiss. "No."

Sy looked at her expectantly, as though waiting for her to continue.

"And I'd do it again if given the chance," Maddie said.

Leon chose that exact moment to come in. Fucking Leon. Blown fuses and needing to add some splits to the breaker box. Definitely something that needed her input but still.

She offered Sy an apologetic smile and got a playful salute in return. She couldn't be certain it equated to agreement, but she decided to take it that way. At least for now.

❖

Maddie blew out a breath. "I'm sorry we didn't get two minutes to ourselves today."

Sy shrugged, enjoying the energy of a slightly off-balance Maddie. "Me, too. But I can't be mad because damn, we made a lot of progress."

Maddie smiled, the comment about progress seeming to center her. "It's always like that. There's this tipping point between ripping stuff apart and putting it back together that finally starts to feel like momentum."

"Well, if this is momentum, sign me up. I feel like we might actually finish."

"Of course we'll finish. I don't leave projects unfinished."

"Oh, I have no doubt." Maddie's efficient confidence was one of the things Sy found most attractive about her. Along with her laugh. And the way kissing her managed to leave Sy somehow satisfied and longing for more all at the same time.

"Good. I'd be offended otherwise." Maddie's posture softened. "I'm glad you're pleased."

"It's starting to feel like home." Sy lifted a hand. "Which feels weird to say because it's even more of a shell than it was. But it's like I can see myself, my stuff, in the space. Does that make sense?"

"Total sense," Maddie said.

"Anyway." As easy as it was to talk about the house, it left the kissing elephant sitting right between them.

"Yes?" Maddie looked expectant, like maybe she didn't share that view.

"About last night."

"Right."

When Maddie didn't continue, Sy took it as her cue to press on. "Are you feeling okay about it?"

"It was a damn good kiss, if that's what you're asking."

It wasn't, but she didn't make a habit of turning down compliments. "That's a start."

Maddie angled her head. "Are you worried that I regret it?"

"Um, a little. I couldn't really get a read on you today." And she was pretty good at reading people. Women. Women she kissed in particular.

"Sorry about that. It was weird, you know, with all the guys around." She waved a hand in a circle over her head. "They're like busy little ants, but with ears."

Sy laughed. "That's fair. And now that they're gone?"

Maddie looked her up and down, a slow sort of assessment that left Sy wondering if she was picturing her naked. "I'm thinking about kissing you again."

It felt like a "but" might be hiding at the end of Maddie's assertion. When it didn't come, Sy took a chance. "I should tell you, then, that I've been thinking about kissing you all day."

Maddie lifted her chin—an utterly perfect, sexy, playful challenge. "What are you going to do about it?"

They needed to talk, to sort out whether they were dating or hooking up or something in between. But with that delicious invitation dropped right in front of her, talking would have to wait. "I'm going to kiss you again."

Maddie smirked. "I'm pretty sure I kissed you first."

"I guess that means it's my turn. Assuming you're cool with that. Kissing again, I mean. But I guess the taking turns part, too."

"Yeah?" Maddie seemed intrigued, if slightly surprised.

"I'm not sure what you're thinking right now, so I'm just going to lay my cards on the table."

Maddie regarded her with something that channeled both curiosity and concern. "Okay."

"I like you."

A smile tugged at the corner of Maddie's mouth. "I like you, too."

"Not to be too dorky about it, but I like you, like you. I'd like to kiss you more. More than kiss."

Maddie nodded, a full smile blooming. "We're on the same page."

"And I'm not looking to U-Haul or anything, but I want to take you on a date and see where that goes, too." She felt silly saying it like that, but she'd been burned more than once when she hadn't been beyond clear with her intentions.

"I'd like that." Maddie twitched her lips to one side, then the other. "The date part, but the prohibition on U-Hauling, too."

She grinned at Maddie's choice of phrase.

"It doesn't bother you that we're working together?" Maddie asked.

"Me? No, not at all. Assuming we're on the same page." And won't wind up yelling at each other in the walk-in cooler like she'd done with that fiery pastry chef she'd gotten herself mixed up with that one time.

"Huh," Maddie said, her expression as noncommittal as her reply.

"Does it bother you?" Please say no.

"A little."

Damn.

"Not bother so much as worry," Maddie said.

That she could live with. "That makes sense. This is your career, your crew who might pick up on things."

Maddie stuck out her arms. "It's your house."

Sy shrugged. "But you're a consummate professional with deep integrity. Even if you decided you couldn't stand the sight of me, I have no doubt that you'd finish the job and finish it well."

Maddie's whole demeanor softened. "Thank you."

Clearly it was the right thing to say, but she happened to mean it. They'd danced around their attraction long enough to build that basic level of trust. "I don't expect that to happen, obviously, but I'd rather not get anywhere close. That's why I asked you out like a sweaty-palmed teenager."

Realization dawned in Maddie's eyes. "To make sure we were on the same page."

"Yeah. If I wanted to date and you just wanted a hookup, we don't get the luxury of going our separate ways and never having to bump into each other." Which she'd learned the hard way after things with the pastry chef went south. The whole staff took sides and pretty much no one picked hers. She'd only lasted in the job a couple of weeks after that.

"For the record, it's pretty impossible not to bump into each other in a town the size of Bedlington."

"And my boss is your best friend."

"Right." Maddie nodded slowly, as if that fact had only just dawned on her.

"Which is all to say that's why I'm proceeding cautiously." She quirked a brow. "And awkwardly."

Maddie stepped forward, bringing their bodies distractingly close. "I appreciate your caution."

"Thank you."

Maddie pressed her lips to Sy's—briefly, but it was enough to send a zinging sensation down her spine. "And your awkward."

Sy smiled. "You might be the first woman who's ever said that to me."

Another kiss. "Well, I know you're not awkward when it comes to the things that count."

"Oh? And what are those?"

"Your work." Kiss. "The way you talk about your mom." Kiss. "Henry."

"I see." Why'd she been so worried? This was fun. Easy.

"Kissing." Maddie didn't kiss her again. She simply stared at Sy's mouth.

Anticipation? Invitation? Whatever it was had yes please written all over it. And it was all the encouragement Sy needed. She slipped one hand into Maddie's hair, the other to the base of Maddie's neck.

Maddie was already close, but she moved in closer. Close enough for Sy to feel the warmth of her body. Close enough for Maddie's scent—an oddly intoxicating combination of cherry blossoms, vanilla, and freshly cut lumber—to invade her senses once more.

She took her time. It had nothing to do with consent or making sure they were on the same page. No, they'd taken care of that already, and then some. This was about enjoying herself, enjoying Maddie. And showing Maddie just how intensely she was wanted.

She expected the perfection of Maddie's lips, soft without yielding entirely. What she didn't expect was the intoxication of certainty, of knowing Maddie wanted this—wanted more than this—just as much as she did. It stoked the fire burning low in her belly, promising to ignite anything and everything she let it.

Would she let it? Only time would tell. But if the simple act of kissing Maddie was anything to go on, she'd have a hard time resisting.

Maddie pulled back first, though her reluctance was palpable. "Definitely nothing awkward about the kissing."

Sy let herself feel just the tiniest bit smug. "Ditto."

"I'm having dinner with Jack and Logan, or I'd stick around."

Given her choice, she'd absolutely have Maddie stay. Still, there was something to be said for anticipation. For that prolonged state of slightly aroused and wanting more. Especially when it was shared. "I can be patient."

"I can too, though I'll say straight up it's not my preference."

"Good to know." Sy waited a beat, pushing aside all the ways it could go wrong and letting herself bask in the possibility it could go so very right. "So, we're going to give this a go?"

Maddie's smile was slow but not the least bit hesitant. "I think we are."

CHAPTER TWELVE

Maddie knocked on Sy's side door, stomping her feet against the frosty morning air. For all her teasing Sy about winter, she wasn't entirely ready for it herself. When Sy opened the door, looking unreasonably hot in jeans and a flannel, Maddie lifted the bakery bag. "Good morning, sunshine. I brought breakfast."

"You're a goddess, but since when do you knock?" Sy stepped back, shutting the door the second Maddie was inside.

"Goddess. I like that. And yeah, but I'm a few minutes early. I didn't want to catch you naked." She imagined the possibility. "Let me rephrase. I wouldn't mind seeing you naked, but I wouldn't want to catch you unaware."

"I see." Sy tucked her tongue in her cheek and nodded slowly.

"It's important not to lie about such things, especially since we've decided we like each other." Which was still strange to admit but also, maybe, refreshing?

"Sure, sure." More nodding. "Full disclosure, then. I've thought about you naked a lot."

"Have you?" Was it silly to be delighted by that, even as lingering doubts lurked around the edges of her mind?

"Among other things." Sy's gaze managed to be piercing and playful at the same time.

"Other things?" She had an idea, obviously, but wondered how far Sy would take it.

"Things I probably shouldn't say out loud before we have an actual date." Sy tipped her head toward the table she'd set up as a makeshift kitchen. "Or coffee."

If part of her wanted to know exactly what sexy and salacious fantasies Sy's imagination had cooked up, the more reasonable part prevailed. Besides, the mere implication said plenty. "When are we going on that date, again?"

"Impatient?" Sy raised a brow, all playful now.

"Efficient. If we can't do…other things…until we've gone on a date, I want to make sure we get that taken care of." Not that she was only interested in sex, but that seemed like the most likely foundation for anything beyond friendship and she didn't want to pretend otherwise. Especially since neither of them were looking for a capital-R relationship.

Sy laughed. "You sound like such a dude right now."

She shrugged. "I mean, technically, we've had dinner together. And driven several places together. And kissed. Twice. That has to add up to a date and a half at least."

Sy, who'd gone over to pour coffee, turned, pot in hand. "Are you saying you don't want to go on a date with me?"

"Oh, no. That sounds really nice, actually."

"But?" Sy fixed both their cups and handed her one.

She spared a second to appreciate that Sy knew—had noticed and paid attention and remembered—how she liked her coffee. "But I don't think it necessarily needs to be the prerequisite to…"

"Other things?"

Maddie laughed, at herself as much as anything. "Exactly."

"Good to know." Sy nodded at the couch. "Shall we?"

"Of course."

Maddie sat and shifted her butt back and forth. "This is nice."

"Right? I think it's only a few years old. My neighbor just wanted a new one." Sy grabbed a roll of paper towels from the table and joined Maddie. "If only she'd do the same with a coffee table, a nice mattress, and a dining set."

"There's always hope."

"There's always a drive to IKEA, too."

Maddie laughed. "I should warn you that you'll be doing that solo."

Sy smirked. "Too good for IKEA?"

"Oh, no." She shook her head. "I just end up spending an obscene amount of money on things I don't actually need every time I go there."

"Is it wrong to find that comforting but also kind of sexy?"

Maddie laughed. "Strange, maybe. But I'd never say wrong."

"Good enough for me. So, what did you bring?" Sy dropped her chin and angled her head like it was a high stakes situation.

Maddie mimicked the gesture. "Danishes."

Sy shifted her head the other way. "What kind?"

"Cherry, cream cheese, and maple bacon."

Sy, who'd nodded her approval after the first two, let her mouth fall open. "What the what?"

"You either love it or you hate it. I happen to love it. 'Cause you know, maple is kind of a thing around here."

"Gimme." Sy grabbed for the bag.

She laughed and handed it over happily. She'd gotten two of each even though it was overkill, so there were plenty to go around. "I take it you approve."

Sy stuck her hand in the bag. "I've had a maple bacon donut. It was the trend a few years back. But Danish? I'm not even sure how that would work."

"Think bear claw, but maple-y and with bacon on top instead of nuts."

"Yes. Yes." Sy fished one out and didn't waste a second taking a bite. "Oh, yes."

Maddie giggled at the sexual-but-not tone. "If I'd known that was going to be your reaction, I have brought them sooner."

Sy licked glaze from her fingers. "If I'd known they existed, I'd have asked you to."

They demolished two Danishes each, agreeing that restraint was overrated and ranking the relative awesomeness of pastry and breakfast foods in general. It would have been almost too easy to while away the rest of the morning, drinking coffee and flirting. But it wouldn't get Sy's shower tiled. "Shall we get to work?" Maddie asked.

Sy nodded with an eagerness Maddie couldn't help but find endearing. "Yes. But seriously, are you sure you don't mind spending your Saturday with me?"

Maddie folded her arms. "Are you sure you want to ask me that for a tenth time?"

Sy pointed her fingers into her chest. "I'm not doubting the appeal of my company. I just feel bad that I'm making you work on your day off."

She appreciated the consideration, even if whole days off weren't exactly her jam. "We won't work too hard. And I plan on being mostly lazy tomorrow."

"I didn't think you had that setting."

She was pretty sure Sy didn't, either. "It's relative, no?"

Sy tipped her head back and forth. "That's one way of looking at it."

They gathered supplies and got set up in the bathroom. Maddie explained the process of gridding off the wall to ensure things were level and centered, but did it herself rather than wasting time teaching Sy the idiosyncrasies of her laser level. Once it was ready to go, she smeared thinset over the backer board in one of the quadrants, then combed it with the notched trowel. "Like this."

"Too bad I squeaked by in pastry class. Between the spackle yesterday and this today, those frosting skills would come in handy."

"I think you'll do just fine. Walls are more forgiving than cake." A lesson she'd learned the hard way that one time she'd attempted a fancy icing technique for Logan's birthday.

"We'll see about that," Sy said.

"For now, you just need to place the tile." She handed one of the white rectangles to Sy.

"How?"

"Just press it on. Use the lines as your guide." She indicated the crisscrossing green marks.

Sy frowned. "It feels like there should be more of a technique involved."

"Just do it. If you do it wrong, we'll start over."

Sy huffed. "I don't want to do it wrong."

"You can't," she said.

"You just said I might. Like, literally."

Since merely standing in the tub together had them practically touching, she gave Sy's hip a bump with her own. "I was trying to take the pressure off."

Sy gave her a look of amused exasperation. "It's not working."

She snagged one of the tiles and fixed it to the wall. "Press it on like this. Firm pressure and a gentle back and forth. Try not to twist it, though."

"Thank you. That's actually helpful." Sy squinted at the wall, then the tile in her hand. Then she mimicked Maddie's movements, placing her tile to the right of Maddie's.

Maddie gestured to the pair. "See? Easy."

"It kind of was." Even as she agreed, Sy seemed suspicious.

"Don't worry. It'll get harder when we have to start cutting tiles and doing corners."

Sy made a face. "Yay?"

Easy or hard, the whole project took only a few hours. Maddie explained the need for everything to cure before grouting and promised that Sy would have a working shower again within the week.

"Music to my ears."

She had Sy help carry their dirty tools downstairs and wash them in the laundry sink in the basement. "We'll do the same thing with the floor Monday, then install the bead board for you to paint and it'll be good to go."

"I'm not going to lie. Living without a kitchen has sucked. But having to use that sketchy shower in the basement? Definitely worse."

It was functional but that was about it. "I know. You've been a good sport."

Sy smiled. "So have you. Thanks again for giving me your Saturday."

They'd made their way back to the living room, where Henry busied himself with the plastic ring from a milk jug. She chuckled at the fierce determination before turning her attention back to Sy, and to the conversation from earlier. "So, about that date."

To her credit, Sy didn't smirk. "Yes. The date."

"Are you going to ask me out or what?" She wasn't opposed to going on said date, though at this point, she'd be just as happy with "or what." Assuming, of course, the "or what" landed them between the sheets together sooner rather than later.

"Right, right." Sy nodded. "Hey, Maddie?"

"Mm-hmm?"

Despite the silliness of this exercise, Sy's expression remained sincere. "Would you like to go on a date with me?"

She projected all the earnestness she could muster. "I would love to."

"Dinner this evening, perhaps? Fagan's?"

Pretty much the only restaurant in town. "If we have dinner there together, half the town will be talking about it tomorrow."

Sy angled her head. "Does that bother you?"

She didn't love that aspect of living in a small town, but she'd made peace with it. And while a few tongues might wag at the prospect of her dating someone who was technically a client, she'd learned to pay the owners of those tongues no heed. She knew her mind and maintained her boundaries, and that was that. "Not in the least. But it seemed like I should give you fair warning."

"I could do worse than be tied to the likes of you."

Barely a compliment, but it sent Maddie's stomach on a Tilt-a-Whirl of anticipation. "Same."

"So, it's settled. How about I pick you up at seven?"

They'd finished the tiling and it was barely three. And as nice as dinner sounded, she had more interest in what would come after. "Make it six?"

"Done."

She could leave it at that, but they'd been open enough about their intentions—their desires—to beat around the bush. And since Sy was still crashing on an air mattress here, it left her place as the more likely final destination for the night. She decided to take a page out of Sy's book. "Hey, Sy?"

Sy quirked a brow, just as she had. "Mm-hmm?"

"Would you like to go ahead and pack a bag?"

Confusion, understanding, and arousal flitted across Sy's features in little more than a second. Then she schooled her features into the same guileless expression as before. "I'd love to."

❖

Sy padded up the basement stairs in her robe and flip-flops, towel slung over her shoulder. It felt strangely like culinary school, when she'd shared a double in a five-bedroom house that might as well have been a dorm, though she couldn't decide whether that had more to do with having such a trek to her bedroom or feeling compelled to wear shower shoes in the first place. Or maybe it had to do with showering at five in the afternoon, in anticipation of a hot date.

Not that she hadn't dated after graduating. But working in restaurants left her with a weird schedule and an even weirder social life. She'd grown tired of the toxic culture, but the two a.m. hookups and halfhearted attempts to woo women with normal jobs over brunch left so much to be desired.

France had been better, at least when it came to the culture. The schedule skewed earlier, but almost painfully so, with morning milking starting every day at dawn. Between that and fumbling her way through the language barrier, she hadn't socialized much.

She'd expected more of the same in Bedlington. Tiny town, not technically in the middle of nowhere but not too far off. Pretty white, pretty conservative, at least from what she could tell. But then Maddie had shown up and turned everything on its head. She could still hear the disbelief in Mama's voice when she'd explained that the woman she'd asked on a date was also the contractor working on her house.

She hadn't mentioned that said contractor had told her to pack a bag. She and her mother might be close, but they weren't that close. Though it wouldn't take Mama long to put the pieces together if she and Maddie started seeing each other. They'd cross that bridge when they got to it.

In her makeshift bedroom off the kitchen, Sy got dressed and packed that bag. She fussed a little more than usual over her hair, working in some pomade to coax her waves into some semblance of a style. A spritz of cologne and a check of her look in the mirror. Casual, but a little more polished than what Maddie usually saw.

Satisfied, she pressed a kiss to her thumb before touching the medal of Saint Sylvia that lived on a thin gold chain around her neck. Not for luck, exactly. Not really a prayer, either. But it had belonged to her grandmother and the gesture always made her feel more prepared for whatever she needed to face. That or grateful for whatever gift the universe had just given her. Strangely, in the case of her date with Maddie, both fit the bill.

Sy drove over to Maddie's, and Maddie came out the second Sy pulled in the driveway, wearing tall gray boots over black tights. Or maybe leggings. A few inches of houndstooth skirt peeked out from the hem of her coat, and she wore her hair down. She slipped into the passenger seat before Sy had a chance to stop staring and get out to greet her.

"Hi." Maddie smiled, her cheeks flushed from even that short time in the cold.

"Hi." Sy swallowed. "You look fantastic."

Maddie waved her off, then seemed to catch herself. "Thanks. You're not too shabby yourself."

"Thanks." Sy put the car in reverse to give herself something to do besides stare. Maddie didn't wear makeup to work, and she wasn't wearing all that much now, but the mascara and lip gloss gave her that look of carefree, low maintenance beauty—that was usually anything but.

The restaurant wasn't too crowded, and they were seated at a table tucked cozily into a corner. Despite spending the day together, they chatted enough that the poor waiter had to come back a third time to get their order. She ordered at random, more interested in the conversation than the food and figuring she'd end up here often enough to try everything.

When the food came, they sampled from each other's plates and went down a rabbit hole of the best and worst meals they'd ever had. When the plates were cleared, they both declined dessert a little too quickly, then laughed because the reason was obvious, and mutual. Sy picked up the check after a bit of protest, promising she was a take turns sort of butch and not a stubbornly old-fashioned one.

The drive back to Maddie's was short, but the air seemed to hum with anticipation. The sort of pent-up energy that came right as a thunderstorm cracked open and drenched ground left dusty and parched by a summer drought. She chuckled at the flowery language that came with the memory and made her feel older than her thirty-four years.

"What?"

She couldn't really tell the story without talking about the impetus for the train of thought. And since she wasn't the sort of woman to assume—even when the cards were pretty clearly on the table—she bluffed with a tidbit of their dinner conversation. That got them safely to Maddie's driveway, and Maddie didn't seem interested in dissecting things further.

Inside, they shed coats and boots. Maddie's cat Kira came over for sniffs and rubs. Sy instinctively bent to give her attention.

"I love that you've become a cat person," Maddie said.

"Henry has me pretty well trained." She stood, but Kira continued to circle Sy's ankles, purring and pressing her face into Sy's pant legs.

"Well, it's paying off. Kira is finicky, but you've clearly passed the test."

Maddie headed from the entryway to the living room. Sy joined her, stepping gingerly, but it was enough to send Kira darting away and up the stairs. Sy's eyes followed. She'd been to Maddie's house, but not past the living room and kitchen. It made her wonder what Maddie's bedroom might reveal about her style, her personality.

"Would you like something to drink?"

"Huh?" Meaning registered a fraction of a second later. "Sorry. I actually did hear you. Do you want a drink?"

Maddie's smile was slow, suggestive, and enough to make Sy's mouth water. "Not really. It just seemed like I should offer."

"I do find myself intrigued by anything you have to offer."

"Careful. I might offer you a weekend of stripping furniture I've picked up from the side of the road."

It was her turn to rock the suggestive smile. "You had me at stripping."

Maddie snorted, slapped a hand over her mouth, then pointed right at Sy. "That was terrible. Don't think I'm laughing. I'm not."

"Kind of looks like you are."

Maddie dropped her hand. "Okay, fine. But it was still terrible. I should make you strip paint just for making such a bad joke."

The funny thing was, there wasn't much she didn't want to do with Maddie. That included sex, DIY, and everything in between. She couldn't remember the last time she felt that way about a woman. "I'm willing to take this punishment, as long as you're not doling it out tonight. There are other things I'd rather do with you."

"Is that so?" Maddie angled her head, playful with a hint of challenge.

"Oh, yeah," Sy said.

"Like what?" She shifted, adding a hip jut to her stance.

"I'd rather show you." Sy closed the distance between them. "Upstairs, maybe. Where we can get comfortable."

"Mmm. Smart." Maddie tipped her head the other way. "Follow me."

CHAPTER THIRTEEN

Maddie had left her bedroom lamp on, the desire to be prepared outweighing any worries over jinxing herself. Duvet turned down, pillows fluffed. She stepped in and turned, wanting to get her hands on Sy and wanting to make sure that feeling was mutual.

"I like your space," Sy said, looking around. "More feminine than I was expecting, but so you."

"Are you seriously making small talk about my sense of style right now?"

Sy's lips twitched. "Impatient?"

"Maybe." That sounded better than borderline desperate.

Sy spun in a slow circle. "You can tell a lot about a person by the way they keep their space. Especially the bedroom."

"And what does mine say about me?" Maddie asked.

Sy angled her head. "You're efficient, but with a soft side. Classic, but not stuffy."

"I see."

"And like I said before, more feminine than one might guess on first glance." Sy lifted a finger. "Not that I'm complaining."

Maddie folded her arms. If Sy wanted to tease, two could play that game. "Do I get to make observations about you based on your air mattress and cardboard box aesthetic?"

"No, because that's a temporary state, not my inherent style. You'll see."

"Will I?"

Sy lifted her chin, seeming to take the question as a challenge. "If you play your cards right."

"I'll do my best."

"Now, where were we?" Sy asked.

Without waiting for an answer, Sy came to stand directly in front of her, close enough that Maddie caught a whiff of whatever scent she wore. Sandalwood, maybe? And sea salt? Maddie breathed it in, letting that and the feeling of Sy's proximity envelop her.

"Here, maybe?" Sy lightly kissed her jaw. "Or was it here?"

When Sy's lips brushed over hers, it was all Maddie could do not to jump her right there in the middle of the room. "If it isn't, it should be."

"Mmm."

Sy trailed a line of kisses down Maddie's neck, sending a tingling sensation along her spine and a rash of goose bumps over her entire torso. Impressive, considering she was still fully clothed. "Yep, that, too," Maddie said.

Sy lifted her head. "Before things get too hot and heavy, we should, you know, do the safe sex talk."

Maddie laughed. "Yes. We should."

"I always wish I'd had it already when the moment arises. But then I imagine having it over dinner and that's even weirder."

Maddie imagined the waiter arriving at the table with their entrees just as she asked Sy about dental dams. "I think we made poor Jerry suffer enough."

"Fair. So, okay. Obviously, I spent the last year in France. I slept with two women while I was there and got tested right before I left."

Maddie nodded at the frank disclosure. "All right. I dated a woman last year. I thought we were exclusive, she didn't. I got tested after that."

Sy cringed. "Sorry about that."

Maddie waved her off. "No, no. We weren't serious. But she was having a lot of extra-curricular activities without telling me, wasn't careful about it, and ended up telling me only after a chlamydia scare."

"Yikes."

"Yeah." She rolled her eyes. "Sorry. Didn't mean to break the mood."

"You didn't." Despite Sy's words, she scowled.

"You're not a very good liar."

Sy shook her head, then looked at Maddie with intense eyes and a genuine smile. "I'm not, but you really didn't. I was just thinking I wanted to know more, if you're open to talking about it. Though not right now."

"Eh. Not much to tell." Maddie shrugged. Not about that one at least. "She bruised my ego more than my heart. Anyway."

"Anyway." Sy continued to smile. "Where were we?"

"Here, I think." She kissed Sy tentatively, not trusting that she hadn't TMIed them right out of the moment.

"Oh. Yes. That's right." Sy kissed her back, and there was nothing tentative about it.

"And here?" She slipped her hands under the hem of Sy's sweater and scratched lightly across her lower back.

"That's very nice. Here, let me show you." Sy mimicked the move, but instead of scratching Maddie's back, she grazed her fingers up Maddie's sides and along her ribs to the underside of her breasts.

"I like where you're going with that." The rather inane conversation seemed only to highlight the heat growing between them. "Let me give you some better access."

She lifted her arms and Sy didn't hesitate to tug her sweater up and over her head. Rather than dropping it to the floor, Sy scanned the room and tossed it onto a chair in the corner. A small gesture, but one Maddie noticed.

Maddie pointed at Sy's torso and made an up and down motion with her finger. "You too."

She thought Sy might take off her own sweater, but she lifted her arms, just as Maddie had. Not that she felt like they were on anything but even footing, but the move seemed to draw attention to it, made it fun rather than earnest. Sy might have her share of butch swagger, but she didn't seem set on wielding it indiscriminately. Yet another surprise that technically didn't surprise her all that much.

With Sy's sweater joining hers on the chair, Maddie took a moment to appreciate Sy's broad shoulders and muscular arms. Her breasts were small, made even less pronounced by the tank top she wore instead of a bra, and she was a little thick in the middle.

"What?" Sy's question made her realize she'd been staring.

"Sorry. I confess I was objectifying you. Not to be superficial, but you're so my type."

Sy smiled. "Nothing wrong with that. And if it makes you feel better, I was objectifying you, too."

"Much better." Maddie tugged at the hem of the tank top, freeing it from Sy's pants. "Is this okay?"

Sy nodded. Maddie helped her out of the shirt, then nodded when Sy's fingers hovered over the clasp of her bra. The desire to be completely naked warred with the desire to tumble into bed as quickly as possible. In the end, both lost out to the kind of skin-on-skin kissing that threatened to ignite her from the inside.

When Sy's mouth covered one of Maddie's nipples, her whole body arched. She gripped Sy's shoulders, wanting more but desperately wanting her not to stop. They tumbled to the bed, Sy sort of on top with a thigh pressed between Maddie's. Maddie's hips took the invitation, rising to meet Sy. Again, wanting more.

More. More. More.

It became sort of a chorus in her mind, spurring her on. She fumbled with the button of Sy's jeans, finally popping it loose and sliding her hand inside. When her fingers found Sy's clit, hard and hot and slick with her wetness, Maddie groaned. To be fair, Sy groaned, too.

"Why are you wearing pants?" Maddie asked with a laugh.

"Why are you?"

"Beats me. Though, technically, I'm wearing leggings. I'm still on the fence about whether they count as pants."

"Too. Much. Fabric." Sy came onto her knees and with far more finesse than Maddie demonstrated a moment before, shimmied both Maddie's skirt and leggings down.

As soon as they were gone, Maddie sat up and went for Sy's jeans. "Those, too."

Sy shed them and returned, blanketing Maddie's body with her own. "Fuck, you feel good."

Maddie grinned. "I was just thinking the same thing. I was also thinking I'd like to get back to what I was doing before that fiasco to get naked."

Sy shifted onto her side, caressing Maddie's breast as she went. "I wouldn't call it a fiasco."

Maddie rolled as well, slipping her hand back between Sy's legs. "Brouhaha?"

Sy's head dropped back. "I don't care what you call it as long as you keep touching me like that."

Maddie continued the lazy strokes over Sy's clit and took one of Sy's nipples into her mouth.

Sy sucked in a breath. "And that. Yep. So much that."

She had every intention of taking her time, but Sy's hips started to pump and the sounds and mumbled yeses coming from her lips became increasingly urgent. Maddie increased the speed rather than the pressure, her own body rocking in time with Sy's.

"Yes. Fuck. Yes." Sy tensed, bucked a couple of times, then slumped into the mattress. "Fuck."

Maddie eased her hand from between Sy's legs and caressed lazy circles on Sy's abdomen. "That was hot."

Sy lifted her head. "Understatement."

She let out a contented sigh, despite the buzz of arousal pulsing through her. "It's so awkward the first time, usually."

"Is it?" Sy rolled onto her side.

"Usually. Not now."

"Well, let's see if we can keep that going." Sy kissed Maddie's shoulder, then planted a circle of kisses around Maddie's nipple before sucking it between her lips.

"Yep. All good. No awkward."

Sy chuckled softly, creating a delicious vibration with her mouth. Her hand grazed over Maddie's belly, across her hips. Maddie opened her legs in invitation.

She teetered on the cusp of coming, but Sy managed to slow her down, coaxing her slowly to the edge. She had the feeling Sy could do that again and again, taking her time and drawing out a single orgasm for God knew how long. But Maddie had been wound up for weeks and finally being in bed with Sy had her pouncing on the prospect of release.

She let the orgasm take her, holding onto Sy and letting out a groan. It lingered, reverberating through every muscle and fiber. Sy stayed with her, holding her hand in place until Maddie nudged her away.

"Damn," she said, doing her best to suck in oxygen and get her pulse to slow.

Sy kissed her jaw. "Not awkward?"

Since lifting her head felt like way too much effort, Maddie rolled it to the side so she could look into Sy's eyes. "Not awkward."

"We should probably do it again, though. You know, make sure we have a good rhythm, good rapport."

Maddie snickered. "Rapport?"

"Don't be making fun of my vocabulary, brouhaha."

She laughed in earnest then. "I'm not sure I've ever been this goofy having sex with someone the first time."

Sy's eyes narrowed. "Wait. Is that a good thing?"

"So good." She rolled onto her side and draped an arm over Sy, rubbing her back lightly. "Easy and fun and so fucking hot. All at the same time."

"In that case, we should definitely keep going."

Maddie brought her hand to the front of Sy's shoulder and nudged her onto her back. She swung one leg over Sy's and hoisted herself up to straddle Sy's hips. "Look at you, full of opinions and good ideas."

Sy smirked. "It's much easier to have an opinion about a gorgeous woman, naked and on top of me, than bathroom tiles."

She circled her hips a few times, enjoying the sensation almost as much as Sy's reaction. "You know, at this exact moment, I feel obliged to agree."

"Though I think we could improve on the position ever so slightly."

Maddie stilled. "What do you mean?"

"You." Sy pointed to where their bodies met, then tapped the finger to her lips. "Here."

Understanding flashed, but arousal immediately took over. "So many good ideas."

She came onto her knees and made her way up Sy's torso, settling them on either side of Sy's shoulders rather than her hips. Sy's arms threaded through, wrapping around her thighs from behind. "This might be my best one yet."

Sy gently but assertively guided Maddie, pulling her close. Between the orgasm she'd already had and the anticipation pulsing through her, Maddie was literally dripping. At the first slick of Sy's tongue over her clit, she swore. It seemed silly to say she'd forgotten how good that felt, but damn.

"Feel free to give me direction," Sy said, tipping her head back just far enough to speak. "I want to learn exactly what you like."

All Maddie could do was nod. Well, nod, grab hold of the headboard, and enjoy the ride. Sy returned her attention to Maddie's clit—long strokes, slow circles. Sometimes an orgasm left her overly sensitive, but Sy coaxed her back up in no time. She rocked back and forth, and Sy's grip on her tightened, holding her steady while nudging her to lean in, let go.

Not that she had much choice. Her body responded instinctively, leaving her brain free to focus on each sensation and swell of another orgasm building deep in her abdomen. It was too busy doing that to form words, but Sy didn't seem to need them. She increased the pressure and the pace and sent Maddie careening into the sort of release that ricocheted through her entire body, leaving her both sated and spent.

Her body sagged and she tried to shift away so she wouldn't suffocate Sy in the process, but Sy held her tight. "Don't go. Not yet."

She worked to catch her breath, to get her bearings. All the while Sy stroked her thighs lazily, like she didn't have a care in the world. "Please tell me I get to do that to you next."

Sy loosened her hold and Maddie eased away, sitting on her heels next to Sy rather than on top of her. "If you insist," Sy said.

Maddie ran her hand down Sy's torso. "I mean, if you're comfortable where you are, I can work with that, too."

"Is that so?" Sy lifted her head, a look of playful challenge in her eyes.

"I pride myself on being adaptable." She crawled backwards without breaking eye contact, then nudged Sy's legs apart with her knee. "Sensitive to my client's needs."

Sy nodded. "But what if I was open to suggestion, wanted to defer to your expertise?"

She settled herself between Sy's thighs, breathed in her musky scent. "I'd say feel free to give me directions. I want to learn exactly what you like."

Sy chuckled at having the words given back to her but stopped laughing the second Maddie's tongue pressed into her. "You," she said, brushing Maddie's hair from her face. "I like you."

❖

Sy sat in Maddie's bed, covers pulled up to her chest for warmth more than modesty. Maddie, who'd ventured downstairs for water, returned with a pair of glasses. Sy took the one she extended. "Thank you."

"No, no. Thank you." Maddie's salacious tone made Sy laugh.

"I was talking about the water."

Maddie joined her in bed and tugged the covers up to cover her torso. "Oh. You're welcome, then."

"But if you wanted to thank me for earlier, I wouldn't mind."

Maddie quirked a brow. "Thank you for earlier."

"You're welcome. And ditto. That was seriously amazing." Sy took a sip from her glass. "Damn, that's good. Why is cold water so good after sex?"

"Because you're hot and sweaty."

She wagged a finger. "Yeah, but I'm hot and sweaty after working out and it's good, but never this good."

Maddie didn't miss a beat. "Oh, that's because sex endorphins are way better than exercise endorphins. I don't care what the runners or the Cross Fitters say."

Sy laughed. "Have I told you that you're funny? Because you are. Funny and smart and sexy. It's a heavy-hitting combination."

Maddie finished downing her own water. "Don't forget really good with tools."

"Are you good with all the tools?" She might have waited a time or two before bringing up toy preferences, but they'd just had sex six ways from Sunday, so it didn't seem like an overstep. And, technically speaking, Maddie brought it up.

"I know my way around most of them." Maddie tipped her head, a look of pure mischief in her eyes. "Though I don't have to be the one wielding them."

Sy's imagination didn't need a lot to go on when it came to sex fantasies involving Maddie. Having something so concrete was going to have her revved up for days, even with the amount of sex they'd just had. "Good to know."

"You?" Maddie bit her lip in this way that had Sy itching to bend her over. Respectfully, of course. And with enthusiastic consent.

"You may be surprised to hear this, given my track record with drills and sanders, but there are a few tools I've had loads of practice with." She angled her head, mirroring Maddie's gesture from a moment before. "Kitchen tools, obviously. But others, too."

Maddie nodded slowly, making Sy wonder if she'd rendered her speechless.

"I could show you sometime. You know, if you're interested in a demonstration." If it weren't after midnight already, she'd offer to drive home now and come right back.

"I'd like that very much." Maddie continued to nod. "Very soon."

"Well, it is your turn to buy dinner." Which she didn't actually care about but was happy to use as an excuse for another date.

"You could let me cook for you this time. Assuming you trust me in the kitchen."

She'd be hard-pressed to think of a scenario where she didn't trust Maddie. Maybe that should have felt weird, but it didn't. And the prospect of a whole night in together—with or without dinner—sounded pretty much perfect. "Sold. But only if you promise not to go to too much trouble."

That earned her a withering stare. "After the meal you made me, you're telling me to go basic?"

Sy set her glass on the nightstand. She took the empty one from Maddie and did the same with it. Then she shifted her body so they sat facing each other, closer than before. "I'm saying that, unlike last time, dinner won't be my top priority, and I'd prefer you keep the majority of your energy for other things."

"Oh."

"Assuming that's not overstepping." She was pretty sure from the look on Maddie's face it wasn't, but it was always better to be certain.

"Nope. Not overstepping at all," Maddie said.

"To be honest, I'd be happy with pizza."

Maddie smirked. "Suddenly the chef is easy."

"Easy has nothing to do with it." She looked Maddie up and down, nice and slow. "I just already know I'll be more interested in taking you to bed than whatever we end up having for dinner."

"Hard to complain about that."

"For the record, I'd like to have another round with you now, but it's late and we both have early mornings."

Maddie scrunched up her face—way more adorable than it should have been. "I'm supposed to appreciate you being considerate and mature about that, aren't I?"

It helped to know that the can't get enough sensation needling at her was mutual. "You don't have to. You could talk me into being downright reckless if you wanted to."

Maddie sighed. "No, you're right. I've got to run an excavator tomorrow."

Of course she did. Sy leaned in and kissed her. "Safety first."

Maddie rolled her eyes. "Safety first."

Sy winked. "But sex a close second."

CHAPTER FOURTEEN

Despite every intention of getting Sy back in her bed as soon as possible, a string of job site mishaps and a series of cryptic check-ins from her uncle in Florida took up all of Maddie's unscheduled time. Sy seemed just as busy, wanting to get several batches of brie aging in time to be ready for the Christmas rush and signing up for a last-minute jaunt to Northampton with Clover with the hope of securing their first retail outlet outside of Vermont.

The prospect of that last bit—Sy and Clover cooped up in a car for several hours—had her begging Clover for a coffee date before they left. She didn't expect Sy to spill her guts about her sex life to the woman who was technically her boss, but she didn't want to take any chances. She and Clover didn't keep secrets from each other and she wasn't about to start now.

Clover got to the coffee shop about a minute after Maddie did and wasted no time launching herself at Maddie with a giant hug. "Why do I feel like I haven't seen you in forever?"

Maddie couldn't help but smile. "Because you haven't seen me in over a week and, for us, that's practically forever."

"Unacceptable." Clover hooked her arm into the crook of Maddie's and marched them to the counter. "Let's get some caffeine and make up for lost time."

A few minutes later, they sat at their usual table overlooking Main Street with hot drinks and a pair of pumpkin muffins. Maddie fussed with the lid of her disposable coffee cup, remembering yet another reason she always carried a travel mug with her. She forced her fingers to still and looked across the table at Clover, who'd been studying her fidgeting over the rim of her chai.

"There's something I need to tell you," Maddie said.

Clover set down her cup. "It's obvious something's bothering you. What's up?"

She winced. "I slept with Sy."

Clover leaned forward, elbows on the small cafe table between them. "And it was terrible?"

"What? No. Why would you think it was terrible?"

"Because you made that pained face you do whenever you have to do something unpleasant." Clover stuck out both hands, though Maddie couldn't tell whether it came from confusion or a desire to emphasize her point.

"Oh. No. It was good. Like, ridiculously good, if I'm being honest." Merely alluding to it had some select images dancing suggestively through her mind.

Clover's expression morphed into one of confusion. "So why did you get all cringey about it."

"Because I feel awkward telling you, since Sy is your employee. But obviously I'm not going to not tell you." Though now she felt more foolish than awkward.

Clover narrowed her eyes, probably trying to make sense of Maddie's logic, or maybe just her penchant for using double negatives when flustered. "What does Sy working for me have to do with you sleeping with her?"

"It doesn't." She frowned, now questioning her logic herself. "It's just that now you know Sy's personal business. I told her I was going to tell you because you're my best friend, and she seemed cool with it, but I wasn't so sure I'd feel the same if the tables were turned. So it just seems kind of complicated."

Clover sipped her chai, as though waiting to see if Maddie was done or merely taking a breath. When Maddie pressed her lips together, indicating she'd blathered enough, Clover simply tutted. "Girl, I'm pansexual and poly in a town of less than ten thousand people. Don't even get me started on complicated."

For some reason, Clover's reference to her own love life took away some of the tension that had been twisting in her stomach since getting out of bed that morning. "You definitely win the complicated game."

"You say that like it's a bad thing," Clover said with a smirk.

Wasn't it? "Not bad. Hard."

"Eh? Challenging sometimes, sure. But if the ante is bigger, the payoff is, too."

Maddie laughed at the poker reference, mostly because Clover found gambling to be a universal waste of time and money. Even the nickel, dime, quarter version she played with her siblings and a few of their friends. But then she thought about using gambling references to talk about relationships and the idea sobered her. "So is the risk of loss."

"Like most worthwhile things, wouldn't you say?" Clover asked.

Honestly, she wasn't sure. Most of her life and career involved playing it safe. Not because she was afraid of a challenge, but because the path that appealed most happened to be laid out neatly in front of her. Well, that and the fact that the one woman she'd given her heart to decided Bedlington—and by extension Maddie— were too provincial for her and her ambitions.

Clover nudged her foot under the table. "Come on, you love tackling impossible jobs, making things that are falling apart sturdy and beautiful again."

"I'm not sure that counts." How often had she really gone out on a limb? Professionally? Nothing like what Clover was doing— taking the run-down co-op she'd inherited and revamping the entire business model to make Grumpy Old Goat a viable and successful company. Romantically? Never. She'd learned her lesson—people didn't move to places like Bedlington permanently. Pretending Sy would stick around more than a few years would be foolish. And she'd been fooled once before.

"So, maybe Sy is your opportunity to take a chance."

Whatever relief she'd felt talking about it evaporated in a new swell of anxiety. "Pressure much?"

"I'm not saying you're going to marry her," Clover said.

"Gee, thanks." No matter how good the sex was, she was a hell of a long way off from thoughts of forever. Because of the whole sticking around thing, sure. But lots of other reasons, too. Like Sy's ambition. Her worldliness. It wasn't just that Bedlington would turn out to be too small-town. It was that Maddie would, too.

"Stop. What I'm saying is Sy might get you out of your comfort zone, help you shake things up in a good way."

Maddie pressed a thumb to that spot between her eyes where worry lines liked to appear. "You don't think it's Rebecca all over again?"

"Oh." Clover let the word hang. "You're worried about that."

She blew out a breath. "Among other things."

"Well, if you're just looking to have a little fun, does it matter?"

"How can you say that when you're hanging the future of Grumpy Old Goat on what Sy does with it?"

Clover blew out a breath in return, though it was more of a huffy sigh. "One, I'm not hanging the future of anyone or anything on one person, personally or professionally."

She knew there would be at least a two, but she couldn't stop herself. "That is such a poly thing to say."

Clover lifted her chin. "Yeah, you should try it."

"I—"

"I don't mean being poly. I mean not putting all your eggs in one basket but maybe putting a couple of them in a basket besides your own every now and then."

She opened her mouth to argue, but none came. Because counting on people—besides her family and maybe Clover—wasn't her jam. Keeping the most important parts of herself to herself was. That went for the wins, the losses, the hopes, the dreams, and everything in between. Perhaps most especially the decisions.

"I promise it's worth it."

"Yeah." She didn't buy into that entirely but could appreciate where Clover was coming from. Besides, agreeing would spare her one of Clover's "life is for living" speeches.

"That's the spirit."

She hadn't thought she needed a shakeup, but maybe Clover was right. At least in the let loose department. "You're sure you're cool with me seeing her?"

Clover rolled her eyes, then regarded Maddie with mischief. "I had a bet going in my mind over how long it would take you two to jump in the sack."

Maddie frowned. "I thought you didn't make bets."

"Yeah, but this was more of a when than an if. It's different wagering on a sure thing."

She'd come up with a lot of words to describe Sy, to describe being with her. Sure thing definitely hadn't made the list. But maybe that was okay. Clover sensing their chemistry, thinking it was a good idea, made it feel a little less rash. Busting out of her comfort zone or not, she wasn't one for rash decisions or reckless behavior.

"So, it was good?" Clover waggled her eyebrows with the subtlety of a Marx brother.

With that one silly gesture, the weirdness melted away. Complications and questions about where things might go vanished. In their place, her best friend and a longstanding tradition of swapping stories about their sexual adventures. And the occasional misadventure. "You have no idea."

❖

"I can't believe you got us a meeting at Fromager. I went there all the time when I was in college." Clover took her eyes off the road just long enough to glance at Sy. "I couldn't afford anything, mind you, but I still went."

Sy chuckled. "The plight of poor college student foodies everywhere—triple cream tastes on a sharp cheddar budget."

Clover let out a snort laugh that made Sy laugh in return. "I hadn't heard that one."

"That's because I made it up."

"Oh. Well, it should be a saying, then." Clover shrugged. "And, again, I can't believe we're going to Fromager."

Fromager was an institution in Northampton, Massachusetts. Sy hadn't known that, or technically even heard of it, when Biaggio, the owner, stopped by Le Coteau on a tour of France the previous spring. Between being American, queer, and both obsessed with cheese, they'd hit it off, and Biaggio had insisted Sy reach out if she ever found herself in New England. "The owner is super nice. And always looking for something no one else has."

Clover blew out a breath. "That's us."

Sy lifted a finger. "But not for long."

"Not for long." Clover nodded her agreement. "Have I told you lately I'm glad you're here?"

"Yes." Something that rarely happened in the kitchens where she'd worked and something she had no intention of taking for granted. "And in case I haven't said so enough, I'm glad I'm here, too."

Clover's shoulders lifted and dropped in a way that conveyed contentment. "I thought it might be touch-and-go for a while there, with everything going on with your house."

She shook her head. "I wouldn't have quit, but I definitely questioned some of my life choices."

"Are you still regretting the house?"

"I'm not sure I ever really did, except maybe those first few days. Now that my roof doesn't leak and I'm on the brink of a functional bathroom and a new kitchen, I'm feeling pretty good about things. Having Maddie on my side made all the difference." In the house, of course, but in so many other ways, too.

Clover's smile was sly. "She does have that effect on people."

The suggestive tone made her think Clover had more to say, but she left it at that. Sy waited a beat, then another. "You two had coffee this morning?"

"We did."

She definitely didn't need to discuss her sex life with her boss, even if they were sort of friends at this point. But not acknowledging that she knew Clover knew felt weird. And now, thanks to her cryptic question, Clover knew that Sy knew she knew. Great.

"For what it's worth, I think it's fantastic. A potato would be able to sense the spark between you two."

Whether it was the unequivocal vote of confidence or the personification of a potato, Sy didn't know. But a guffaw tumbled out gracelessly and she didn't even try to stop the laughter that followed. "Thanks, I think."

"I'm happy to talk about it, or not talk about it. Whatever's more comfortable for you. I just want you to know I'm cool with it." Clover glanced over again. "And by cool, I mean mildly ecstatic."

"Really?" Sy asked, not incredulous exactly, but not expecting such a superlative, even with the qualifier.

"Absolutely. I mean, I could give you the protective best friend routine, but I don't think you're any more likely to hurt her than she is to hurt you, so it seems disingenuous."

A sound argument, but of course it put the idea in her head that she and Maddie might hurt one another. "Well, we managed to pause long enough to make sure we were on the same page."

"Did you, now?" Clover regarded her with curiosity, which made her wonder what exactly she and Maddie had discussed.

"Like, we like each other and want to date. Not have a random hookup." And now she'd officially talked about it more than she'd planned.

"Oh." Clover let the word hang, leaving Sy to wonder if that was news to her or merely a clarification of something she already knew.

Sy shifted in her seat, officially crossing into uncomfortable territory. "Yeah. I mean, not serious relationship talks or anything. Just, you know, we respect each other and wanted to be adults about it."

Clover smirked. "It is good to be adults when doing adult things."

Sy coughed at both the phrasing and Clover's casual delivery, and she used the opportunity to chug water from her bottle rather than put her foot any further into her mouth.

Clover's gaze returned squarely to the road. "Like I said, mildly ecstatic."

CHAPTER FIFTEEN

Since the door to the cheese room was closed, Maddie peered through the small window rather than barging in. What she found was Sy, donned in her white coat, galoshes, and a hair net, studying a wheel of cheese like it held the secrets of the universe. She knocked lightly and cracked the door, knowing better than to barge in during production without the appropriate protective gear.

Sy turned at the sound, wielding what appeared to be a torture device. "Hi."

"Hi." Maddie smiled. "You look like a mad scientist right now."

"Thank you." Sy frowned. "Was I supposed to be expecting you and forgot?"

"No." Maddie tipped her head. "Do you often forget you're expecting people?"

"I wouldn't say often." Since Maddie couldn't come in, she set down her tools and crossed the room for a quick kiss. "But I've been known to get lost in my work."

"Happens to the best of us."

"So, since I didn't forget plans, why are you here?" Sy winced. "That sounded like I'm not happy to see you. I totally am."

Maddie waved away the explanation. "I took a chance coming unannounced."

"Well, your timing happens to be perfect. I just finished needling." Sy lifted a finger. "Actually, let me go put them in the cooler and I can stop for a bit."

"Are you sure?" Maddie asked.

"Yep. Give me two minutes." Sy hurried over to the table and loaded the wheels onto a tray. She carried them to the cooler, then returned. "Thanks."

"Needling?" She'd been sitting on that and wasn't about to let it go.

"Poking tiny holes to encourage air flow so the molds can get in. It's how blue cheese is made."

"Oh. Yum. Weird, but yum." She'd spent enough time with Clover to embrace such things in theory but hadn't given much thought to the process.

"It will hopefully be exceptionally yum by the time I'm done with it."

"I have no doubt." She didn't bother trying to suppress her grin. "And I have something that will help."

"You do?" Sy asked.

"Well, some things, to be more precise. I brought the rest of the boards for the aging room."

Sy had seemed happy enough to see Maddie, but now her whole face lit up. "I thought you said it would be after Christmas."

"I thought it would be. But I pulled a few strings and was able to pick them up this morning."

"You have no idea how excited that makes me. That means I can get them treated and installed, and they can acclimate and get inoculated before I'm even ready to fill them." Sy did the sort of happy dance Maddie associated with football players scoring touchdowns.

"You're more excited for this than the stove, aren't you?"

Sy's hip jiggle stilled. "Do I have to choose?"

"No, but I get to be amused by the fact that it would be a hard decision."

Sy tipped her head. "I'm okay with that."

They stood for a moment, right in the middle of the packing room, giving each other goofy looks. Like maybe they were both trying to decide whether sleeping together meant they should be more flirty with each other or less. Eventually, Maddie rocked back on her heels. "So, do you want to go get them?"

Sy started. "Yes. Of course. Absolutely."

Sy changed her shoes and pulled off the hairnet, and they got the boards unloaded and into the packing room. Sy changed her shoes again, Maddie slid protective booties over hers, and they both donned the requisite hairnets to bring the boards the rest of the way in. Sy had Maddie help her arrange them on the worktable so she could clean and treat them before putting them in place.

More goofy looks ensued.

"I can come back in a day or two if you want help getting them in place," Maddie said.

"I think I can manage. I know you have plenty else on your plate."

Mention of plates jarred her brain in a different direction. "Oh."

"What?" Sy asked.

"I feel like a jerk for not asking sooner, but what are you doing for Thanksgiving?"

Sy gave her a curious look. "Why do you feel like a jerk?"

"Because it's next week."

"Shit. It is?" Sy looked genuinely surprised.

She laughed. "I'm glad I'm not the only one it snuck up on."

"I count days in here, but I've lost all track of dates. That's my story and I'm sticking to it," Sy said with more humor than conviction.

"I don't even have that excuse and I lost track. Anyway, do you have plans?"

Sy lifted a shoulder, a casual gesture that didn't match the gloomy look that crept into her eyes. "Nah. I can't afford two trips and seeing my mom for Christmas is more important."

Maddie frowned, feeling even worse that she'd let it slip her mind. "I'm sorry you have to choose."

"I didn't even make it home for Christmas the year I was in France, so this isn't too bad."

Still, it sucked. Sure, some families didn't celebrate or weren't close, but that wasn't the vibe she got from Sy. "You should come to dinner with my family."

"Yeah?" Sy perked up but seemed incredulous. "I wouldn't want to crash."

"You wouldn't be crashing," Maddie said perhaps a little too quickly. "My mom asked me if you had plans like two weeks ago and said I should invite you if you didn't."

"Oh."

Sy's vaguely disappointed tone made her realize the explanation made the invitation seem forced. "I mean, I totally want you there, but my mom is the thoughtful sort of person who'd think about it."

That got her a chuckle. "I see."

"It's my whole family, but also whoever is around. Friends, the occasional neighbor. Clover will be there."

"Are you sure?"

"Absolutely." She almost added a caveat about it not being a girlfriend sort of invitation but changed her mind. She didn't want that to influence Sy one way or the other. And truth be told, she wasn't so sure how she felt about it herself. Not Sy coming to dinner, but the question of whether it implied they were in girlfriend territory. "The more, the merrier."

Sy hesitated, leaving Maddie to wonder if she'd given away the weird flux of emotions. But just as Maddie prepared to offer a gentle out, Sy smiled. "I'd love to."

It was her turn to offer a cautiously optimistic, "Yeah?"

"Only if you let me bring something. And help once I'm there."

For all that it hadn't even been on her radar an hour before, Sy's acceptance filled her with delight. And relief. Mom would have been none too pleased if she'd flaked completely. "Oh, yay. I'll check with my mom, but I'm pretty sure her answer will be cheese."

Sy smirked. "Won't Clover be bringing that?"

"Hmm." She had a point.

"If it's cool with your mom, let me bring corn pudding. It's something my mom always makes."

Even if the family buffet wasn't already a smorgasbord situation, she wouldn't dream of turning down a dish that might make Sy feel like she had a taste of home. "I have no idea what's in that, but I'm excited already. Sold."

"You can tell me if your family is super traditional, or it would be weird or whatever."

She grabbed Sy's hand, an unsettling wave of sentimentality swelling in her chest. "I'm sure it's amazing. Bring it. Please."

Sy laughed. "It's good, but not life changing or anything. Don't get too excited."

Maddie blushed but decided she didn't actually mind Sy's way of teasing her. "I've had your cooking. I'm always going to get excited."

"I bet you say that to all the women."

"I really, really don't." She indulged in looking Sy up and down. "Though, that's not the only thing you do that excites me."

Sy raised a brow. "Is that so?"

"I could list quite a few things." None of them SFW. And yet all of them safer than getting into the weeds of family traditions and the ones they'd shared with other women.

"What if you came over tonight?" Sy asked. "We could walk through them in detail."

Now it was her turn to raise a brow. "Your place?"

"I finally got a new mattress delivered, and it needs some breaking in."

A totally different sort of swell spread through her, and a totally different sort of blush. "An important household task. I'd love to give you a hand."

"More than a hand, I hope."

"So much more." She'd been thinking about getting naked with Sy again, definitely more than she'd been thinking about small talk over turkey.

"I'd like both my hands on you," Sy said. "Among other things."

"Your mouth?" Maddie asked.

Sy nodded.

"What about your cock?"

A flash of surprise, but Sy nodded again. "That could be arranged."

Maddie grinned. "I'll be there."

❖

Sy made her way around the room, placing candles. Between the dresser and the side table she picked up, there were enough surfaces to get a nice romantic glow going once they were all lit. Overkill, probably, given that Maddie's coming over after work was basically a booty call. Or was it a reverse booty call, since Maddie had basically propositioned her?

Not that it mattered. Sy finally had a real bed of her own and Maddie was on her way over. Or at least Sy thought she was. Maddie hadn't texted after leaving the farm. They'd made plans, though, so there technically wasn't anything to confirm.

She came downstairs to the sound of tires in the driveway and opened the door to find a smiling but bedraggled Maddie clutching a pizza box. "Hi," Sy said.

Maddie held it out to her. "Hi. Did you eat yet?"

"Late lunch." And an afternoon of sampling her work. "I figured we'd get around to takeout at some point."

Maddie rolled her eyes. "I had oatmeal at seven this morning."

"Maddie." The scolding tone reminded her of her mother. Sy cleared her throat. "Sorry. Are you okay? What happened?"

Maddie stepped inside and bent over to untie her boots. "Long story. I'll tell you all about it after I carb load."

"What else do you need? Wine?"

Maddie shed her coat and hung it on the coat tree. Sy tried not to notice how adorable she looked in work clothes and socked feet. "A hot shower and even hotter sex."

Okay, then. "That, I can do."

She grabbed bottles of water and paper towels from the makeshift kitchen. By the time she returned, Maddie had already started on her first piece. "Sorry. I couldn't wait."

"I'm glad you didn't." She joined Maddie on the sofa and snagged a piece for herself because hot, fresh pizza had a way of inspiring an appetite.

After polishing off half her first slice, Maddie dropped her head onto the back of the couch. "I feel so much better."

"Good." Sy waited a beat. "Do you want to talk about it?"

Maddie lifted her head and rolled her eyes. "My uncle has fallen in love, decided to move to Florida, and wants to sell his half of the business."

"Oh." She'd been expecting some sort of debacle at one of Maddie's job sites. A flood or a fire or a whole house painted the wrong color. "And that's bad?"

"Well, it means my uncle is even more of an idiot slash ass than we all thought." Maddie blew out a breath. "And it means we have to find a way to buy him out or risk some random person owning half the business."

"Oh." She let the word drag with understanding.

"I spent the afternoon at the office with my siblings and parents talking about what we were going to do."

Sy grasped at the line between supportive and nosing her way into family drama that was none of her business. "Did you sort anything out?"

Maddie took another bite of pizza and shook her head, chewing slowly.

"Well, I'm happy to listen or distract. Just tell me which you'd prefer."

"He's just so fucking selfish. Like, we all figured the day would come eventually. His kids have no interest and we all knew they'd want money over a share of the business. But now he wants to abandon his whole life here and prance around Coral Beach like some retiree Casanova."

Sy laughed at the description because how could she not, but then schooled her expression into something serious. "That sucks."

"I mean, the good news is that I don't think there's anyone chomping at the bit to buy half of a family-owned construction business in rural Vermont. So even if he wants a fat check and a quick exit, he's not going to get it."

"That's good."

"It buys us some time if nothing else. But we're going to need a plan." Maddie shook her head and rolled her eyes again. "Idiot."

She hated seeing Maddie upset, but appreciated her straightforward—with just a hint of snark—approach to dealing with a crappy situation. "I'm sure you'll figure something out. You're very smart."

Maddie's features softened. "Thanks."

"I mean it. Like, you know your stuff, but you're also good at thinking outside the box. Not everybody can do that."

Maddie nodded, a look of resolve taking over. "Well, between the lot of us, I think we'll come up with a solution."

She thought about her trip to Northampton with Clover. Not family, maybe, but it was starting to feel like they were a team. She'd wanted that in the restaurant world and struggled to find it. "I'm sure you will. I'm happy to be a sounding board, if you want to bounce ideas or anything."

"I might take you up on that. It would be good to get some outside perspective."

"In the meantime, you sure you don't want that glass of wine?"

Maddie considered and helped herself to a second slice of pizza. "I'm good. I want all my faculties for later."

Sy half expected Maddie to eat and crash. She might still, but Sy liked the prospect of her switching gears and being in the mood. "I do enjoy your faculties."

Maddie smirked. "My faculties need some ibuprofen and a shower and then they're all yours."

Chapter Sixteen

S y sent Maddie off to enjoy her gloriously finished and fully functional bathroom and went to the bedroom to get ready. She lit the candles so the vanilla fragrance could start working its magic while she got her harness and favorite cock from the little chest she kept tucked in the closet. The smell of leather made her smile. And turned her on.

After situating the harness where she liked it on her hips, she tightened the buckles and did a few test thrusts. The silicone bobbed, like it shared Sy's enthusiasm for what came next. She contemplated a pair of boxers but decided against it. She could get under the covers and save the trouble of having to wiggle out of them later.

"Well, there's a sight for sore eyes."

Sy spun, the cock bouncing up and down in friendly greeting. "I didn't hear the water go off."

Maddie, towel around her and tucked between her breasts, smirked. "Because your house is properly insulated now. You're not supposed to hear the water through the walls."

"I'm not complaining. Just explaining why you caught me standing in the middle of the room naked."

Maddie looked her up and down. "Not completely naked."

"You know what I mean." She liked wearing a cock, but it felt strange to parade around in it.

"Here." Maddie gave the towel a gentle tug and it fell to the floor. "Now we're both naked. Feel better?"

She returned the once-over. "Seeing you naked always makes me feel better."

Maddie lifted her chin. "I'm looking forward to seeing what you can do with that."

"I'm looking forward to learning what you like."

"I like touching." Maddie wrapped her fingers around the cock.

Sy might have wished for a clever comeback. All she managed was a groan.

"I like to taste, too."

Sy's mouth opened, but no sound came out, much less words.

"But what I really need is to have you inside me. The sooner, the better."

Without letting go of the cock Maddie leaned in and kissed her. Between the feel of Maddie's mouth on hers, the brush of her breasts, and the exquisite pressure she'd placed on Sy's clit, any hope of coherent thought evaporated. "Yes. That."

Maddie laughed. She released the cock and took Sy's hand. "Come on, hot stuff."

They turned toward the bed, but Maddie stopped in her tracks. "Your bed is here."

It was her turn to laugh. "That is the reason we're at my place instead of yours."

"Yeah, but you distracted me being sexy. I haven't taken it all in." She turned a slow circle. "It looks really good."

Sy smiled, weirdly proud. "I wasn't sure about the duvet because I ordered it online, but it's nice."

"You painted the dresser you picked up." Maddie trailed her fingers over the surface. "And you lit candles."

"Seemed like the least I could do was set the mood." Given that Maddie had helped to make it a usable room in the first place.

Maddie returned to her. "You did an excellent job."

"I need a rug, I think. I just can't decide what kind."

"For sure. It'll look good, but more importantly, it'll make the floor feel warmer in winter."

It hit her then that they were standing in the middle of her room, naked, having a conversation about interior design. "You can help me pick one out. But later. Right now there's something else I'd rather be doing."

"Right. Yes." Maddie sauntered over to the bed and perched on the edge. "You did promise to ravish me."

"Ravish, huh?"

Maddie angled her head. "Does that word bother you? I was with a woman once who found it way too aggressive."

Sy slowly closed the distance between them. "It's a great word, as long as it's consensual."

Maddie tipped her head back, holding Sy's gaze with hers. "I consent to being ravished."

"Perfect." She nudged Maddie onto her back, directing her to swing her legs up so she'd be comfortable. When Maddie obliged with a coy smile, the low thud already pulsing between her legs intensified. She climbed in, settling one knee between Maddie's thighs and bracing on one elbow. She used her free hand to sweep a damp curl from Maddie's forehead. "Hi."

"Hi." Maddie wiggled beneath her. "It's nice. Super comfy."

"Thanks for helping me break it in."

"It's my full service package. Comes with all the big reno jobs." Maddie started with a straight face, but cracked a grin by the end.

"Does it, now? And here I thought I got the sweat equity special."

"Sure, sure." Maddie nodded. "I'm just making sure you really get the sweat part down."

"I see."

Maddie wiggled again. "Clearly, I've had a long day. I'm going off the rails, here. Help a girl out."

Sy laughed. It had gone a little sideways. "Let me see what I can do."

She slid a hand between them, thinking it would take a minute to get Maddie's brain and body on the same page. What she found was Maddie hot and slick and practically begging to be fucked. She sucked in a breath, happily surprised.

"Oh, I want you. I'm just all over the place up here." Maddie laughed and tapped her index finger to her forehead.

That, she could work with. She kissed Maddie's forehead, then each temple. One cheek, then the other. Her chin, her jaw. When Maddie let out a sigh, Sy captured her mouth, kissing her long and deep. All the while, tracing lazy circles over Maddie's clit. Maddie's arms came up and around Sy's neck, her nails scratching lightly at the base of her fade.

Sy pulled just far enough back to study Maddie's face. Maddie's eyes fluttered open, the green already a few shades darker with desire. "That's better."

Maddie nodded slowly. "So much better."

"And this?" Sy slipped a finger into Maddie's tightness.

"It's good." Maddie smiled. "But I definitely need more."

Sy was only too happy to oblige. She added a second finger, reveling in the way Maddie's body molded around her. Maddie's hand returned to the cock, starting a slow push and pull that mirrored the rhythm of Sy's hand.

"Yes?" Maddie asked.

Sy grinned. "It's good. But I definitely need more."

"I've got just the thing."

Their bodies were close, but Maddie managed to maneuver the cock to the vicinity of Sy's hand. Sy got onto her knees to get both the leverage and position she wanted and Maddie opened her legs in invitation. She snagged the bottle of lube she'd left on the nightstand and worked a little onto the silicone.

Sy positioned the cock, eased the tip in. "How's that?"

Maddie smirked. "I feel like I'm starting to sound like a broken record here."

"Let me guess. More?"

Maddie arched her hips, taking half the length in. "More."

The pressure on her clit, the way Maddie opened for her but seemed to pull her in at the same time. It addled her brain in the best possible way. She let Maddie set the pace, at least for now, loving the way Maddie's eyes drifted closed, and she seemed to truly let go of everything but the moment. Especially after the day Maddie had, how she started the night so stuck in her head.

And then there were the sounds. Good God, the sounds alone were enough to push Sy to the edge. Little moans, whimpers barely above a whisper. She increased the tempo and the sounds followed, along with the arch of Maddie's body to meet her.

Maddie's legs snaked around Sy's waist, pulling Sy against her with more force. "Yes. Oh, yes. Right there."

"That's it. I've got you." She continued thrusting.

"Sy. Fuck. Yes."

The orgasm had already been building deep in Sy's abdomen. Maddie's words—so simple and yet so powerful—set the flicker aflame and it tore through her the way a fire consumes dry brush. Her body bucked. Maddie's quaked but stayed with her, holding on tight.

She did her best not to collapse on top of Maddie completely, but Maddie's legs had yet to loosen their grip. "I don't want to crush you."

"You're not. Just stay here a second."

She didn't believe Maddie but wasn't about to tell her no. They stayed like that for a moment, still save Sy trying to catch her breath and Maddie trembling with the occasional aftershock. The sort of blissed out stupor that came with, well, coming.

Aside from her hand falling asleep, it was damn near perfect. Until Maddie smacked her bicep. Not hard, but not nothing, either. Sy lifted her head and searched Maddie's face. "What was that for?"

"Simultaneous orgasms are a myth."

Sy laughed. Seriously? "They're elusive. That's not the same thing."

"Fake news."

"So, you're saying what just happened didn't happen?" Sy asked.

"No." Maddie pouted for a second, but it quickly morphed into a smirk.

"Good. Because I thought it was pretty fucking amazing." She nipped Maddie's jaw and eased the cock out before flopping next to her. "And there was nothing fake about it."

"Yeah." Maddie let out a happy sigh. With Sy off of her, she stared up at the ceiling, allowing her focus to soften and her vision to blur. "I really needed that. I thought I knew how bad, but I was wrong. I needed it way more."

Sy rolled onto her side and propped on her elbow. "If it's any consolation, I needed it, too. And I didn't even have a shitty day."

She mirrored Sy's position and posture. "It wasn't all that shitty. I'm sorry I showed up in a mood."

Sy shook her head and smiled. "You don't need to apologize. You're allowed to have stressful days and need to unwind."

"Yeah, but I don't want to be the girlfriend who unloads, either."

Sy raised a brow. "You saying you want to be my girlfriend?"

Maddie winced. Not the can of worms she wanted to open. "I didn't mean it like that."

"Oh, so you don't want to be my girlfriend."

The gleam in Sy's eye made it clear she was teasing. Still. Saying she didn't would surely kill the mood. Maddie covered her face with her hand. "I didn't mean that either."

Sy seemed to take pity on her, planting a slew of kisses on her shoulder. "As the person who chose the absolute dorkiest way to say she liked a woman, you get a pass on this one."

She could take the pass and leave it at that, but something made her want to give Sy a more truthful answer. "How's this? I like you a lot. And, as we've established, the sex is off the charts. I'm really not in the market for anything too serious, but I could see us getting to mutually agreeable girlfriend territory. Assuming you'd be into that, of course."

Sy nodded slowly. "More elegant than what I managed before our first date. You get all the points."

Maddie pumped her fist in a pretend display of victory. "Yes."

"And I feel the same way." Sy angled her head. "For the record."

Just like that conversation before their first date, Sy took a moment that could have been awkward and made it playful. Weirdly refreshing. Which was maybe the point of not taking everything so seriously. When had dating gotten so boring? Delighted by the prospect of succeeding at it, Maddie nudged Sy onto her back and rolled on top of her. "The sex part or the girlfriend part?"

Sy's hips pressed up and into hers. "Yes."

"I see." She thrust her own pelvis down.

"Careful or you're going to have me all turned on again."

She could think of worse things. "Yeah?"

Sy's hands went to her hips. "Yeah."

Maddie repeated the motion, adding a circular grind at the end. "Oh, no. Whatever will I do?"

"You're cute when you're full of sass." Sy's grip tightened.

"Sass? What are you, seventy?"

In a single fluid motion, Sy reversed their positions, pinning Maddie's arms over her head. "Keep it up and I'll have to fuck that sass right out of you."

She'd never been one for power play—in bed or otherwise— but something about the sternness had her pulse tripping and her clit twitching back to attention. "Promise?"

Sy's eyes went dark. Not exactly dangerous, but not entirely innocent, either. "Is that what you want?"

By the laws of physics and whatever other natural sciences controlled the universe, she shouldn't be capable of being turned on again. And yet, being with Sy didn't seem to obey any of the rules. Why should this be any different? Maddie spread her legs, inviting Sy in. "Yes."

Sy slid a hand between them, fingers sliding over Maddie's thrumming clit and plunging into her wetness. "Fuck. How can you be that wet again?"

She laughed. At least she wasn't the only one not quite sure how it was all possible. "You. You do this to me."

Sy positioned the cock and eased it into her slowly. Considerate, yes. But more than that. She took the sort of care that made feelings way beyond desire quiver in Maddie's chest. "Is this okay?" Sy asked.

Maddie nodded.

Sy fucked her slowly this time, with intention. Purpose. Funny, she'd expected hard and fast. Maybe a little smug. Okay, to be fair, Sy's smile bordered on smug. Maddie couldn't bring herself to mind. She was too busy basking in every exquisite sensation—the thrust of the cock, the weight of Sy's body. Even the sheen of sweat that formed between Sy's breasts captured her attention and coalesced into something that would be imprinted on her forever.

She didn't think she could come again, but she did. Less intense than before, like a vessel filled to the brim and then some, spilling over the top in a perfect cascade, leaving her drenched and weak. Sy continued to move inside her but soon followed, collapsing beside her, breath ragged.

"Remind me to sass you more often," she said when the ability to form words eventually returned.

"If that's what happens when you do, I'm going to have to concur."

She rolled into Sy's outstretched arm and rested her head on Sy's shoulder. "Look at us, agreeing on something."

Sy pinched her lightly beneath the ribs. "I think we agree on most stuff. The stuff that counts, at least."

She wouldn't have said so at first. Of course, she wouldn't have said she and Sy would have tumbled into bed together, either. Or that they'd manage to have so much fun along the way—in bed and out. "I suppose you're right."

Sy lifted her chin. "It's hot when you say that."

It was her turn to do the pinching, only she wasn't overly gentle about it. "Don't press your luck."

CHAPTER SEVENTEEN

Sy fretted over her attire, explaining to Henry the double jeopardy of meeting Maddie's parents for the first time and going for a holiday dinner. "But they're down to earth, too, you know? I can't imagine anyone getting super fancy, so I don't want to look like I'm trying to be better than anyone, either."

Henry yawned from his spot on the foot of the bed.

"Really? I'm boring you? This is high stakes, man."

He stretched, lay down, and immediately began to nod off.

"You're no help." She let out a humph and turned back to her closet. "I sure hope everyone talks to their cats."

She settled on a pair of caramel-colored pants and a button-down but rolled the sleeves and pulled on boots rather than dress shoes. Technically an outfit she'd wear on a date, but also one she'd take her mother to dinner in. A compromise if ever there was one.

She drove over to Maddie's parents' house, running about fifteen minutes early but fully prepared to park up the block and wait it out. But by the time she arrived, there were at least eight cars—well, mostly trucks—already in the driveway. That, in turn, gave her a stab of paranoia that she'd misread the time and was actually late, so she grabbed the casserole dish from the front seat and hustled to the front door.

It opened before she could knock, and Maddie stood on the other side. "Hi."

She took a moment to appreciate the deeply scooped neckline of Maddie's sweater, along with the plaid wool skirt that showed off her gorgeous calves, even if they were covered in tights. "I'm not late, am I?"

"You're early, silly. Come in." Maddie pulled her inside and held the dish while Sy hung her coat.

"I thought so, but then there were so many cars already."

Maddie rolled her eyes. "Five of those are immediate family. You think we'd learn to carpool or something. Your timing is perfect."

"Okay, good." Sy nodded, nerves about timing reverting to nerves about meeting the family.

Maddie flicked her head. "This way."

She followed Maddie down a short hall and into a large, open concept kitchen and den. For some reason, she expected something with the look of a recent remodel. Instead, the space felt comfortable and lived in, like it had been gussied up but at least a decade ago. It instantly made her relax.

"Sy's here," Maddie said, not quite at a yell but close.

She recognized Logan, of course, and quickly pegged Jack, the middle sibling. They seriously looked like a matching set—hair in different shades of red, green eyes, varying degrees of freckles. Maddie's mom, Cathy, gave her a warm hug, and Maddie's dad offered a friendly wave from his recliner. "I split some wood this morning and overdid it a little. I'm sworn to taking it easy till dinner."

She crossed the room to shake his hand. "I'd do what I'm told, too, when it comes to that crew."

Fred roared with laughter and took over the introductions: Cathy's mother, Fred's buddy from the Moose Lodge, and the octogenarian who lived next door.

"Martha." The woman stood to shake Sy's hand. "He calls me the octogenarian because it makes him feel young."

"And he likes proving he knows some big words." Jack came over and put an arm around Martha's shoulders. "Martha is a doll and humors him."

Martha laughed, clearly enjoying Jack's attentions. "That, too."

Clover came in from the sliding door to the backyard and grinned. "I'm so glad you came."

More hugs and a friendly argument about when to switch the television from the parade to football. Utterly unlike Thanksgiving with her mom, but somehow it felt familiar and homey anyway. Maddie offered her a seat on the sofa, but she opted to join the kitchen crew. Force of habit, probably, paired with wanting to be helpful.

Cathy pointed at the wooden cutting board next to the sink. "How do you feel about chopping duty?"

"Mom." Maddie let out a huff that would have gotten Sy into trouble—as a teenager for sure, but as an adult, too. "Don't put her to work. She's a guest. I told her she'd have the day off."

Sy lifted a hand. "I'm happy to help."

Maddie gave her a look of exasperation. "Really? You're taking her side?"

Sy shrugged. "It's her kitchen. She gets to call the shots."

"That is such a chef thing to say," Maddie said, shaking her head.

"Guilty as charged."

Cathy came over and bumped her shoulder lightly to Sy's. "And we're thrilled to have your skills. Almost as thrilled as we are to have your company."

"I'm thrilled to be here." Polite, but true, too.

Logan strolled in. "Am I missing a meeting of the mutual admiration society?"

Maddie hip checked her. "Yeah. You weren't invited."

"You wound me." Logan pressed a hand to her chest.

Maddie rolled her eyes and Sy couldn't help but laugh. She looked to Cathy. "Since those two are useless, you should definitely put me to work."

Cathy gave her a conspiratorial wink. "A woman after my own heart."

Since most of the cooking was already underway, Sy got assigned ingredients for the fruit salad—chopping apples, and adding them to a bowl of walnuts, raisins, and miniature marshmallows. Sort of a riff on Waldorf. Well, aside from the marshmallows, but quirky additions were what made family recipes special.

Maddie came over with a smaller bowl and poured the contents on top. "Nineteen seventy-six called and would like its salad back."

Sy stirred to give everything an even coat of the dressing, which did appear to be mayonnaise-based. "That's exactly how Thanksgiving should be."

"I'm going to remind you you said that when the green bean casserole comes around."

She laughed. "Okay, seriously. We never had that when I was a kid, and I was so jealous of my friends who did. Those crispy onions? Sign me up."

Maddie shook her head but laughed as well. "Please don't tell me you feel that way about Stove Top, too."

Sy wagged a finger. "No, that always freaked me out. Like, bread is not supposed to be like that."

"My mom's stuffing is legit, but you won't hurt her feelings if you don't try it."

"Girl, I went to culinary school. I'll try anything." Though, the year in France stretched her taste buds just as much.

"I keep forgetting that. Clearly, you should cook for me more often so I remember."

She thought about cozy winter nights, snow swirling and something hearty simmering on the stove. Maddie coming over after she finished her workday, and the two of them curling up together. It wouldn't be hard to get used to that, on a lot of levels. "You finish my kitchen and I'll cook for you all you want."

Maddie groaned. "I'm working on it."

No one was watching them, so Sy snuck a kiss onto her cheek. "I know. You can't control the supply chain."

"If it doesn't come soon, I'll chop down a tree and make the butcher block myself."

She knew it didn't work that way, but it was sweet of Maddie to offer. "It'll come when it comes and it will be awesome. Because everything you make is awesome."

Maddie grinned, a flush creeping into her cheeks and making Sy want to kiss her in earnest. "I'm glad you're here."

Sy returned the grin. "Me, too."

❖

Maddie had Sy go ahead of her in the buffet line set up along the kitchen counter and breakfast bar, which meant Sy filled her plate first and made it to the kitchen table a step ahead of her. She took the seat next to Logan, the one Maddie had been planning to snag to create a buffer between them. Not that she expected Logan to be mean. No, if anything, Logan would be over-the-top nice, insinuating Sy was part of the family now.

Sy glanced at the larger dining room table, where all the older members of the family and guests sat. "Can I say how much I love that you guys are still at the kiddie table?"

Clover, who'd settled in opposite Maddie, laughed. "I know, right? It makes me feel like I'm twelve and I'm not going to lie, I'm into it."

Logan leaned over and lifted her chin at Sy's plate. "You don't have to eat the Jell-O mold. It's family tradition, but I don't think anyone but my grandma actually likes it. And the adults aren't paying attention."

Sy forked a bite into her mouth. "Yum."

Maddie snickered. For an only child, Sy didn't seem to have any trouble holding her own in a sibling situation.

Logan shook her head. "Suck up."

Sy shrugged. "I learned to appreciate all sorts of things in culinary school. And in France. If it's made with love and matters to someone, that makes it good enough for me."

Holding her own or not, Maddie leaned over Sy and poked Logan on the shoulder. "Stop harassing my date."

"I'm not harassing her. I'm telling her she doesn't need to worry about brownie points." Logan shrugged. "But she's not listening to me."

Maddie shifted her focus to Sy. "Do you feel like you need brownie points?"

"I want to make a good impression," Sy said. "It was very generous of your family to include me."

Logan flicked a hand her way. "See?"

Maddie gave Sy's leg a squeeze. "I promise you're more than welcome."

"Yeah, but that's because your family is nice, not because they've decided I'm nice. I want them to like me enough that they'd invite me again," Sy said like it was the most logical thing in the world.

Logan rested the hand she'd just flicked on Sy's arm. "Consider this a standing invitation to all holiday dinners henceforth."

"Henceforth?" Maddie rolled her eyes. "Who are you? Dad?"

Logan batted her eyes at Sy. "Though you'd probably prefer that invitation come from my sister."

And there it was. She not so subtly kicked Logan under the table. Only it was Jack who let out an "ow" and glared at her. Logan deduced what had happened and laughed. Sy looked confused. Maddie cleared her throat. "How about we talk about something else?"

Clover raised her hand. "Let's talk about how Sy got us into Fromager."

Maddie smiled. She could always count on Clover.

"What's Fromager?" Jack asked.

"Only the swankiest cheese store in Northampton," Clover said triumphantly.

Logan whistled and Jack said, "Nice."

Rather than puff up, Sy seemed to get modest at the attention. "I met the owner when he was on a scouting trip in France."

Logan picked up one of the crackers she'd smeared with Sy's cranberry and fennel chèvre. "You mean this cheese is now sitting next to some chichi French stuff in a shop?"

Sy angled her head. "It will be when I drive their first order down next week. Along with our rose petal and pink peppercorn."

"And he wants brie as soon as Sy can get it to him," Clover said.

Maddie didn't give a lot of thought to taking pride in other people's efforts, but her chest swelled nonetheless. Maybe because it had to do with Clover as much as Sy, how long Clover had been dreaming about making cheese the legacy of Falling Barn Farm.

Maybe it was because raising the profile of Grumpy Old Goat had the potential to rub off on Bedlington as a whole. Turn it into one of the places people went out of their way to visit on their weekend jaunts up to Vermont.

But even as she made the case to herself, Sy remained front and center. She'd had so many doubts when Sy arrived—about her reasons for coming, about her ability to settle in an area so far removed from her scope of experience. And that didn't even touch on her train wreck of a house.

In spite of all that, Sy had stayed. Stayed and, in short order, was turning both Grumpy Old Goat and her home into something special. She still didn't put a lot of stock in Sy sticking around in the long term, or whether this thing between them would grow into something she'd need to manage or simply fizzle. But in this moment, it was more than Maddie had bargained for and pretty high on the list of things she was grateful for. She'd worry about the rest later.

CHAPTER EIGHTEEN

W ait, what?" Sy pinched the bridge of her nose and paced the length of the cheese room. She'd talked with her mother literally the day before and everything had been normal. Happy Thanksgiving. What did you cook? Who did you see?

Mama waited a beat before saying, "I said, your father reached out to me and we've been talking. I want to invite him for Christmas."

Been talking. Sy stopped pacing and let her head fall back, phone still pressed to her ear. The words were identical but still failed to make sense. "I thought you didn't even know where he was."

"I didn't."

"So, he tracked you down out of the blue?" As far as she was concerned, that had stalker written all over it. Especially concerning after the disappearing act he pulled even before Sy was born.

"He recently got divorced and it got him thinking about the past and he looked me up on social media," Mama said, as though it was the most logical thing in the world.

Great, so a stalker having a midlife crisis. "Why would you want to talk to him after all this time? He broke your heart."

Mama sighed one of those sighs that could be a show of patience or exasperation—a frustrating skill she had. "Going away wasn't his choice. It was his parents' doing."

She knew the story well enough. They'd been high school sweethearts. His parents were stereotypical rich white folk. Classist, racist, and they certainly didn't approve of their golden boy son running around with the daughter of Mexican immigrants. And when her mother got pregnant, their solution was to move to another town and send their son to private school. She'd grown up with more anger toward his parents than him, but she didn't have all that much use for him, either. Because if he'd wanted to find them—at any point in the last thirty years—he could have.

"Sy."

Since Mama wasn't there to see, she scowled.

"Don't make a face. I can tell even through the phone."

She laughed in spite of herself and scrubbed a hand over her face. "You're an adult and can do what you want. I just don't want you to get hurt."

"I'm perfectly capable of taking care of myself," Mama said.

"I know." Like, she really did know. Her mother was smart and tough and had an irrepressible spirit. Ironically, it's what made Sy feel all the more protective of her.

"How would you feel if we came to you?"

"Are you serious?" She'd started needling her mom to come for a visit but expected it to happen late spring or summer, when the weather was nice and her house was done and she had a handle on how long she planned to stick around Vermont.

"Well, I know money is tight for you."

"It's tight for you, too." And if money was the point, she could have just as easily offered to help Sy with her ticket.

"John and I were thinking about taking the trip together. I've never seen New York, and he says it's one of his favorite places."

Just when she thought things couldn't get more bizarre. "Mama, are you and John dating?"

"We aren't putting a label on things."

Definitely code for dating, if not more. "Why didn't you tell me?"

Mama sighed again. "Because I didn't know how I felt about it at first. I didn't know how it was going to go. I didn't want to worry you for nothing."

She knew better than to tell her mother too fucking late, so she bit her tongue. "Obviously I want to see you. And I want you to visit. If you're telling me this is what you want, that it will make you happy, of course it's fine."

"Sylvia Marie, are you patronizing me?"

Technically, the answer was yes, a little. But she knew better than to say that, too. "No. I'm just trying to process all of this. It's a lot."

"I know. It's a lot for me, too. It's just…"

"Just what?" As much as she didn't like this, she hated the prospect of her mother not being open with her even more.

"It feels like it used to feel, back when we were seventeen and nothing seemed impossible. And of course we're older and wiser and know that isn't true, but the feeling, Sy. The feeling is still there."

She didn't often experience ambivalence, but that was the only word she could come up with to describe the heavy knot in the pit of her stomach. Her mother didn't suffer fools, nor was she prone to acting like one herself. But had sentimentality gotten the best of her? Sy hated not being able to see her face, her body language. "You're not going to run off and elope on me are you?"

She'd meant for the question to break the tension—an absurd notion they could both laugh about. Her mother did laugh, but it had that vaguely uncomfortable cadence that came with something hitting a little too close to home. "Of course not, mija."

Sy wanted to call her out on it but wasn't sure she wanted the answer. "So, you're both coming. Will you both stay with me?"

"Only if you're okay with it."

Did she have a choice? "It might be awkward, but the closest hotel is almost an hour away, so I think that's what we're stuck with."

"You're upset." Mama didn't make it sound like a question.

"Surprised. And I have feelings, but they aren't bad necessarily. It's a lot to take in." Sy swallowed. She'd already said that last bit.

"I know. Maybe I should have said something sooner."

One of the things Sy loved about her mother was that she didn't play that guilt card bullshit so many mothers did, especially the

Catholic ones. What it meant, though, was that when she sounded dejected, she legit was. "I mean, yes, but only because I love you and I want to know what's going on with you. If this is important to you, it's important to me."

"He's very anxious to meet you. I hope you'll give him a chance. I think you'll like him."

She'd gotten so caught up in the rabbit hole of her mother dating and getting involved with a man seemingly out of the blue, she'd almost—almost—lost track of the fact that the man in question was her father. A man she'd never met and never expected to meet. "I'll try."

"Thank you."

Resigned, at least for the moment, to the massive change of plans, her mind kicked into gear on the logistics front. "So, what's the plan? How long will you stay?"

"I think we're going to do New York first so I can see it all decked out for Christmas. We'll head north on the twenty-third maybe? Stay with you a few days and fly out in time to be home for New Year's." She rattled off the details like she'd already made all the arrangements.

"Okay," Sy said, because what else could she say?

"I know you'll have to work after the holiday. We can entertain ourselves. Even go to Boston for a day or two if you're busy."

Her mother did all right for herself, but not so well she could readily bankroll a few days in two of the most expensive cities in the country on a whim. She opened her mouth to ask about that part, but closed it just as quickly. John came from money. That was part of his parents' objection to him hooking up with Bonita in the first place. She had no idea what he did now, but that sort of money tended to perpetuate itself. Ugh. "I'm flexible. It's the beauty of being the only one doing the work right now. I get to set my own hours."

"Oh, I can't wait to see it. And your house, of course. I'm so very proud of you."

Mama often said things like that, but it felt like she was laying it on extra thick. Normally, Sy would poke fun and they'd tease one another a bit. This time, she just wanted to end the call and take a minute to process. "It should be done by then. As long as the kitchen counters show up."

"So exciting."

Sy shifted her weight from foot to foot, the antsy feeling taking over. "I need to check my curd to see if it's ready for cutting. Can I call you over the weekend?"

"Go, go. I'll be here. Call anytime."

It was something she often said, but for the first time, Sy wondered how true it really was. Not that she needed—or wanted—her mother to be available at the drop of a hat. But if she was planning a trip with this guy, they must be spending a lot of time together. Reality struck her again. Not some guy. Her dad.

"Sy?"

"Sorry, distracted by the cheese." Often the case, if not in this instance. "I love you."

"Love you, too. Bye."

The call ended and Sy stuck her phone in her pocket. She looked at the empty vat, wishing she did have curd waiting to suck up all her energy and focus. She'd have to settle for packaging the latest batch of chèvre. Fussy, but satisfying in its own way. Which was more than she could say for that conversation.

After spending Friday with her family, and missing Sy more than was reasonable after a mere two nights apart, Maddie was almost giddy pulling into Sy's driveway late Saturday morning. Though, realistically, that had as much to do with getting her tree as anything else. She loved Christmas tree shopping. Loved.

This year, she got that on top of taking Sy to her very first Christmas tree farm ever.

Only when Sy slid into Maddie's truck, she seemed both distracted and disinterested in the whole process. Sullen silence, staring out the window—the whole bit. Maddie clicked off the classic Christmas playlist she always broke out to set the mood. "Are you not into this?"

The abrupt silence got Sy's attention as much as the question. "Into what? Getting trees?"

"It's okay if the answer is no. I can admit my enthusiasm for the whole process is a lot. Maybe you feel compelled to play along so you don't hurt my feelings. Maybe you don't even want a real tree in your house."

Sy shook her head vigorously. "No. Sorry. I do want to go."

Maddie would give her an A for effort, but it still didn't explain her mood. "Then what's bugging you?"

Sy waited a beat, like she was deciding what—or maybe how much—to say. "My mother is dating my father."

The mere oddity of the statement threw her for a second, but meaning followed. "I thought you'd never even met your father."

"I haven't. But he tracked down my mother, is recently divorced, and now they're seeing each other."

"Whoa." It was one thing not to have a dad. It was another thing entirely to have him show up out of the blue after thirty-some years.

Sy let out a huff of exasperation. "Yeah. And now they're coming here for Christmas. What am I supposed to do with that?"

"Jesus, Sy. Why didn't you say something?"

"Because it just happened."

Maddie braked for a stop sign and decided to pull all the way over. "Like, just just?"

"Well, yesterday. I processed it with Clover, but I guess I'm still stewing."

"Oh."

Sy shrugged. "And I'm much better at stewing in my own jumble of mixed emotions than talking about them."

She laughed at the honesty but her insides bristled with disappointment that Sy had confided in Clover before her. "Would you like me to let you keep stewing?"

Sy shook her head.

"Do you want to talk about it?" Maddie asked.

Sy sat up straighter in her seat. "Maybe, but not now. Right now I'd like to compartmentalize the shit out of it and have a good day with you."

"You sure?"

"Positive."

She could appreciate that, so she decided to do the same, if for no other reason than getting her feelings bent out of shape was the exact opposite of what she wanted to do with Sy. "You got it."

"Thanks."

Maddie turned the music back on and pulled back onto the road. "Do you want hot chocolate or mulled cider?"

To her credit, Sy played along and took the question seriously. "Tough call."

"Wait until you have to choose a tree."

Sy nodded but didn't seem to get what she was saying. Not really. But rather than explaining the expanse of a twenty-acre tree farm, Maddie decided to let it speak for itself. She pulled into the lot, finding a spot in a long row of pickup trucks and SUVs. Today was the day for tree getting. The little shed the owners set up with wreaths and refreshments was out of cider, so they snagged cups of cocoa, complete with candy cane stirrers. Maddie picked up a saw and they made their way into the sea of trees.

"It's like a movie," Sy said, turning a slow circle deep in one of the rows.

The flurries that had started certainly set the scene, as did the distant sound of children laughing and squealing with delight. It wasn't always that perfect—sometimes there was mud and tantrums—but she opted not to burst Sy's bubble.

She settled on hers pretty quickly, as she always did. Eight-foot Fraser fir that she could wrap her arms at least halfway around. Sy, on the other hand, was like a kid in a candy store, wanting everything all at once. She hopped from one to another, obsessed with the idea of getting one with character over one that fit more traditional beauty standards.

The only problem? Sy seemed to have absolutely no sense of scale.

For at least the fourth time, Maddie shook her head and gave her best disapproving look. "Raise your arm."

Sy pouted but did as she was told.

"Now, how far above your reach can you go?" Maddie asked.

Another sigh. "No more than a foot."

"And how much taller is that tree?"

Sy squinted and looked up, shading her eyes with her free hand. "Two?"

"Try three."

Sy dropped both hands. "You're mean."

"Mean is letting you buy a tree I know won't fit in your house and watching you learn that lesson the hard way." Maddie grabbed her hand and tugged her in the direction of a more modest row. "Come on."

Sy eventually picked one, Maddie agreed it would fit through the front door, and Sy cut it down herself. They loaded both onto one of the sleds the farm provided and got them down the hill and into the back of Maddie's truck. They also bought Sy a stand, since she didn't own one.

They headed to Sy's first, since Maddie had the tools and ability to put a fresh cut on hers the next day, and wrestled it into the house. No mean feat, with Henry underfoot and Sy having no clue what she was doing. After some huffing and puffing, a little swearing, and legit giggling, they got it in and upright.

Sy took a step back and planted her fists on her hips. "I think it looks good."

"It looks fantastic." Maddie threaded her arm through Sy's. "Congratulations on your first ever real Christmas tree."

Sy smiled briefly, but then her expression sobered. "To go along with my first Christmas with a dad."

She pursed her lips, wishing she knew what to say. "You can meet him and decide he's a perfectly nice guy and still not want him to be a father to you."

Sy shrugged. "I don't even know if he wants that."

"True." Though she'd bet money he did, based on the current plan of flying across the country to meet her.

Sy shook her head. "Sorry. I know I keep rehashing it. I'm sure it's beyond annoying at this point."

"It's not." She slid her arm around Sy's waist and gave it a squeeze. "Family drama is hard. Trust me, I know."

Sy squeezed her back. "Any developments on that front?"

"Nada." Which was better than a bad development, she supposed, but uncertainty was not her favorite thing by a long shot.

"Well, what do you say we crack open a bottle of wine and pretend our families aren't major sources of consternation?"

She laughed at the assessment. "Don't you want to get the lights on?"

"I want the lights to be on. Getting them there is another story, one I'm pretty sure will go better with a glass of wine."

"Can't argue with that," Maddie said.

"Except, I don't actually own any Christmas lights."

"You don't?" Who didn't own Christmas lights? Well, of the people who celebrated Christmas anyway.

"I got rid of the cheapy ones I had when I put everything in storage to go to France," Sy said.

Ah. That made her feel better. "Are there any kind other than the cheapy kind?"

Sy shrugged. "Not the person to ask."

"Then I guess we get to have that wine and decorate tomorrow. Assuming you want help decorating." She shouldn't presume. About lights or anything else. And she'd do well to remember that.

"Oh, I want help. Four hands is the only way to do lights in my book." Sy stuck hers out as if to prove the insufficiency of two. "And you have to teach me this method of wiring things to the wall. If the tree fell on Henry, I'd never forgive myself."

Maddie chuckled, then kissed Sy's cheek. "It's cute that you said it that way."

"What other way is there?" Sy asked.

See, this was what she wanted. Light. Easy banter and good sex. The rest was more trouble than it was worth. "Um, if Henry knocked down the Christmas tree, I'd never forgive him."

Sy laughed then. Like, really laughed. "Thank you. I needed that."

"Happy to oblige. Now where's this wine I was promised?"

"I'll grab it. Do you want dinner now? Later?"

She considered her options. They hadn't discussed her spending the night, but it might prove a good reset as much as a good time. "Honestly?"

Sy gave her a look. "Well, I don't want you to answer dishonestly."

"Honestly, I'd love to take a hot shower with you, crawl into bed for a bit, then have food and wine and cuddles." Which was pretty fucking domestic now that she said it out loud. Oh, well.

Either Sy didn't get that vibe, or she did and didn't mind. Whichever way, she let out a contented sigh and said, "Sold."

Chapter Nineteen

W ith the cabinet doors hung and the appliances in place, the only things remaining to complete Sy's kitchen were the countertops and kitchen sink. Maddie told Sy the counters would be a few days still, courtesy of the ongoing backlog with the supplier. In truth, she wanted Sy to have at least one "big reveal" moment, and the kitchen would obviously pack the biggest punch.

So, she sent Sy off to work, promising to feed Henry when she stopped over to take a final round of measurements. What she did instead was arrange for Logan to meet her there to get the butcher block cut and set and to install the massive under-mount sink she'd scored at a liquidation sale.

"Thank you so much for coming over," she said as she and Logan slid the last piece into place.

"I think it's cute that you want your girlfriend to have an HGTV moment."

She could argue either the girlfriend reference or the HGTV one—or both—but didn't. She was in a good mood and, honestly, she didn't mind the idea of Sy as her girlfriend, especially since she kept a clear image in her mind of what that meant. They had fun together. They had enough shared interests to do things together, without crossing that weird line of becoming the same person. And the sex. Dear God, the sex. What more could she want?

"You're thinking about seeing her face, aren't you?" Logan, hands now free, gave her shoulder a friendly shove.

Her face. Her hands. Broad shoulders. The sexy swell of her chest. Not that Logan needed to know any of that. "She deserves something nice."

"And what's nicer than a surprise finished kitchen courtesy of your girlfriend?"

Coming home to find said girlfriend standing in the kitchen naked? "Exactly."

Logan shook her head. "I can't believe you're not even protesting the fact that I keep calling her your girlfriend."

Maddie squirted a line of epoxy around the lip of the sink before crawling into the cabinet where it would go. "Only because I know, if I did, you'd pull out some nonsense about protesting too much."

Logan tipped her head. "True."

"For the record, I'd say we're dating." And fucking. So much fucking.

"Do you really differentiate?"

"Of course. Girlfriend implies exclusive, unless it's a poly thing, obviously. Girlfriend implies some mutual agreement that you're together, that you want to be together." That you're at least contemplating staying together.

Logan peered through the hole, her face looming large over Maddie's. "I should have known you'd have all these lines and boxes and definitions."

"It's called clarity, kid. Clarity of expectations and clarity in communication." Not that she'd told Sy every single thought she'd had, but certainly the essentials. What was the point of being in a relationship with someone without that?

"Ooh, aren't we the paragon of all grown up and emotionally mature?"

Maddie dragged the sink into the space and positioned it on her chest. "Jealous?"

"No, because I know you talk a good game but screw up your love life just as much as the rest of us."

Touché. "Grab the clamp, will you? And that board."

Logan did what Maddie asked but waggled the clamp in the air like a giant foam finger. "Don't change the subject."

"The subject is sink installation. You're the one doing the distracting."

"You're the one doing the distracting." Logan echoed the words in her most annoying singsong voice.

Since she did consider herself the paragon of all grown up and emotionally mature, at least among her siblings, she didn't take the bait. "You ready?"

"Mm-hmm." Logan, in true Logan fashion, looked annoyed by the question.

Maddie hefted the sink and lifted it into place, lining up the marks she'd made on the underside of the counter earlier. "How does it look up there?"

"Straighter than you, sister," Logan said.

She snorted. Logan might be a pain in her ass, but the girl was funny. "That's a pretty low bar."

"Truth. Still. It's pretty damn straight."

"I'll take it. Fish me the clamp."

Logan stuck the bar of the clamp through the drain hole. Maddie slipped the back jaw into place while Logan held the sink steady from above. She positioned the wood brace and got her end of the setup situated.

"You good?" Logan asked.

"All good." She resumed her hold on the sink while Logan clicked the clamp tight.

"And I think we're done."

Maddie scooted out from inside the cabinet but remained seated on the floor. "God, that's easier with two people."

"Most jobs are." Logan, the consummate extrovert, shrugged.

Since she mostly agreed, she mirrored the gesture. "Except the ones that aren't."

Logan smirked. "And those take twice as long."

Despite the fact that nearly a decade separated them, and Logan could run circles around Maddie when it came to creativity, they remained more alike than not. "Indeed."

Logan stuck out her hand and Maddie took it, letting Logan haul her to her feet. "Anything else you want a second pair of hands with?"

"I mean, if you wanted to do a little staging while I installed the cabinetry hardware, I wouldn't say no."

"Seriously?" Logan's incredulous look said plenty—not about her thoughts on staging but Maddie's own impatience with the level of fussing that went into finishing jobs these days.

"Nothing over the top. I want to get some of Sy's dishes on the open shelving. I picked up some flowers."

Logan blinked slowly, laying it on extra thick. "Flowers."

"If you're going to give me this hard a time, you can leave. Or go play with Henry. Sy says he's always pining for someone to play with."

The teasing look faded and a serious one took over. "Are you in love with this woman?"

"Of course not. We've been seeing each other for like two weeks." She was not the sort of woman to fall in love after two weeks. And, as she continued to remind herself, she was not the sort of woman to fall in love with someone like Sy at all.

Logan tutted. "You have been in each other's pants for two weeks, but you've been in each other's pockets for like two months."

Did she have to be so fucking clever about it? "We were friends. Which is a nice foundation but a far cry from falling for each other."

"If you say so. Where are the dishes?" Logan rolled her eyes. "And these flowers you speak of?"

❖

Sy pulled into her driveway, cut the engine, and took a moment to adjust the bulge straining against the seam of her jeans. It was the age-old butch problem, really. The cocks made for packing didn't stand up to play—quite literally—and the ones she preferred for play were definitely not made to be tucked away. But catching Maddie by surprise would make the momentary discomfort worth it.

And fortunately, no one but Maddie would see what she so clearly had on display.

She'd planned to show up on Maddie's doorstep and see how long it took Maddie to notice. When Maddie texted a change of plans to meet at Sy's place instead, it felt serendipitous that she'd brought the cock with her to work. Maddie really wouldn't be expecting it then.

She strode to the front door faster than she might otherwise. Not that the neighbors would notice, but, well, a couple of them might. Nosy wasn't the half of it. She almost knocked, then remembered it was her house.

"Honey, I'm home." She put on her most affected Ricky Ricardo accent to make it abundantly clear she was joking.

"Honey popped out to the store, so you're stuck with me." Logan stepped from the kitchen but hovered in the doorway.

Sy stopped short. "Logan."

"She told me to tell you she won't be five minutes." Logan hooked a thumb behind her. "And I'm supposed to keep you from going in there."

"Uh, okay. Cool." Sy shifted, mortification mingling with the physical discomfort of the silicone jabbing her in the groin.

"You okay?" Logan regarded her with a mixture of confusion and concern. And then her gaze flicked almost imperceptibly down and realization dawned. "Oh."

Sy winced. "I wasn't expecting anyone but Maddie."

Logan nodded, seemingly more amused than embarrassed. "It's all good, dude."

"You're gonna tease her about this, aren't you?"

"Oh, yeah. Big time."

"Any chance I could prevail upon your good nature? Or maybe play the butch code card?"

Logan's eyes narrowed. "What's it worth to you?"

The haggling made it feel like they were friends more than Logan truly wanting to hang something over Sy's head. "Dinner? I could cook at your place, maybe something you could heat up and use to impress a date?"

Logan nodded slowly, as though mulling the idea. "No women to impress at the moment, I'm afraid. But I do have a soft spot for mole. You do mole?"

Now they were speaking her language. "I do my grandmother's mole."

"I know better than to ask you for the recipe, but one batch, delivered at your convenience."

Were they really trading mole for Logan not giving Maddie flack about her girlfriend showing up with a massive cock on display? Apparently they were. "Deal."

Logan stuck out her hand. "Deal."

They were still shaking on it when Maddie burst through the front door, cheeks flushed from the cold and hair in deliciously wind tossed disarray. "Did you keep her out?" Her gaze flew from Logan to Sy. "Did she keep you out?"

"Out of where?" Sy asked.

"The kitchen," Maddie and Logan said in unison.

Maddie glared at Logan. Logan looked at Maddie with mild exasperation. And as far as Sy could tell, Maddie had yet to notice the bulge that had dominated the conversation before she arrived.

"I kept her out," Logan said.

"I didn't go in," Sy added.

"Okay." Maddie nodded slowly. "Sorry. I wanted it to be a surprise, but then I forgot something, so I left Logan to stand guard."

"And now that that's done, I'm going to make my exit so you two can do your thing." Logan went to the front door and slipped on her coat. "You kids have fun."

Logan left but not before wiggling her eyebrows suggestively at Sy. Sy managed to keep a straight face, but it didn't stop Maddie from giving her a curious look once Logan had gone. "What was that about?"

Sy's gaze flicked down before she could stop it, and Maddie's followed. Her mouth dropped open and she pointed. "Did my sister see that?"

"No?" A decidedly unconvincing answer, weakened further when she cringed.

"She did."

"But she promised to be cool about it." No need to mention the bribe, especially until she was sure Logan would hold up her end of the bargain.

Maddie pinched the bridge of her nose.

"Sorry. I was going to surprise you at your place, then you told me to come here, and I figured I'd do it here instead. I had no idea Logan would be here."

Maddie laughed. "How could you have possibly known that?"

She shrugged, less focused on the logic of that and more on the fact that Maddie didn't seem to be mad. "I'm still sorry. I don't want to make things awkward."

Maddie crossed the room to stand in front of Sy. "They won't be awkward. She'll harass me like she always does, but she'll be cool with you. It'll probably be some weird butch bonding thing."

Sy barely held in the laugh. If Maddie only knew. "Hopefully she won't give you too hard a time."

"If she doesn't over that, she'll find something else. It's our thing."

"Deep affection laced with antagonism?" Sy asked.

"Exactly." Maddie rolled her eyes. "But enough about that. We have more important things to discuss."

"We do?" She still didn't know why she wasn't supposed to go in the kitchen.

Maddie cupped the bulge with her hand. "Yep."

It was tempting to forget all about the kitchen and Logan and getting caught packing. To drag Maddie upstairs to the bedroom that still felt like a pleasant surprise every time she walked through the door. To put the cock to good use. But Maddie obviously had something up her sleeve. "But what about the kitchen?"

Maddie laughed but didn't move her hand. "Do you know how much it says about me wanting to have sex with you that I'm basically willing to forgo a reveal for it?"

She wanted sex, too, but the tail end of Maddie's comment caught her attention. "Reveal?"

"Your counters aren't on backorder. They're here. And in. Along with your sink, though the silicone needs to cure overnight before you can use it. I wanted to surprise you."

"Really? You did that for me?" Getting the kitchen done was pretty much the thing she wanted most, as far as the house was concerned at least. Having that, paired with Maddie wanting to make it a surprise, had her pulse tripping with excitement. But something deeper, too. Something bigger. Something she'd have to tease apart eventually, but not today.

"Come on." Maddie grabbed her hand but didn't move. "Close your eyes?"

The apprehension in Maddie's voice, like maybe she wasn't sure Sy would obey, only intensified the hum of emotion. Sy closed her eyes. "Don't let me run into a wall."

"I won't." Maddie laughed and grabbed her other hand. "It's only a few feet."

"I trust you." Even with that trust, her steps were halting and hesitant.

"Okay, open."

She did and, for the first time, got how people on those home shows could be so blown away by a remodel, even when they'd been part of the process right up until the end. She'd literally been in her kitchen that morning, and the difference was night and day. The counters and sink, the pulls on the cabinet doors and drawers—it all looked perfect.

It was more than that, though. The shelves held her dishes, and one of her kitchen towels hung from the oven door handle. A mason jar of flowers sat on the island, along with a cutting board holding a baguette and a log of chèvre. Even with the clamps still holding the sink in place, the room felt complete. More, it felt like home.

"I can't believe you did this for me." Emotion made her voice catch, and tears pricked at her eyes. "It's so beautiful."

Maddie's arm slid around her waist. "I'm glad you like it. You did plenty of the work yourself. I just put on the finishing touches."

Sy spun Maddie to face her. "It's thoughtful and sweet and perfect."

Maddie grinned. "Good. The counters still need to be oiled a couple of times before you use them, but it will be fit for purpose this time tomorrow."

"Thank you." Sy pulled Maddie close and kissed her. "Thank you, thank you, thank you."

"You know how you could really thank me?" Maddie asked.

She imagined an elaborate dinner, spending a whole day waiting on Maddie hand and foot. Maybe a massage. "How?"

Maddie's hand returned to the cock.

"Ah." Or there was that.

CHAPTER TWENTY

Maddie cupped the cock through Sy's jeans, already imagining it inside her. "You gonna take me upstairs or what?"

Sy seemed to consider the question, or maybe more accurately, her options. "We'll get there."

She quirked a brow, as much at the gleam in Sy's eyes as her words. "I have no idea what you're thinking right now, but I have the feeling it's hot."

Sy's arms came around her. "I'm hoping you'll indulge me in a little experiment."

"What kind of—" Before she could finish the question, Sy lifted her off the ground. She instinctively hooked her legs around Sy, ankles landing on Sy's butt more than her waist. Sy carried her a few steps and deposited her on the counter. She let go of Sy and let her legs dangle. "Okay."

"A little tall for what I had in mind, but nothing we can't work around."

Understanding zipped through her, chased by a surge of arousal. "I see."

"I mean, I can kiss you easy enough." As if to prove her point, Sy did. Only she took her time about it, sucking Maddie's bottom lip into her mouth and biting it gently.

When Sy pulled away, Maddie nodded, slightly dazed. "Yep, yep. That definitely works."

"And your breasts are at literally the perfect height." Sy made quick work of the buttons on Maddie's flannel and covered them with her hands.

"It's not the sort of thing you should estimate, though." Maddie worked the shirt down her arms and yanked the tank top she wore underneath over her head.

Sy reached behind her and flicked open the clasp of her bra. "You did teach me to measure twice."

"Suck once?" Maddie snickered at her joke, but it turned into a gasp when Sy pulled a nipple into her mouth.

"How was that?" Sy asked after working it thoroughly.

"I don't know. You might need to suck twice, too."

"You're the boss." Sy turned her attention to the other nipple.

Maddie ran her fingers through Sy's hair and let her head fall back. "Mm-hmm, mm-hmm."

Sy continued to work her breasts, sucking and biting at one nipple while pinching and tugging the other with her fingers. Maddie wound her legs around Sy once more, pulling her close and feeling the hardness of the cock against her. She rocked her hips, getting wetter even through the layers of cotton and denim.

Sy tugged at the button of Maddie's jeans, yanked the zipper down. It happened to be one of her looser pairs and Sy had no trouble working her hand into them, shoving past Maddie's panties and finding her throbbing clit. Maddie swore and gripped Sy's shoulders, not wanting to come yet but knowing she was close.

"You going to come for me like that? Half-dressed and perched on the pretty counters you just put in?"

At Sy's question, Maddie erupted. The orgasm ripped through her like a tornado, winding her tight and spinning her out of control at the same time. Her body bucked and her grasp on Sy tightened, desperate to hold on even as she let herself go.

But rather than sating, the whole thing spurred her desire to new heights. She needed Sy inside her, and she needed it now.

Maddie slid off the counter and wasted no time shimmying out of her jeans, thinking she'd happily have Sy fuck her right there on the kitchen floor. Unfortunately, that plan hadn't included the time to take off her boots. The result left her hopping around on one foot, attempting to yank them off while her pants bunched around her ankles.

"Please let me help," Sy said, clearly trying to hold back laughter.

She stopped, mostly because she'd started to laugh as well and, at the rate she was going, there was every chance she'd end up on her ass. "Fine."

"Thank you. You know what's not sexy? A sprained ankle." Sy got down on one knee and went to work on the laces.

"This would be a terrible way to propose," she mused, not really meaning to say it out loud.

Sy tapped one foot for Maddie to lift, then slid the boot off. "Noted."

That got her laughing again and she had to hold onto Sy's shoulder for balance. After entirely too long, Sy managed to rid her of her second boot, both socks, her jeans, and the black cotton bikinis that she liked under work clothes. "Phew."

Sy stood. "Better?"

"Much."

"Good." Sy spun her around and pressed a hand between her shoulder blades. "Because now that you're standing, I have other ideas."

The pressure of Sy's hand was gentle but firm. Maddie took the hint, bending at the waist and resting her palms on the smooth wood. She looked over her shoulder with a smile. "Like this?"

Sy ran a hand over one ass cheek, then the other. "It's like we're of one mind."

"Okay, I'm thinking about something really intensely. See if you can sense what it is." She shimmied her hips.

Sy undid the button of her jeans, then the fly. "Does it go something like this?"

Maddie bit her lip and nodded. "How'd you guess?"

Sy freed the cock and stroked it a few times. "Like I said. One mind."

"You better get over here and fuck me with that or I might not be able to think straight for much longer."

Sy smirked. "Who wants to think straight anyway? So overrated."

Maddie laughed. "Fair. But still."

Sy came closer. One hand remained on the cock. The other disappeared between Maddie's legs. A slow circle of Maddie's clit before sliding a finger inside her had Maddie's knees threatening to buckle. "If you're thinking straight while I'm doing this, I'm afraid I might not be doing it right."

Maddie's brain blurred and she struggled to form thoughts of any kind. "You're. Doing. It. Right."

"Oh, good. Would you like to tell me exactly how you'd like it done?"

Sy added a second finger and Maddie groaned. "Slow. Fast. Hard. All of it."

"All of it, huh?" Sy eased her hand away.

Even though she knew what came next, her pussy clenched at the loss. "All of it."

Sy positioned the cock but didn't press into her. She just held it there, a taste and a tease at the same time. "I don't have any lube down here."

Maddie took a chance, thrusting her hips back and taking the length of silicone in all at once. She let out another groan at how exquisitely Sy filled her. Sy let out a groan of her own. She tossed another smile over her shoulder. "I'm good without."

Sy's hands came to Maddie's hips, holding her steady while she stroked in and out a few times. "So, so good."

Maddie rested her cheek on the counter between her splayed hands. "I was just thinking the same thing."

She let Sy set the rhythm, giving herself over to how delicious it felt to be taken like this. Because consent and respect and all those things were always present with Sy, but being fucked like this had that and an edge of something else. Something raw and possessive, something that made her feel like she could push Sy to the limits of her self-control, test them, and not be afraid of what might be lurking on the other side.

As if sensing that in her, Sy increased the speed and force of her thrusts. Her fingers dug into Maddie's hips, and she started to mumble, a sexy and incoherent string of expletives and encouragement, punctuated with a warning that Maddie was going to make her come. Maddie mumbled some encouragement of her own, wanting to push Sy over the edge even more than she wanted another orgasm of her own.

She lifted her head and braced her hands more firmly, matching the pumping of Sy's pelvis thrust for thrust. Sy let out a primal sound, pushing into Maddie hard enough that her hands gave out from under her. She sagged against the counter, and Sy collapsed on top of her. She let out a happy sigh, feeling like a lusty sex goddess.

Until she didn't.

"I don't want to break the mood, but you're squishing my boobs."

"Oh. God. Sorry." Sy stood.

"Don't worry. It was totally worth it."

Sy nodded, looking too full of sex endorphins to argue. "Yeah."

They stood, leaning against adjacent counters, breathing heavy. Sy's slumped posture and slightly dazed expression mirrored her sentiments perfectly. "So, happy new kitchen," Maddie said.

Sy gave her a lopsided, sex-addled grin. "Happy new kitchen indeed."

"I'm sorry you came home to my sister." Though, in this current state, she had a hard time being anything but smug.

"I'll get over it. I hope she will."

Maddie waved away Sy's worry. "She'll be fine. I'll assure her I can take a little teasing when the sex I'm being teased about is so good."

"So good, huh?" Sy asked.

Damn it all if self-satisfied wasn't the sexiest look on her. "You know it is."

"I'm just glad the feeling is mutual." Sy pushed herself to a fully upright position. The cock bounced between her legs, as though expressing alacrity for whatever might come next. "Did you want dinner?"

"Eventually." As sexy as the cock was, she had other things in mind. "First, I'd like to get you out of that thing and get my mouth on you."

Sy's head fell back. "Are you trying to kill me, woman?"

"No. But a sex coma isn't off the table."

Sy took her hand. "If I do die, it will have been a good way to go."

❖

"Do you have to go?" Sy mumbled into the pillow, pulling Maddie's warm and naked backside tighter against her.

"Yes." Maddie groaned her answer, though, and that counted for something.

"What if you were just a little bit late?" She cupped the underside of Maddie's breast. The weight and warmth in her hand had her body zipping from snuggly to sexy in under a second. "I could be quick."

Maddie wiggled against her. "I've been with you. There's nothing quick about it."

She rolled Maddie's nipple between her finger and thumb. "I'm not saying I prefer to be fast. I'm saying I can be when I'm up against a deadline."

"Is that so?" Maddie reversed positions so they were face-to-face.

"Totally." She dipped her head to take that same nipple into her mouth.

"Mmm." Maddie arched into her, then slung a leg over both of Sy's, giving Sy a delicious hint of the heat between her thighs.

"See? We're halfway there already." She could practically taste Maddie.

Maddie used her new position to roll Sy onto her back. She rolled on top, straddling Sy's hips and gyrating against her suggestively. "Halfway, huh?"

"Make that three-quarters." It certainly wouldn't take her long to come if Maddie kept that up. And she was pretty sure she'd be able to return the favor just as efficiently.

"Well, then." Maddie made a few more circles, then practically hopped out of bed. "I'll remember that next time I have a few minutes to spare."

Sy groaned, but ended it with a laugh. "You're a tease, Maddie Barrow."

Maddie, who was already to the door, glanced back with a wink. "Sometimes."

She groaned again but hauled herself from bed. "At least tell me we get to shower together."

They did, and even managed to cop a few feels while sharing the soap. Maddie pulled on her clothes from the day before, borrowing a pair of boxer briefs from Sy and promising to return them clean. After thanking Maddie for a mental image she'd get to keep with her all day, Sy told her she might as well keep them. "It's weird, but they make your ass look fantastic."

Maddie gave an extra wiggle as she pulled up her jeans. "Not as good as they make yours look, I'm sure, but thank you."

"Oh, no. Thank you." Sy gave one of Maddie's butt cheeks a squeeze.

"I could give you a pair of mine if you want. A thong, maybe?" Maddie asked with a straight face.

"Do you even own a thong?"

Maddie lifted a shoulder. "I guess you'll have to wait and see."

"I'd rather see you in it than borrow it. Maybe you could give me a little fashion show."

For all that Maddie had started it, she now blushed. "I think that could be arranged."

"I'll look forward to it," Sy said and meant it, especially if it gave Maddie a thrill to put herself on display.

"But right now, I have to go. We've got a staff meeting this morning and if I'm late, Logan's going to know exactly why and find a way to make sure everyone else does, too."

As nice as it would have been to continue the quest to have sex with Maddie in every room of the house, she wasn't about to be the reason Logan gave her a hard time. Again.

Besides, she respected that Maddie had other projects demanding her time and attention. She did too, technically, with holiday orders for chèvre still rolling in and at least half a dozen new cheese varieties in various stages of the aging process. But she also had kitchen counters to seal and the downstairs guest room left to paint and decorate before her mom arrived, so that's how she decided to spend her morning before heading to the farm.

Paint first, if for no other reason than it was the less pleasant task. And the first coat could dry while she worked on the counters. She prepped the roller and tray, then remembered she was supposed to do the edging first, so dumped the paint into her little handheld cup instead. Up and down the ladder, along the ceiling and around the windows. Hands and knees for the baseboard, carefully dragging the angled brush the way Maddie had taught her.

What had started as a tedious and frustrating process three or four rooms ago had taken on almost meditative status, each satisfying sweep covering dusty peach with the soft sea green she'd chosen with her mother in mind. She'd imagined it would be months before Mama had the chance to visit, to sleep in the first guest room Sy could boast having.

The excitement of having her come so much sooner warred with the ambivalence that still churned in her chest at the prospect of meeting her father. Seriously, a couple of weeks ago, she couldn't even fathom using that phrase. And now it was happening.

Like so many other unexpected things that had played out over the last couple of years. Complete career shift, year in France, moving to a tiny town in the middle of Vermont. Maddie. Oh, and buying her first house.

As intense as the career change and year abroad had been, it was the last two that stuck with her now. The rather impulsive decision to buy a house had been the reason she connected with Maddie in the first place. She'd had more than her fair share of doubts at the start of the reno, convinced she'd bought a money pit and been saddled with a contractor who thought she was a complete idiot. Fortunately, she'd been wrong on both fronts. Okay, maybe Maddie had thought she was an idiot at first, but she'd come around.

She still didn't know if Vermont was for her for the long haul, but things were going better than she ever could have expected. And when was the last time she'd been able to say that?

Chapter Twenty-one

After a quick stop to check on the delivery of new hardwood flooring for a project that happened to be on her way, Maddie headed to the office.

"The vultures are circling," Logan said the second Maddie walked through the door.

Maddie glanced from Logan to Jack to her parents, looking for clarification. Her mom let out a sigh. "Your uncle and cousins. They've asked for an outside appraisal and audit."

"Are you serious?" Maddie dropped her messenger bag into her chair and stalked over to the little table they used for coffee breaks as much as meetings.

"He wants two hundred fifty grand." Dad shook his head with what looked like a mixture of disbelief and disappointment.

"So do I." Jack gave a dismissive head toss.

Maddie smiled, trying to find a trace of humor in this whole mess. "I mean, if someone is handing it out. You?"

"Obviously," Logan said without further elaboration.

"He knows he's being ridiculous, right?" Maddie tossed the question out rhetorically but looked to her father in case he had a real answer.

"Everything about him is ridiculous these days." Dad huffed out a breath. "Marrying some woman he just met. Retiring at sixty. Moving to Florida. Florida!"

She laughed at the way he practically screamed it the second time, even if it was no laughing matter. "Maybe he's having a delayed midlife crisis."

Jack let out a snort. "And wants us to bankroll it."

"And his kids would gladly take a payout sooner rather than later." Mom let out a tsk of disappointment.

"Really, though, what good does the business do them otherwise?" Jack asked.

She didn't begrudge them preferring money to a stake in a business they didn't care about. She did begrudge her uncle throwing them all into upheaval so he could chase tail. "Well, if they wait till Uncle Rich kicks the bucket, there will be a bigger share left for them than if he cuts and runs now."

"Two hundred fifty thousand dollars." Dad mumbled it this time, shaking his head.

Logan, who'd been uncharacteristically quiet, shrugged. "It's not that unreasonable, if you think about our client base and brand on top of the physical assets."

Maddie glared at her. "Not helping."

Jack's shoulders dropped. "Not wrong, either."

On one hand, it was thrilling to think the business was worth half a million dollars, on top of the labor they put in alongside the crew they hired. What had started out as little more than a pair of brothers with some tools and a horse-drawn buggy had turned into one of Bedlington's biggest businesses. But Rich deciding to cash out his half without notice put the rest of them in a terrible bind. "I've got maybe twenty grand in savings," Maddie said.

"Twenty-five here." Jack shrugged.

"Damn, you two. I've barely got ten." Logan frowned.

Maddie slung an arm around her sister's shoulders. "Yeah, but you went to fancy college and Jack and I just got our associate's."

"A lot of good it'll do me if there's no business for me to work at." Logan folded her arms, giving in to a full pout.

Dad waved both hands in the air. "None of that nihilistic nonsense. The business isn't going anywhere."

He could always be counted on to pull them back to the matter at hand. Doing so with fifty-cent words was new. Maddie lifted her chin, deciding to use that fact to diffuse some of the tension. "You been studying for the SAT while you're laid up?"

"Crosswords," he said, sitting up a little straighter. "Impressed?"
She couldn't help but smile. "Very."

"But it doesn't solve our problem." Logan continued to pout.

Jack, ever the practical one of the bunch, began to nod. "It doesn't. But like Dad said when this first dropped, unless he's got a buyer hanging out in his back pocket, he's going to be stuck with us. And that means he'll be inclined to accept a reasonable offer. We just have to figure out what's a reasonable offer."

"That we can reasonably offer," Maddie added, since those weren't necessarily the same thing.

Jack tapped his finger to the surface of his desk. "And now that we know what he wants, we have a starting point for a counter offer."

All of this was true. And, in theory, it made her feel better. Offers and counter offers, seller's concessions. This was a language she spoke, even if real estate technically sat adjacent to her world. "Jack's right."

He put on a sugary smile. "I do love when you say that."

"Don't get used to it." He might be less overtly stubborn than Logan, but those particular still waters ran deep in him.

And like he'd read her thoughts, he offered a satisfied smile. "I don't need you to say it for it to be true."

Logan raised a hand. "Can we talk about something else now? This is stressing me out."

"Yes." Dad smacked a hand on the table with more enthusiasm than force. "What's on the docket this week?"

"I got sign-off from the Kesslers for the design on their addition," Logan said.

Dad gave a decisive nod. "Excellent. Maddie, when can we start demo?"

She looked to her mother, who kept both the calendars and the books in working order. "Mom?"

Mom clicked her mouse a few times. "Penciled you in for Tuesday, assuming we can get the excavator lined up to dig the foundation."

"We really should get one of our own." Something she said every time they needed one, even though it wasn't nearly often enough to justify the investment.

Mom didn't miss a beat. "You get contracts for five new builds in the next six months, and I'll sign the check myself."

Everyone laughed except for Maddie. Because new builds were a rarity in Bedlington and everyone knew it, including Maddie. "That's just mean."

"No, it's just business." Mom shrugged, confident there were no hard feelings.

"If I get two, can we look at used ones?" She'd never tried bargaining before.

"Three," Mom countered.

"Fine." It was funny. Everyone assumed Fred and Rich called the shots because they were the current generation of Barrow brothers. But the truth was that her mother held the purse strings and that's where the power was. It was why she and her siblings had already agreed to hire an impartial manager and bookkeeper when Mom retired. That was a ways off, though. They needed to navigate Uncle Rich's Peter Pan phase first, and see where it left them.

"Besides bargaining for new toys, what else do we have?" Dad laughed. "Lord knows we've gone off the rails when I'm the one who has to keep us in line."

Jack noted a few projects that were strictly electrical. Logan briefed two meetings she'd done with potential clients, one of which had gone well and one of which hadn't. When all eyes turned to Maddie, she gave status updates on all the larger projects they had underway and ended with, "And I think we can call Sy Travino's house completed. She's finishing up the last of the painting, and I'm going to put the trim up as soon as that's done."

Dad nodded his approval. "Oh, good. I know that's a feel good finish more than a professional ta-da, but they all count."

Logan snorted. "If by 'feel good' you mean stay the night to celebrate."

She had no illusions that everyone in her family knew she and Sy were sleeping together. But that was crass, even for Logan. She glared, deciding whether to bother with a retort.

Mom didn't give her the chance. "Logan Colleen, you watch your tongue at this table."

Logan resumed pouting, clearly cowed. "Sorry."

Mom tipped her head. "Well, your sister made it particularly easy to tease her when she started seeing a client, but you've got to give your parents the benefit of not too many details."

Maddie, who'd succumbed to gloating, cleared her throat. "Well, her check's cleared and the work is done, so—"

Mom lifted a hand. "You're fine." She looked to Logan. "And you're fine, too."

"What about me?" Jack asked.

"And you're fine, three," Mom said.

Maddie laughed and pulled out her laptop. "I'm going to do some work now, if we're done here. Someone's got to."

That got her eye rolls from everyone before the meeting officially adjourned. She booted up and pulled the contract for the Kesslers so she could start the materials list for the construction phase. Logan would handle the finishes for this one, and she was only too happy to let her. That was the beauty of their business. Everyone got to play to their strengths, but they all managed to work together. She couldn't imagine working any other way. Even if it meant enduring the occasional harassment.

Thoughts of being harangued had her thinking about Sy. It would be great to get the last of the trim done. With her mom arriving in the next couple of days, it would be a weight off Sy's shoulders for sure. As for the spending the night part? Well, haranguing or not, she was looking forward to that part just as much.

Despite Sy's best intentions to finish the painting, she headed to Maddie's after finishing at the farm and didn't make it back to her house until the next morning. Fortunately, two more mornings of painting and finishing touches, paired with slightly later evenings in the cheese room, did the trick. And honestly, not a second too soon.

Her mother was due to arrive in two days. Well, her mother and her father. Gah. She still couldn't wrap her head around that.

Instead of trying—because reality would clobber her soon enough—she invited Maddie over to tack up the last of the trim and celebrate the official end of the work. At least as much of the work as she could swing for the foreseeable future. She had some ideas for the garage. Backyard, too. But they'd keep until spring. Maybe by then she'd have some pennies back in her piggy bank. And maybe by then she'd come to terms with being the butch who wanted a nice deck with a grill on it, and a place she could putter away on this project or that.

Thoughts for another time. Tonight, a few baseboards and a fancy ass dinner to thank Maddie for all the lessons and extra hours she put in to make Sy's house a reality for a price Sy could manage. And then hopefully, taking Maddie to bed for enough sex to tide them over until the flurry of Christmas was over.

She'd no sooner gotten the rub on the ribeye she'd splurged on when a knock came at the side door. Maddie's voice quickly followed. "Just so you know, even though I'm not going to be working here anymore, I'm at the stage where I let myself in."

Sy wiped her hands on a kitchen towel. "I like you at that stage."

Maddie held up a paper bag and a chunky power tool. "I brought wine and my finish nailer, as instructed."

She slipped her arms around Maddie's middle and pulled her in for a kiss. "You sure know your way to a woman's heart."

"Well, this one at least." Maddie smirked and peered over Sy's shoulder. "Hey, is that red meat?"

Sy chuckled. "It is. I figured we deserved a celebration steak."

Maddie's eyes went wide with delight. "We do. I should get a steak every time I finish a big project."

She wasn't exactly sure how often that was, but it couldn't be too many. "That could probably be arranged."

"You spoil me," Maddie said without seeming overly bothered by the prospect. Bashful, maybe.

"You deserve to be spoiled. With simple pleasures at least. I'm not really a fancy jewelry, designer bag gifter."

Maddie took a step back and moved her hands up and down to indicate herself. "And what exactly about this makes you think I'm into any of that?"

"Just because you're practical doesn't mean you shouldn't have something fun and frivolous every now and then." She hadn't meant to go down that path, but it felt important all of a sudden.

"I do. Steak and a nice bottle of wine on a weeknight counts. New drill bits before they're technically needed." Maddie stuck a finger in the air. "Or a massage. I love a good massage."

Of course she did. "I feel like that counts as routine maintenance in your line of work, but I'll take it. Especially since I've never had a professional massage."

"You haven't?" Maddie looked genuinely scandalized. "We have to go. It's amazing. And worth every penny."

She imagined them in plush white robes, a couple of beefy Nordic-looking men asking about the pressure they liked. She could think of worse things. "Deal."

"How do you like to be spoiled?" Maddie's arms folded in what Sy had come to think of as her signature stance.

"Good people, good food. Maybe a new gadget for the kitchen or cheese room." There hadn't been money for much else, so she'd learned to really appreciate those things. Though at this point, she wasn't sure having more money would change much.

"So, basically, exactly what I said." Maddie added a satisfied smile to the arms and jutted her hip.

She hadn't thought of it that way, but now that Maddie pointed it out, it felt like one more thing they had in common. "I guess it is."

Maddie's features softened. "I like that."

Sy smiled. "Me, too."

They stood there for a minute, giving each other goofy smiles. Eventually, Maddie said, "So, how about I get to work and you make me an amazing dinner so we can relax later?"

"If by 'relax' you mean 'take you to bed,' then yes."

Maddie laughed. "Yes."

She jerked her head in the direction of the guest room. "Well, what are you waiting for?"

CHAPTER TWENTY-TWO

Sy added another log to the fire and adjusted the throw blanket on the back of the couch. Then she straightened the stack of books on the side table. Henry, happily loafed on the top perch of his cat tree, regarded her with curiosity. "I know. I'm fussing. I can't help it. I'm nervous."

Henry yawned.

"Thank you. You're good at keeping everything in perspective." At the sound of a knock on the front door, she jumped. Henry looked equally startled. "You're a terrible guard cat."

He stretched and yawned again.

She laughed at herself as much as him and went to open the door. Her mother stood on the other side, a big, if slightly nervous, smile on her face. Just behind her, a middle-aged white guy she'd never seen before who managed to look vaguely familiar. It was the nose, she realized, and the chin. She might not have known it until that moment, but she got both from him.

"Sy."

She shifted her attention back to her mother, who'd opened her arms wide. Sy stepped into the embrace without hesitation. No matter what weirdness the next few days would bring, nothing could diminish the magic of her mama's hugs. "I'm glad you're here."

"Me, too, mija." Mama released her and stepped to the side. "Sy, this is John."

To his credit, John looked even more nervous about the introduction than Sy felt. He extended a hand. "It's really good to meet you."

Sy couldn't quite echo the sentiment, but she nodded. "Come on in out of the cold."

She took coats and showed them around, as much to give them something to do as show off. Mama delighted at everything and John seemed to delight at watching her. Sy put on coffee, then served it in the living room. Mama and John took the couch and Sy sat in one of the mismatched consignment store chairs opposite.

Mama kept the conversation going, sharing tidbits of personal information about each of them without making it feel forced. She bragged about Sy's year in France, shared that John never had other children. Sy asked about John's work and learned that corporate law paid well but fed the soul even less than one might think.

"I'm too boring to start from scratch, but I'm working on getting some hobbies," he said with a chuckle. Then his expression sobered. "And on relationships."

Mama gave his hand a squeeze and regarded him with affection. "It's a good use of your midlife crisis. Much better than that sports car."

John shook his head and looked to Sy. "I confess I was quite the cliché. Fortunately, it was my wife who ran off with her assistant rather than me. It was the kick in the rear I needed to come to my senses and start thinking about what actually matters in life."

Sy filed away the new details, feeling slightly better if still by and large suspicious. "And that led you to find my mom?"

"Among other things." John looked down at his hands. "My parents passed away a year ago. It made me realize that life is short, and that I'd wasted way too much of mine doing what they wanted me to do."

It was hard to find fault with that sort of come to Jesus moment. Or with some schlubby guy realizing that her mother was the best thing that had ever happened to him.

"Anyway." John shook his head and looked up. "Trying to do better and make up for lost time and all that jazz."

Even if he was the sort of guy who said "all that jazz."

Mama, as though sensing they'd had a moment and shouldn't push things, cleared her throat. "Is that posole I smell?"

"It's Christmas Eve, isn't it?" And having posole had been a tradition as long as she could remember. "I should go check on it."

She used the moment alone to stir the pot, but also to shoot a text to Maddie, who'd been really sweet about being available for check-ins. She'd no sooner hit send when Mom appeared, this time without John in tow.

"Are you doing okay?" Mama asked.

"Yeah. Totally. Of course." Though saying yes three ways somehow felt less sure than if she'd gone with one. "It's fine. Good. Weird but good."

Mama nodded but didn't say anything.

"You? Are you doing okay?" Sy asked.

"I feel like God has answered a prayer I didn't even know I had."

Sy considered herself agnostic, but her mother took her religion and her relationship with God very seriously. If she was bringing divine intervention into the conversation, she meant business. "Wow. Okay."

"Thank you for giving him a chance."

When push came to shove, that's what it was—giving him a chance because it was important to her mama. "He seems to be trying. I respect that."

Mama nodded briskly. "How about I set the table?"

Sy smiled. "Thanks."

She called John to help and he hustled in, looking more like an eager to please puppy than a corporate lawyer. Sy watched him out of the corner of her eye while she finished preparing the limes and radishes and other soup toppings. He stole surreptitious glances at her, but mostly had eyes for Bonita. If the whole situation hadn't been so damn weird, it would have been downright adorable.

Even in its weirdness, it managed to be kind of endearing. Like the way Mama pretended to withhold the hot sauce after Sy had filled bowls or the way John joked about leaving New Mexico but always keeping part of it with him. Sy had said essentially the same thing more than once.

"It's good, mija," Mama said after her first bite.

Sy took a bite, pleased with the flavor. "But never as good as yours."

John angled his head. "It's pretty damn close."

Rather than look offended, Mama beamed. "You should see her making her fancy restaurant food. Knocks your socks right off."

"I bet." John took another bite. "But I have to admit I'm partial to this."

It was the right thing to say, no doubt. Just like the questions he asked about her work and the self-deprecating comments he made about his career as an attorney. She wanted to find him too polished, too ingratiating. But he managed to be just awkward enough that she couldn't see him as anything but sincere. And unless he was putting on some Oscar-worthy performance, he was utterly smitten with her mother.

When they'd finished eating, Mama shooed them both to the living room while she put on a pot of decaf. Sy wondered if she'd orchestrated the moment for the two of them to be alone, and seeing John fidget confirmed her suspicion.

"Thank you for opening your home to me," John said. "For being willing to meet me in the first place."

She felt compelled to be generous but couldn't bring herself to lie. "It's important to my mother and she's the most important person to me."

He nodded, seeming to understand the line she was attempting to walk as much as the words. "I don't have any expectations, if that makes sense. I'm just grateful to be here, to be able to spend even a small bit of time with you."

As much as she'd intended to keep her guard up, a kernel deep in her gut told her he meant it, that his words were sincere and his intentions good. She might not be ready to embrace him as a dad, but she could at least give him that. "It still feels kind of surreal, but I'm glad you're here, too."

He nodded, as though acknowledging the significance of that.

She considered saying more, but couldn't settle on what. Before she got the chance, Mama bustled in from the kitchen like she owned the place, plate of cookies in hand. "Who wants dessert?"

❖

Maddie and her siblings might not be kids anymore, but since none of them had kids yet, Christmas hadn't changed much. Christmas Eve, too, for that matter. They piled into one car and went to the candlelight service at the Methodist church in town, unwrapped and put on the matching pajamas Mom had picked out, and drank cocoa around the fire until bed. Truly, the only real difference was that everyone got their cocoa spiked with whiskey now.

Christmas morning came, and maybe everyone was a little more excited for coffee and cinnamon rolls than stockings, but it was a close call. Tools took the place of toys, but they elicited the same level of delight. And no one grumbled about getting a pair of new wool socks.

After the flurry of torn wrapping paper and hugs, she sat on the couch, perfectly cozy in her flannel pj's covered in sleds and sloths, keeping Dad company while Logan and Jack helped get dinner started in the kitchen. She texted Sy without expecting a response but kept looking at her phone anyway. Since doing that annoyed her, she set it facedown on the coffee table and made a point of staring at the tree. It was a spectacular tree, so not a heavy lift.

"You're looking extra reflective this morning," Dad said. "That's usually my job."

Maddie turned her gaze from the twinkling lights. "I was just thinking about how much I love our little holiday traditions. And how at some point it's not going to be like this anymore."

Dad chuckled. "Plotting my demise, eh?"

"No. As far as I'm concerned, you're going to live forever." Or at least a good long while. "I was imagining that at some point, one or more of us is going to get married, have a couple of kids. And it'll be amazing and all that, but different."

"Reflective and sentimental?" He lifted his chin. "Who are you and what have you done with my daughter?"

"Ha ha." She could always count on him to keep things light.

"Seriously, though. What's got you all caught up in ghosts of Christmas future?"

"You remember Sy, right?" Maddie asked.

He looked mildly insulted by the question. "You mean the woman you brought to Thanksgiving? The one making cheese down at Clover's? Whose house you did? And who you've been dating?"

Touché. "That's the one."

"Seems like things might be getting serious," he said in that completely casual way he had.

Were they? More serious than anything she'd had recently, but those hadn't amounted to more than a handful of dates. Sy was more than that for sure, but how much more? Maddie had put a tidy little fence around that question and anything it might imply. Because as much as she liked everything about spending time with Sy, she harbored no illusions about the likelihood Sy would stay more than a few years. Clover had said as much and didn't begrudge Sy for making her mark and moving on. Maddie didn't either, even if the reality of it was becoming harder and harder to stomach.

"What about her?" Dad asked.

"Huh?" Maddie asked back, buying time to scramble out of the rabbit hole she'd fallen down.

"I asked what about her?"

She'd happily field that question over ones about how serious things might be. "Well, her mom came up for the holidays. And it's a long story, but her dad who she's never met came, too."

"She's never met her father?"

Even saying it out loud felt strange and left her with a pang of worry over how it was all going. "Like I said, long story. But he's turned up, and it seems like he wants to be part of Sy's and her mom's lives now."

"Ah." Dad nodded.

"And I was just thinking about how much of a bombshell that is. I mean, we've got our share of drama. Thanks, Uncle Rich." She rolled her eyes. "But I know who's who and what's what."

That got a chuckle. "Well, you do until you don't, right? That's how bombshells work."

Maddie lifted her chin, ninety-nine percent sure he was joking. "Got a big secret you're about to drop?"

"Nah." He gave a dismissive wave. "What you see is what you get."

"That's what I mean. Sy thought she did and now it's all up in the air. I don't take that for granted, but I don't appreciate it as much as I should."

He lifted his chin. "You know a great way to show someone you appreciate them?"

"What's that?" She prepared herself for some next level Fred Barrow wisdom.

"Get them a fresh cup of coffee when they're nicely settled in front of the Christmas tree."

Next level wisdom, all right. She hefted herself off the sofa and took the empty cup he held out to her. She bent to kiss his cheek. "One cup of appreciation, coming right up."

Chapter Twenty-three

Christmas Day passed quietly enough. Sy made a light breakfast and built a fire. Henry provided entertainment while she, her mother, and John self-consciously unwrapped the gifts they'd gotten one another. Her mother had insisted on cooking the traditional spread for dinner and Sy hadn't argued. Tradition was tradition, after all. Even in a new place and with a new person thrown into the mix.

Sy slipped into sous chef mode seamlessly. She had more training with that after all, especially when it came to being in the kitchen with her mother. Between the cooking and a few classic movies on in the background, there wasn't too much pressure to make constant conversation. It almost managed to be relaxing, which was a hell of a lot more than she'd expected.

The next morning, Sy offered to show them the farm before they hit the road. Mama delighted in every detail—from the aging room to the labels Sy had designed for their limited edition runs—just as Sy knew she would. But John seemed delighted, too. Impressed the way professionally successful people were when they got a glimpse at a world utterly out of their wheelhouse.

When she walked them out to the gravel pad she and Clover used as a parking lot, Sy's mom squeezed both her hands tight. "I'm so proud of you."

"Thanks, Mama."

John stood to the side, not comfortable exactly, but a hell of a lot less awkward than when he arrived. "I know it's not my place to be proud, but you've got quite an operation here. It's definitely something to be proud of."

Sy nodded, not quite comfortable herself but getting there. "Thanks."

"You'll come home for Easter, yes?" Mama may have phrased it in the form of a question, but it was really more of a statement.

"I'll do my best."

Mama nodded. "And maybe we'll come back in the summer, enjoy a nice break from the heat."

Her use of "we" wasn't lost on Sy, but she didn't mind it as much as she thought she might. "The door is always open."

"That's a two-way street, you know. Just because we came here doesn't mean you can't visit, too."

It occurred to her she had no idea where John lived. Or if living together was something they'd put on the table. As much as it screamed way too much, way too soon in her mind, little would surprise her at this point. "I will. I promise."

John gave her one of those handshakes that turned into a hug. With their hands clasped between them, he pressed an envelope into her palm. But when he let go, he didn't wait for her to acknowledge it. He offered a parting wave and climbed into the car, ostensibly giving the two of them a moment alone to say their good-byes. She studied it for a moment. Mama merely raised a brow and shrugged. She stuffed it into her pocket and focused on the task at hand—hugging her mother as tightly as she could.

Mama hugged her just as hard, but the second she pulled away, the stern finger came out. "You be good now."

Sy spared a quick glance at John, who went from watching them to fiddling with something in the console. "You, too."

"He's a good man. He just lost his way for a while."

She was more inclined to believe that than she had been a few days ago. "Well, aside from the fact that no one could possibly be good enough for you, I'm glad he's making you happy. Just make sure he keeps doing that if you decide to let him stick around."

Mama nodded. "Look at you with the wise words."

Sy shrugged. "I learned from the best."

One more hug and Mama hurried to the car. Sy waited until they'd pulled onto the road and out of sight before heading back inside. She switched back to her indoor boots and returned to the cheese room. Maybe she'd get a batch of milk going in the pasteurizer before lunch. That way she could spend the afternoon in the cave.

She piped the milk in and set the timers and controls before patting her pockets in search of a pen to note the details. In the process, her hand landed on the envelope John had slipped her. She pulled it out and tore into it. No card or fancy stationary, but a simple piece of paper that looked to be torn from a journal, along with a check that had been folded in half.

Sy,

I couldn't think of a way to give you this without making it awkward, but I couldn't leave without acknowledging that I was absent from your childhood financially as much as personally. This is a tiny fraction of what I should have contributed, but it's a start. I have your mother's blessing to do this and I hope you'll accept it for what it is—a gesture of love, with no strings attached. I hope we can continue getting to know one another, but I leave that decision squarely with you.

John

Sy opened the check, not sure how she felt or what to expect. She looked at the number of zeros, read the amount written out on the line. Twenty-five thousand dollars. "You've got to be shitting me."

"What's wrong?"

She spun to find Clover hovering in the doorway, a look of concern on her face. "Have you ever held a check for twenty-five grand?"

Clover laughed. "No. But I held a bill for ten times that much when I refinanced the farm."

Sy crossed the room and handed her the check. "Well, now you have."

Clover looked at the check, then back at Sy. "What is this?"

"My father's attempt to make up for being absent the last thirty or so years."

"For real?" Clover asked.

Nothing about any of this surprised her at this point. "Apparently."

"Damn. What are you going to do with it?"

"First I have to decide if I'm going to keep it."

Clover handed the check back. "Why wouldn't you? He's rich, right?"

"Yeah." But if he owed anyone anything, it was her mother. "It's weird, though."

"Do you think he's trying to buy your affection?"

Possibly, but she kept coming back to how fucking sincere he seemed. "I think it's more trying to ease his guilt for not being there for so many years."

Clover nodded. "Raising a kid as a single parent is no joke. And being the kid of a single parent isn't, either."

She'd wanted for plenty of things through the years but had never gone without anything she needed. The same couldn't be said of her mother, who sacrificed plenty to make sure Sy didn't go without. Obvious things like nice clothes and houses full of the little luxuries that made life easier and more comfortable. But also things Sy had only begun to appreciate now that she was grown. Things like time and space for herself or, at the other end of the spectrum, the companionship of another adult. "Yeah."

Maddie picked up her phone and found no fewer than ten texts from Sy. A flirty one. Four about her dad giving her a stupid amount of money before he left. A couple musing about being practical or irresponsible with it. And finally, one asking if she was okay.

Overwhelmed by the prospect of answering them all, she asked if Sy wanted company for dinner, even if said company didn't come with a big fat check. Sy's answer—that she'd have soup on the stove and a bottle of wine open—gave her more certainty than anything else that day. Not to mention something to look forward to.

She showed up at Sy's, empty-handed and emptied out from a day of one problem on top of another. Nothing devastating, just the sort of day where every little thing that could go wrong did. The wrong cabinets delivered from the factory to a kitchen job she'd hoped to finish within the week, one of her guys showing up to work hungover after getting dumped by his girlfriend. When Sy opened the door, looking freshly showered and happy to see her, the last little bit of fight she had in her faded. "Hi."

"Hi." Sy's head angled. "Are you okay?"

Maddie nodded, suddenly and strangely on the verge of tears. "I will be."

Sy grabbed her hand and pulled her inside. "Let me see what I can do."

A dozen or so kisses, getting to pull off her boots, and a glass of zin worked wonders. By the time she peered over Sy's shoulder into the pot of simmering posole, she'd almost forgotten about the day of minor disasters. "That looks so good."

"I'd apologize for serving you leftovers, but it's actually better after a few days in the fridge."

She inhaled deeply. "Never apologize for anything that smells that heavenly."

Sy pointed to a basket of chips and a plate piled with radishes, shredded cabbage, and lime wedges. "Bring those to the table?"

Maddie kissed the back of Sy's neck. "Yep."

"And please do that again when we're done eating."

Since the table was otherwise set, Maddie settled into what she'd started to think of as her chair. "Only that?"

"Oh, no. Start with that." Sy wagged her brows with zero subtlety. "I just meant that in particular would be a good place to start."

"I do like the way you think." She cleared her throat. "Speaking of, how are you? We haven't talked about your weird day yet."

Sy ladled soup into bowls and carried them to the table. "I'm fine. Weird but fine."

Maddie shook her head. "I still can't believe he wrote you a check for twenty-five thousand dollars."

"To be fair, it's probably like one year's worth of child support, given what he makes."

"True." After watching Sy, she helped herself to a handful of chips and crumbled them in. "I hope he's being that generous with your mother."

"Not with cash, according to her, because that would feel icky." Sy laughed. "I was glad to hear she's doing things on her terms even if it was almost too much information."

"Yeah." There was spoiled and there was kept. Not that she had a problem with either if it worked for all parties involved, but she could appreciate the distinction. "How are you feeling about that?"

"My mother dating my father or my father plying me with guilt money?"

Maddie cringed. "Either?"

Sy waved a hand. "It's better now that I've met him. I think he's genuine. Like, knows he was a schmuck and wants to do better."

Sy deserved that. And though she hadn't met Sy's mom on this trip, it wasn't a stretch to say Bonita did, too. "I'm glad."

Sy shrugged. "I am too, I guess. I'm also glad for things to get back to normal."

"Back to normal?" she asked with a smirk.

"Ha ha. Fine. I'm ready for things to settle down into some semblance of normal. Get into my cheese groove, enjoy my finished house, spend as many nights as I can with my sexy girlfriend."

Maddie pointed her spoon at Sy. "No fair. I want to make fun of you for saying cheese groove, but the rest of what you said is so sweet, I don't think I can."

"You still can." Sy brushed her foot up Maddie's ankle under the table. "Especially if you spend the night."

"Obvi." She rolled her eyes but didn't try to hide her smile. "Just don't forget you're helping me throw a New Year's party in two days."

Sy rested her elbows on the table and leaned forward. "Do I get to kiss you at midnight?"

She'd never put a lot of stock in that sort of thing, so it didn't have the significance it might otherwise. A fact that made it easier to digest the idea of hosting a party together. "You damn well better."

CHAPTER TWENTY-FOUR

Maddie eyed the spread of food and slipped into the kitchen. She'd teased Sy for prepping four pans of puff pastry hors d'oeuvres to be baked throughout the party, but only one remained. She slid the cookie sheet into the oven and set the timer, thinking she'd need to snag one of the gouda and tomato jam ones before they all disappeared. She turned to find Clover hovering in the doorway.

"Need any help?" Clover asked.

She shook her head. "None, thanks to Sy."

"The woman knows her way around the kitchen." Clover came the rest of the way in. "Among other things."

Maddie laughed. "That's one way of putting it."

"I'm serious. You two throw a good party."

She cracked the oven door and gave the pastries a peek. "She's upped my appetizer game, that's for sure."

"I'm not talking about the food. I'm talking about the two of you. You're good together."

The simple declaration made her pulse trip. "But we're not supposed to be together, together."

Clover leaned against the counter. "And why is that again?"

She opened her mouth to make her usual arguments, but they felt like commitment-phobic platitudes more than the truth. "Because."

"Because opening your heart is hard." Clover came over and grasped Maddie's hands. "But you're good at hard things, especially when you know they're going to pay off."

That was the problem. She didn't know if things with Sy were going to pay off in the end.

"It's okay to fall in love for a little while, you know."

Maddie took a deep breath and released it slowly. "Not if it hurts like hell when it ends."

"Maybe it does, maybe it doesn't." Clover gave her a sly smile. "But either way is a hell of a lot more fun than sitting on the sidelines."

They'd had this talk a hundred times before—mostly about love in general, but a couple of times about Sy in particular. But once again, her usual arguments fell flat.

Clover's date for the night, a newly minted professor of gender studies at Smith, joined them in the kitchen. "Am I interrupting?" they asked.

"Not at all." Clover gave Maddie's hand a parting squeeze before turning her full attention to her date. "Let's get a glass of bubbly."

They returned to the living room and Maddie tapped her foot, wondering not for the first time if maybe Clover was right.

"Are you okay?"

She turned at the sound of Sy's voice. "Never better."

Sy angled her head. "You looked a million miles away when I came in."

"I'm right here." And, she realized with a start, there was nowhere else she'd rather be.

"That's good." Sy crossed the room. "Because I've been meaning to corner you all night."

"Is that so?" she asked.

"Yeah. I haven't gotten the chance to tell you you're a fox."

It was silly to blush, but she did anyway. "It's fun to have an excuse to get fancy."

Sy closed the distance between them and trailed a finger along the neckline of her dress, all the way to where it dipped between her breasts. "I'll take you out on the town anytime you want if I get to enjoy this view."

She laughed. "Not many places in this town where a girl can get away with this look."

"Maybe I'll have to take you to a different town, then. A weekend in Boston. Or New York."

She blushed again. It wasn't like she never went to the city—either city—but she'd never done it with a girlfriend. Going with Sy felt fanciful, while at the same time screaming serious relationship. Did she want that with Sy? Weren't they most of the way there already?

"No?" Sy raised a brow. "Don't want to run away with me?"

She shook her head. "No. I mean yes. I was just thinking that I haven't done that in ages."

Sy lifted a shoulder. "I haven't at all."

"You've never been?" Maddie asked.

"I flew out of New York, but I've never spent any time there. Or Boston. I spent more time on the West Coast."

"Right, right." She'd never had a burning desire to visit LA, but she could see Sy there. Or at least in the version of LA that lived in her mind. It made the prospect more compelling. She wanted to know that version of Sy, to see her in the worlds she occupied before this one.

"I bet you make an exceptional tour guide."

Maddie smirked. "I could show you a few things."

Sy looked her up and down in a way Maddie was sure she'd never tire of. "I bet you could."

"Unfortunately, the ball is about to drop and a couple dozen people will be expecting at least one of us to make a toast," Maddie said.

"I'm tempted to drag you to bed and let them fend for themselves."

"I'm tempted to let you," Maddie said, surprising herself.

Sy kissed her neck, right below her ear. "Promise me we can kick everyone out before one."

"Promise." She poked Sy in the ribs. "And I won't make us clean up until morning."

❖

Sy closed the door behind the last guests to leave. "Twelve fifty-two. We did it."

Maddie bit her lip and smiled. "As promised, what do you say we leave this till tomorrow and call it a night?"

"I'd say you're the boss."

"Boss, huh? I could get used to that."

"I'm pretty sure you're already used to it." Sy wrapped her arms around Maddie and pulled her close. The black dress she wore was simple but showed off all the right things. And the material was soft enough and thin enough that she could feel the lacy things Maddie wore underneath.

Maddie smirked. "Not with you. And especially not now that your house is done."

She was already imagining Maddie naked and under her, but the banter felt like foreplay, so she was hard-pressed to complain. "Do you miss bossing me around?"

Maddie shook her head.

"Do you want me to boss you around?" Sy asked.

She expected another immediate no, but Maddie seemed to consider the possibility, and her eyes sparkled with mischief. "Not tonight, but maybe sometimes. In bed, I mean."

"I wouldn't dream of you meaning it any other way." She kissed Maddie, long and slow. "What do you want tonight?"

The playful expression faded. In its place, one that melted Sy from the inside. "Just you. This. Us."

She took that to mean being together without pretense rather than spending the night standing in the remnants of the party, but she wanted Maddie to own it, to say it out loud. "I think I need you to be more specific."

Maddie took her hand. "I'd rather show you."

That would work, too. She let Maddie lead the way upstairs and to her room. The soft glow of the lamp by the bed reminded her of their first night together. They'd been tentative then, learning each other's cues as much as each other's bodies. Tonight seemed to hold that same intentionality, that same slow intensity, despite being together literally dozens of times by now.

Maddie started with Sy's shirt, freeing the buttons and pushing it from Sy's shoulders without breaking eye contact. Then Maddie worked her undershirt up and over her head. Sy did the same with Maddie's dress, inching the stretchy fabric up Maddie's thighs, then her torso. Maddie lifted her arms and Sy slid it all the way off, tossing it onto the cedar chest at the foot of Maddie's bed.

She'd gotten a peek at Maddie's underwear when they got dressed, but she took a longer look now. "I appreciate that it's not practical for the work you do, but I have to tell you how fucking hot you look in that lingerie."

Maddie stepped back and turned a slow circle. "I'm glad you like it."

"Like is not a strong enough word."

Maddie looked into her eyes once more and, without looking down, went to work on Sy's belt. "No?"

Sy shook her head, wondering how it was possible to simultaneously want to ravish Maddie and make love to her with infinite care. "Adore, maybe. Venerate. Delight."

"I definitely delight in you." Maddie worked Sy's pants and boxers over her hips, making them pool at her feet.

Sy stepped out of them. "I have to confess, though, I delight even more when you're not wearing a thing."

Maddie tipped her head. "Understandable, seeing as that's how I feel about you."

"I love when we're of like mind." Sy reached behind Maddie to unhook her bra, sliding it down her arms before working the matching panties down her legs. "Yes, definitely better wearing nothing at all."

"Come on." Maddie grabbed her hand. "Take me to bed before we freeze."

Sy was only too happy to oblige. She flipped back the duvet and sat on the bed, surprised to find it warm. "Did you turn the blanket on?"

Maddie, who loved her electric blanket enough to convince Sy to buy one for her place too, grinned. "I flipped it on before the party ended."

"Nice. Now I get to enjoy all that naked without having to navigate a pile of covers to do it." It was her biggest complaint about New England winters—having to have sex under blankets. Well, at least start out that way.

Maddie joined Sy on the bed, nudging her on her back and straddling her hips. "Here, I'll keep your front warm."

"You better get down here then." Sy pulled Maddie to her, and the feel of Maddie's whole body covering the length of her turned Sy's insides molten. "Yep, nice and toasty."

"Yeah, but my butt is cold." Maddie smirked, clearly only minding a little.

"We can't have that." Sy rolled them both, blanketing Maddie's body with hers. "How's that?"

Maddie wiggled deliciously beneath her. "So good."

"Now, where was I?" Sy kissed her way down Maddie's body, taking more time and more care than she ever had. She reveled in Maddie's skin, the way the softness of her belly contrasted with the muscles in her arms, shoulders, and legs. It was a softness, a femininity she didn't let much of the world see.

"That seems about right," Maddie said, running her fingers through Sy's hair.

She flicked her tongue in the crease where hip met thigh, let the tidy patch of hair tickle her nose and chin. "God, you're gorgeous."

She didn't wait for Maddie to respond, slicking her tongue into Maddie's wetness instead. When she found Maddie's clit, Maddie sucked in a breath and arched her hips. Sy moaned her approval, then wrapped her arms around Maddie's thighs to hold her close. Every part of Maddie invaded her senses—touch and taste to be sure, but also the faint musk of her sex and the sight of her breasts swaying slightly as Maddie's body listed.

Sy varied the speed and pressure of her tongue, wanting to draw Maddie out, take her to the brink but hold her there rather than send her tumbling over. After the third time of backing away from the edge, Maddie let out a sound somewhere between a laugh and a groan. "If you don't let me come, I might actually die."

Hyperbole? Yes. But hearing Maddie all but beg sparked a new flame in Sy. One that ignited her soul as much as her body. She wanted to give Maddie everything and then some, sexual and beyond. It was intoxicating to imagine she could, even for just a moment.

She redoubled her efforts, sliding two fingers into Maddie's wetness and coaxing her G-spot. It felt like mere seconds before Maddie called her name. Not the first time Maddie had done so, but it echoed in Sy's mind and sent shock waves of pleasure coursing through her, as intense as any orgasm.

Maddie's body sagged, melting into the bed like chocolate on a ninety-degree day. "I take it back. You keep fucking me like that and I might die of orgasm."

Sy chuckled and draped an arm over Maddie, content to be melty with her. "I promise we'll pace ourselves. I need you sticking around."

Maddie chuckled, too. And in true Maddie form, she didn't waste any time rolling onto her side and slipping a hand between Sy's legs. "That's the beauty of taking turns. Recovery time."

"Hard to argue with that." Sy shifted to give Maddie better access, but Maddie used the movement to reposition herself entirely and settle between Sy's thighs.

"Now let me see if I can make you question your ties to the mortal realm."

"Mortal realm?" Sy lifted her head, prepared to make fun.

Maddie didn't give her the chance, thrusting her tongue into Sy before finding her clit and working her into an absolute frenzy. Only instead of making her come, Maddie gave her a dose of her own medicine, taking her time and leading Sy to beg for release outright.

Maddie took mercy, but instead of a frenetic climax that left her quaking, Maddie sent her into a freefall of pleasure. She tumbled, weightless and unfettered, unable to do anything but let it wash over and through her. It left her breathless with wonder.

"That was perfection," Maddie said after she'd crawled up the bed and into Sy's arms, her voice already showing signs of sleep.

"Perfection." Sy held Maddie close and thought about the number of times in her life she'd used that word. Not that many, when push came to shove. A few dishes she'd tried, a gorgeous and blissfully relaxing day on her last visit home. A couple of cheeses, obviously.

Never about a woman. A relationship.

It was all so much more than she bargained for when she moved here. Certainly more than when Maddie showed up and offered to put her to work to make her house livable for a price she could afford. More, even, than she expected when she and Maddie started sleeping together. And yet this thing with Maddie was turning out to be exactly what she wanted, without ever really realizing it was what she'd been missing.

CHAPTER TWENTY-FIVE

Maddie stretched and let out a sigh that could as easily have been a purr. "This is the most indulgent New Year's Day I've had since, well, ever."

"Please tell me it's because we're being next-level indulgent." Sy lifted her head enough to kiss the top of Maddie's before flopping back on the pillow.

"As opposed to what?" Maddie asked. They'd slept in, made a huge breakfast, showered, then tumbled back into bed for sex and a nap. There was no way to describe it other than next-level indulgent.

"As opposed to indulgence being completely out of the norm. Like, normally, you'd have a smoothie and go for a run before coming home to organize your closet." Sy blew out a breath, as though merely listing those things exhausted her.

She rolled so that she was draped over Sy more than curled against her. "And what if I was that girl?"

"I'd still love you, but I might respect you a little bit less."

Maddie laughed because Sy seemed to mean it, then stopped because she'd processed the respect bit before the love part.

As if sensing her mental stumble, Sy cringed. "Sorry. Definitely didn't mean to drop that all casual."

"Didn't mean to be casual about it or didn't mean to do it at all?" Not that she wanted to put Sy on the spot, but she wanted the answer.

"Well, didn't mean to at all." Sy waited a beat. "But I did mean it."

It would have been easy for Sy to take it back, to play it off as a figure of speech, slip of the tongue moment. Maddie loved that she didn't even as it terrified her. "Yeah?"

Sy's expression turned serious. "Yeah. I mean, it's sort of a slippery thing for me. That line between like and love, or love and being in love. But not slippery in a bad way. More like sliding into feelings. Instead of arriving in a poof."

"A poof. That might be the best emotional metaphor I've ever heard." And one that would have stirred up her own case of the feels if she didn't have them already. Because that's how it was, wasn't it? A slow creep that happened if the stars aligned and you didn't fight it too hard. A creep she'd finally stopped fighting.

"Hey, I never said I was eloquent."

"You're plenty eloquent." She nudged herself forward to press her lips to Sy's. "And sexy." Another kiss. "And I'm on the slippery slope to being in love with you, too."

Sy narrowed her eyes. "Slippery slope?"

"Okay, see? I'm being even less eloquent than you were. I love you, too. And it feels like going ice skating after a long time of not. It's awesome and a little scary at the same time."

Sy grinned. "See? Now you're speaking my language. Well, the awesome and scary part. I've never strapped on a pair of ice skates and don't plan to."

"You haven't?" she asked.

"That can't really surprise you."

"Fine. But are you saying I can't talk you into giving it a try?" She imagined Sy, unsteady on her feet and clutching Maddie for dear life. They'd laugh and kiss and slowly make their way around the rink until Sy got the hang of it. Then come home and warm all the parts that had gotten chilled.

"I'll try after we get to do something I'm good at and you aren't. How's that?" Sy smirked like she'd successfully backed Maddie into a corner and gotten herself off the hook.

Maddie lifted a shoulder. "We just did. You're way better at talking about your feelings than I am."

That got her a dubious look. "Weak."

"It's not. Talking about feelings is hard and I'm notoriously bad at it. Just ask Clover."

"Okay, okay. You talk some more about your feelings, and I'll strap on a pair of death shoes."

"Deal. I may have called it a slippery slope, but I liked where you were going."

Sy's expression got serious. "What part? Me sliding into love with you?"

Her chest tightened, exhilaration laced with trepidation. "Yeah, that part."

"I'm pretty excited you feel the same."

Maddie nodded. She hadn't been looking for love. And there were still plenty of looming questions about what that meant in the long run. She'd worry about those later. For now, she'd bask in the fact that she loved Sy and Sy loved her back. Not a bad cap off to the most indulgent day ever.

❖

Sy stepped out of the aging room and checked her phone, mostly for the time but also to see if she had any messages from Maddie. Silly, really, but in the days following Christmas, it had felt like they'd turned a corner. Talking about feelings, using the L word—it all had her feeling squishy and sentimental, and she wasn't ashamed to admit it.

She had one text, which basically requested being naked together soon. She returned the sentiment, because there was no reason squishy and sentimental couldn't go hand in hand with smoking hot sex.

With that squared away, Sy turned her attention to a voice mail from Biaggio. Hopefully, he'd sold out of chèvre and wanted to place an emergency order before the scheduled February delivery. She wouldn't mind a day trip to Northampton. Maybe she could convince Maddie to take the day off and join her.

The message wasn't about an order, though. Or at least she didn't think it was. He rather cryptically referenced needing a favor but implied he might be the one doing her the favor in the long run. Huh. Maybe it was about a last-minute order and he was just being dramatic.

Since she had a few minutes before her check-in with Clover, she tapped the phone icon, thinking vaguely about how weird it was to call someone who wasn't her mother.

"Darling, thank you for calling me back," Biaggio said in lieu of a hello.

Also weird to be called darling by someone who wasn't her mother. "Hey, Biaggio. What's up?"

"You'll never guess what happened."

With that much to go on, she was pretty sure she wouldn't. "What?"

He let out a dramatic sigh. "Marco broke his leg skiing in Lake Placid."

Nope, never would have guessed that. "Oh, no. Is he okay?"

"He'll be fine, but of course it's his driving foot. He's utterly useless for the next six weeks."

She didn't have a burning desire to ski, but the mere thought quashed any inkling she might have to give it a try. Even more so than ice skating. "That sucks."

"I know. He's miserable and I've got to wait on him hand and foot. I'm not sure who I feel sorrier for."

Sy got a niggling sensation along the back of her neck. One that told her Biaggio was about to ask her to play shopkeeper for the next month. She shoved the dread aside and focused on the fact that he considered her both a friend and a colleague. She could use both in this business. "I feel equally sorry for both of you."

"But you don't even know the worst of it yet."

There was more? "What's the worst?"

"Well, worst for me at least. I'm supposed to be in France next week on a scouting trip."

Was he going to ask her to babysit the shop and his husband? Surely, he wouldn't do that. Would he?

"I know you're a busy little bee up there, making all sorts of new things I can't wait to carry in my shop. But could you possibly tear yourself away for a week?"

Son of a bitch. He was going to ask her. "I'm not sure."

"The accommodations and car are all arranged, of course. And I'd cover the cost of your flight. I could manage to pay you a little something probably, but I'm hoping it's the sort of trip you'd enjoy as much as I would."

Sy stopped trying to formulate a graceful excuse long enough to process Biaggio's words. "Wait. You want me to go on the trip for you?"

"I can't possibly leave Marco alone and I'd hate to cancel it entirely. The expense, but also the relationships. You know how it is. And I can't think of anyone else I'd trust to go in my place."

Excitement quickly eclipsed the surge of guilt, and her brain began calculating logistics of what would need to be done in her absence. "I'm honored that you would ask me."

"Is that your polite way of turning me down?"

"No." She answered a little too loud and a little too fast. "Not at all. I mean, I need to make sure I can get things covered here."

"Of course, of course. But I'm afraid time is of the essence. Everything is booked for the third week of January."

That would be safely before the Valentine's rush. If the modest uptick in sales she anticipated could count as a rush. And she and Maddie didn't have anything big planned. If she worked a couple of sixteen-hour days and could talk Clover into monitoring the aging room, she might be able to pull it off without a dip in production. "I'll need to talk with my boss, but I really want to make it work."

"You're an angel."

Far from it, given how reticent she was to play shopkeeper and nursemaid. But who was she to correct him? "I try."

"It'll be an intense trip. Fifteen cheese makers in six days." Biaggio let out a tsk as though disparaging his own planning.

Intense, perhaps, but the stuff of dreams in her book. "It sounds amazing."

"I'm sure you'll do me proud. Now, go do something nice for your boss so she lets you go."

The line went silent. Sy tapped her foot, debating what to do first. Then she broke into a happy dance.

"Is that your move when a cheese turns out the way you want?" Clover asked.

Sy spun around. "How long have you been standing there?"

"Long enough to enjoy the show."

Okay, that was good. No awkward eavesdropping. "I, uh, just got off the phone with Biaggio."

"Fromager Biaggio?" Clover narrowed her eyes. "He's not trying to woo you away, is he?"

Sy cringed before she could stop herself. "Not exactly."

"But kind of?" Clover came the rest of the way into the cheese room, all business now.

"No, no," Sy said, again a little too quickly. "Nothing like that. He asked me if I'd be interested in doing a scouting trip for him. His husband broke his leg and he needs to stay home to take care of him."

Clover perched on the stool Sy kept in the corner. "Say more."

"He's got all the arrangements made, so the dates are firm. It's soon but would only be a week." Sy tried for a sheepish smile.

Clover pressed a hand to her chest. "Jesus, Sy. You had me scared for a minute. A week? You get three weeks of vacation as part of your job."

There was that. "Yeah, but this is short notice. And I wasn't planning on taking more than a long weekend here and there for the first year."

"That's bullshit corporate speak. We're not about that here." Clover punctuated the statement with a sniff of disdain.

"So, you'd be cool with it? I'd need you to keep an eye on the cheeses that are aging, but I'd frontload everything else." Could it really be as easy at that?

Clover waved a hand. "Piece of cake. I love this. I'm thinking you'll be able to get some inspiration, too, right? Ideas for things we can try here?"

"For sure. It's the kind of thing I hoped to do eventually, once we were really off the ground. Keeping up with trends, scoping the competition." In a friendly way, though. Cheese makers generally were happy to share and support each other, move the whole industry forward. A far cry from the cutthroat world of high-end restaurants and exactly why she loved the career she had instead of the one she'd thought she wanted.

"I can get behind that. Especially if I get to tag along sometimes." Clover shimmied her shoulders in apparent delight at the prospect.

"Hey, you're the face of Grumpy Old Goat. It's a very pretty face, too. I have no plans of changing that." Especially since the farm and the brand and whatever they made of it together would belong to Clover long after Sy had moved on.

"Flattery will get you everywhere." Clover grinned. "Just don't go falling for some other outfit and leave me in the lurch."

"Nah. We're building something special here. I want to see it through." Something she'd have felt even if she didn't have such a strong affection for Clover and her little herd of goats.

"We are, aren't we?" Clover let out a happy sigh. "I'm really glad you came to work here."

"I am, too. Even if, when I first started my apprenticeship, scouting and sourcing was exactly the sort of job I hoped I'd land one day."

"Yeah?" Clover looked genuinely surprised. "I think of you as such a maker."

Sy shrugged. "That's true. But traveling the world with the sole purpose of discovering amazing cheeses, and getting those cheeses into the hands of people who'll appreciate them? I mean, come on."

Clover grinned. "Well, when you put it that way."

CHAPTER TWENTY-SIX

Maddie stopped by the farm after work, mostly to see Clover. But it didn't mean she couldn't snag a kiss from Sy before tagging along for the evening ritual of feeding the goats and tucking them in for the night. She got a lot more than she bargained for, though, when Sy told her about her plan to fly off to France for a week. As much as she wouldn't begrudge anyone a bit of fun, something about it didn't sit right with her. Something that maybe had to do with the almost giddy look on Sy's face. Something that told her Sy would just as happily jet off and not come back.

She tried to convey those feelings to Clover over drinks an hour later and failed epically.

They sat at Fagan's, glasses of wine in hand and a bubbling crock of spinach dip between them. "I just don't know," she said, after Clover raised a brow at her first attempt.

"But, like, what don't you know? Explain it to me." Clover smeared dip over a slice of baguette and stuffed the whole thing in her mouth.

Maddie scowled. "It doesn't feel like a conflict of interest to you?"

"Fuck, that's good." Clover pointed at the dish. "And not at all. If anything, having her schmooze with other cheese makers, as the cheese maker for Grumpy Old Goat, is free publicity. It implies we're one of the big dogs now, holding our own with the fancy French folks."

That was one way of looking at it. The other was that Sy was bored with Bedlington already and eager to pounce on any opportunity to escape.

"You don't think so?" Clover frowned.

"I just think it's more glamorous than the day-to-day here."

Clover let out a snort. "Obviously."

Maddie sighed. "And that worries me."

"Huh." Clover sipped her drink. "You know, Sy kind of said the same thing."

The suspicion Maddie had tried to smother pinged back to life. "What do you mean?"

Clover shrugged like it was no big deal. "Sy said it was kind of a dream job, one she'd thought about during her apprenticeship."

"Seriously?" Definitely a big deal in her book.

"Yeah, but then I said she struck me as too much of a creator to find that satisfying in the long run, and she agreed."

It was her turn to "huh."

"Anyway. This is only a week. It'll satisfy her wanderlust and give her all sorts of inspiration to bring home."

Maddie's hackles went up again. "How do you know she has wanderlust?"

Clover, not big on eye rolls or sarcasm, narrowed her gaze.

"I'm serious." She certainly didn't have the need to roam. Clover didn't seem to, either. Why would she assume Sy did?

Clover shrugged again, only this time with a truth universally acknowledged vibe. "People like Sy always do. It's part of their creative energy or something."

She couldn't decide what was worse—learning that part of Sy would always crave something new or realizing it was something Clover picked up on when she hadn't.

"It's not a bad thing," Clover said.

Maybe not, but she had a hard time seeing it as a good thing, either. At least when it came to people she'd fallen in love with. "Aren't people like that always at least a little dissatisfied with wherever they are?"

"Not necessarily." Clover's expression turned serious. "Is that what you're worried about? That Sy isn't happy here?"

It was her turn to shrug.

"If you are, you should talk to her about it," Clover said.

"Clingy much?" No thank you.

"It's not clingy to be curious. Or vulnerable."

The thing with being vulnerable was that it sounded so mature and self-actualized in theory but, in the moment, usually felt like crap.

"Talk to her. She's actually pretty good at communicating. Better than the last two women I dated, to be honest," Clover said.

"Do you want to date her instead?" She'd meant it as a joke, but the possibility that the answer might be yes niggled the edges of her brain.

"God, no. She's hot but not my type." Clover grinned. "Besides, she's obviously totally into you. I wouldn't want to stand in the way of that, and joining would be a little too much like a throuple with my sister."

"Ew." At Clover's impatient look, she lifted a hand. "The sister part, not the throuple. Your way of doing relationships is just as valid as mine."

Clover tipped her head. "Thank you."

That settled that, but it didn't leave her feeling any better about Sy's imminent departure. If anything, it made her feel worse. Which, of course, made her even less inclined to share her feelings about it with Sy.

That ambivalence carried her through dinner with Clover and all the way to Sy's house, where they'd planned to spend the night. To her credit, Sy picked up on it almost immediately. "I'm sorry I didn't get to tell you when it was just the two of us. I was surprised to see you is all, and still riding the high of Biaggio asking me in the first place."

Determined not to be an utter jerk about it, Maddie quelled her unease. "It's cool that he did."

Sy nodded, her enthusiasm returning. "It's a total honor. Like, the trip is going to be amazing, but the fact that he trusts my eye, my palate. That's huge."

Right. It would be like the owner of some really important building cherry-picking her to do the work on it. That, if nothing else, was the sort of professional feather in the cap she could understand. "You're good at what you do."

"Thanks." Sy nodded but seemed surprised by the comment.

Whether it had to do with the compliment itself or the fact that it came from Maddie wasn't clear, but it made Maddie double down on being supportive. "I'm serious. I'm no expert, but I've eaten my fair share of cheese and yours is freaking fantastic."

Sy grinned then. "I'm going to put that on my business cards."

She folded her arms, letting herself relax into the familiar territory of banter. "You don't have business cards."

"Yeah, but now that I have something good to put on them, I'm going to get some." Sy stuck out her hands, making a pair of mirrored brackets with her fingers and thumbs. "Sy Travino: Freaking Fantastic Cheese."

"While you're at it, you should put great in the sack, too. Wait." She lifted a finger. "Nix that."

Sy made a show of looking scandalized. "Are you not a satisfied customer on that front?"

"Oh, I'm completely satisfied. It just occurred to me I don't want you advertising that fact to the rest of the world." See, this was fine. Everything was fine.

"I'm glad to know you're not disappointed in my…offerings." Sy quirked a brow at the end.

"Not at all. I mean, it wouldn't even feel like a hardship to enjoy your offerings exclusively." Weirdest way ever to broach not seeing other people—not to mention questionable timing—but she had no choice now but to roll with it.

"I'd like that. And for the record, I'm not interested in letting anyone else work on my house."

She laughed. "Okay, your euphemism is even worse than mine."

Sy shrugged. "Yeah, but you started it."

"True. I guess that makes us even." Probably not the conversation Clover had in mind when she told Maddie to talk about her feelings, but it seemed to do the trick. She felt better about Sy leaving and they'd taken yet another step forward in their relationship. Maybe she could rock a little vulnerability after all. "I'm going to miss you, but I'm excited for you."

Sy smiled. "Yeah?"

"Yeah." And the best part? For all her perseverating, she meant it.

❖

After attempting to fold the three nice shirts she owned and placing them in the small suitcase she could use as a carryon, Sy settled on three sweaters that could pass as nice and called it good. Good enough, at least. Most of the places she'd be visiting weren't overly formal, even for guests. Another perk of the cheese industry. She topped off all her three-ounce containers of liquids and gels and got everything situated, making sure she left enough room to bring something fun home for Clover. And Maddie, of course.

Though she and Clover had discussed traveling together to stay current on trends, it was Maddie she imagined sitting with in an outdoor café. Glasses of wine, a board of cheese and a baguette between them. Soaking up some sun and watching the world go by. Then meandering the narrow streets and poking into shops.

Would Maddie like France? Sy liked to think so. Though perhaps the more relevant question might be whether Maddie would ever go with her. Of course, she'd be inclined to take Maddie to New Mexico first. Or California. A nice little winter escape.

The prospect prompted visions of Maddie in a bikini on a beach, basking in the sun and inviting Sy to rub sunscreen onto her back. Sy laughed. Because even in her fantasies, Maddie couldn't help but be practical.

The sound of Sy's phone ringing jarred her back to her bedroom and her suitcase and the fact that a veritable blizzard swirled around outside. She groaned before looking at the screen. Seeing John's name jarred her again—general weirdness laced with immediate worry something was wrong with her mother. "Hello?"

"Sy. Hi. It's John." He coughed. "You probably already knew that."

She laughed because of course she did, but the worry stayed at the front of her mind. "Is everything okay?"

"Oh. Yes. Sorry. Everything is great."

When he didn't elaborate, she wondered if this was his way of trying to stay in touch. Which then made her wonder if she could train him to text.

"I'd like to give you some money," he said abruptly, no lead-in or explanation.

"You already gave me a large sum of money." Sy took the phone away from her ear and put it on speaker, impressed with herself for saying large sum and not crap ton.

"That was a gift. Thirty odd years of missed Christmases and birthdays and graduations."

Even with that math, it was a lot. "Okay. So, I think we're squared away on that front."

"I also missed thirty years of child support."

Were they seriously having this conversation? "Technically, you would have only been on the hook for eighteen of those."

John chuckled. "Look, Sy. I don't want to make you uncomfortable. Or make it seem like I'm made of money. But my ex-wife made even more than me, so I'm not paying alimony. I don't have other kids. And your mother only tolerates me lavishing her so much."

"What are you proposing?" And how did he make it seem like she'd be doing him the favor?

"I'd like to send you a hundred thousand to start. And then the same over each of the next five years. I'm consulting with my financial advisor, but I think I can count it toward my lifetime estate exclusion, and you wouldn't need to deal with any excess tax implications."

Since he'd officially started using phrases beyond her meager financial expertise, her brain raced to other things. Things like how that much money would literally change her life. But those thoughts could send her down rabbit holes even deeper than fantasies of Maddie at the beach, so she forced herself to stay in the moment. "I don't want to say I don't understand, but I don't really understand."

"I'd rather not wait until I'm dead to take care of the people I care about," he said with a disarming mix of bluntness and clarity.

Sound logic, in its own way. "Does my mother know about this, too?"

"Not yet. I don't plan on keeping it from her, but I wanted to discuss it with you first." He coughed again. "I wanted to make sure you'd accept."

On one hand, who in their right mind turned down half a million dollars? On the other, it implied a permanency of her father in her life. In her mother's life. She was feeling more open to that than she thought she might, but that didn't make it a dotted line she was quite ready to sign. Even as possibilities danced through her mind. A bigger operation here in Vermont. An operation of her own somewhere else. All the things she could do to her house. Or a house closer to her mom. Though, with the way things were going, that felt like a moving target.

"Should I take your silence as hesitation?" John asked.

"No. Yes. I mean, you caught me off guard is all." Sy sat on the edge of the bed and pinched the bridge of her nose.

"For what it's worth, there aren't any strings attached. I'm just trying to do the right thing."

Was it jerky of her not to dive right into effusive thanks? "I get that. And I'm pretty sure I'm not looking to turn you down."

"But it's a lot," John said.

She nodded even though no one was there to see. "It's a lot."

"Don't say yes or no yet. Sit with it and we can talk again. I'm not trying to shake up your life."

He probably meant with his presence, but she couldn't help thinking about all the other aspects of her life that would get shaken along the way. "I hope I don't sound ungrateful."

"You don't. And I'm not looking for your gratitude. If anything, I'm grateful to you for letting me into your life at all."

She believed he meant that. Which made the prospect of saying yes all the more appealing. And made her all the more inclined to embrace their fledgling relationship. "I think we can both be grateful."

He chuckled softly. "That works for me."

At the sound of Maddie's truck in the driveway, Sy's brain clicked back to her room and her suitcase, to the fact that she was leaving for France in about twelve hours. "I need to run at the moment, and I'm leaving for a trip tomorrow. Can we connect when I get back?"

"Right, right. The French cheese adventure. Bonita told me."

Of course she had. "I really do want to talk, though. And I'm probably not going to turn you down. I think I need time to let it settle, if that makes any sense."

"Absolutely. And I won't keep you." His tone was all business now, more comfortable and confident than when talking about things like gratitude.

"Okay. Thanks. Um, take care." She almost said "tell my mom hi" before realizing John hadn't told her about the conversation.

"You too. Safe travels. Send us some pictures." John cleared his throat. "Send your mom pictures, I mean. You don't have to send them to me."

His deference continued to disarm her, though she was starting to hope they'd get past it. "I'll start a group text. Seems like we're there."

He laughed. "That would be great. Bye, Sy."

"Bye, John." Would she ever call him dad? Did she want to?

Questions for another day. For now, she needed to finish packing and spend the evening with Maddie. Oh, and decide how much of that conversation to share.

She wasn't one for keeping secrets, especially with someone she loved. But John's proposition gave her so much to think about, so many possibilities to consider. Possibilities that opened doors and made pipe dreams suddenly seem plausible. She needed to wrap her head around that before dumping it at Maddie's feet.

The sheer magnitude of what she could do with that kind of money had her hovering on the precipice of euphoria. But the ripple effects of whatever decisions she made weighed her like sandbags. Because no matter what she decided, things would change. Her relationship with her mom, with Clover and Grumpy Old Goat. And perhaps most of all, with Maddie.

CHAPTER TWENTY-SEVEN

Maddie woke early, though maybe it was more accurate to say she gave up on sleep and got up early. Sy had seemed restless, too, though she'd finally stilled into a sound sleep sometime around four. It made Maddie wonder if she always got like that before travel. Maddie did, even if she couldn't use that as her excuse this time.

Maybe Sy had something weighing on her mind. She'd been squirrelly over dinner and almost distant during sex. And when Maddie had asked, she'd downplayed it and then gone distractedly quiet. Again, leaving Maddie to wonder if it had to do with travel anxiety or something else entirely.

Either way, Sy was about to be gone for a week, and Maddie wanted them to part ways on as good a note as possible. So she padded downstairs and put on coffee before looking to see what she could rustle up from the fridge for breakfast. But of course Sy had cleared things out in anticipation of being away, and the pickings were slim. Fortunately, she could hack a batch of pancakes with the eggs that remained and some watered down half-and-half.

She'd no sooner finished the batter when Sy appeared in the kitchen. "You didn't have to cook."

"I know, but I was up and wanted something to do with my hands." And getting handsy hadn't felt like an option.

Sy came up and wrapped her arms around Maddie from behind. "You're the first woman I've been with who's a busier bee than I am."

Maddie let herself lean into Sy's embrace and the reassurances that seemed to come with it. "Guilty as charged."

Sy kissed her neck. "I like it, though. Makes us evenly matched."

See? That was nice. Normal. Maybe she'd blown the whole thing out of proportion. "Do you want coffee?"

"Do you have to ask?" Sy let her go. "I'll get it."

She warmed a skillet and got the first round going, accepting the cup Sy offered and letting her eyes drift closed with the first sip. "Mmm."

"I love how much you savor that first taste, even if you're doing something else," Sy said.

"I love that you pay attention and fix my coffee exactly the way I like it." A small detail but one she didn't take for granted—not at face value and not for all the things it signified.

Sy leaned against the sink with her own cup. She sighed but didn't say anything more. Maddie couldn't decide whether to attribute it to the early hour or things Sy might be thinking but not wanting to share. She wanted to start an argument even less than she wanted to know, so she focused her attention on the task at hand and sending Sy on her way with something more than coffee in her stomach.

While they ate, she asked Sy about the places she'd be going, whether she'd get to visit the creamery where she'd done her apprenticeship. Sy perked up as she talked, chasing away whatever cobwebs of fatigue or clouds of distraction had enveloped her. It made Maddie feel better until it occurred to her that Sy preferring a life of adventure to the one she'd built here was what she'd been afraid of. Ugh.

"Are you sure I can't take you to the airport?" Maddie asked.

Sy waved her off. "It would literally take up your entire day. And the weather is going to be crap."

Both true. And the last thing she wanted was to come off as clingy. Still. "You are talking to a New England native, you know. Who drives a truck."

"It would still take your entire day. And I know you're juggling projects now that the holidays are done."

A trace of the misgivings she had when Sy first announced her trip returned. "Too girlfriendy for you?"

Sy's whole demeanor changed. "You know that's not true. We literally used the L word with each other. And we decided to be exclusive."

She liked to know where she stood, but she truly wasn't one for keeping score when it came to that sort of thing. Nor was she the sort of woman who felt compelled to declare her feelings a dozen times a day. But something about Sy's energy had her on edge. Worse, she couldn't figure out why.

Or maybe she knew exactly why and that was the problem.

This was useless. She'd get answers when Sy got home, one way or the other. No point having a row and sulking for a week in the meantime.

"Maddie?"

"Sorry. I didn't mean it like that."

Sy's gaze didn't waver. "What's up? Something's bugging you."

Yeah, whatever's bugging you that you don't want to talk about. "Just feeling a little off. Didn't sleep great."

"I'm sorry." Sy's expression went sly. "Is it because you're gonna miss me?"

"That must be it." It was certainly part of it.

"I'm going to miss you," Sy said without hesitation or any trace of teasing.

Maddie squared her shoulders. She was being silly. "It's only a week. Then you'll be home, and it'll still be winter, and it will feel like you never left."

Sy sighed, then got that distant look on her face yet again, though Maddie couldn't tell which of her assertions triggered it.

"Now I feel like something's bugging you." So much for not opening any cans of worms.

Sy waved her off. "Just restless. I'll be fine."

Obvious BS, but she took the out because two could play that game. "Okay. Well, I shouldn't keep you."

"Yeah." Sy gave a shudder like she was shaking off whatever had come over her. "I'll text you when I make it to the airport and when I land."

Maddie nodded. "Send me some pictures and eat lots of cheese for me. Oh, and drink some good wine."

Sy grinned. "That won't be a problem."

❖

Sy landed at Charles de Gaulle just after seven local time. It reminded her of her only other trans-Atlantic flight, the one that set her cheese making career in motion. Just like then, she emerged groggy but wired, simultaneously cursing whoever invented redeye flights and giddy to be in Paris. Because Paris.

Unlike that first trip, she understood how customs worked and didn't feel foolish trying to make out the most basic French words and phrases. She also had a rental car waiting for her and a series of fairly posh accommodations in the towns she'd stop in along the way. Oh, and the pleasure of tasting the fruits of other people's labor rather than doing all the labor herself. Like she'd said to Clover, nice work if you could get it.

She picked up her car and programmed her first destination into her GPS. She got herself checked into the hotel with just enough time to grab a coffee and a shower before her first stop at a cheese maker just south of the city. She'd only been away for a few months, but damn was her French rusty. Though, to be fair, she'd peaked a few levels south of fluent. And very, very specialized.

Fortunately, her fromage lingo remained on point, and she was able to both charm and do business with the various cheese makers and distributors Biaggio had secured meetings with, even with jet lag. She'd forgotten how inspiring it could be to talk shop with people who knew even more about cheese than she did. And she'd forgotten how magical it could be to drive around the French countryside to get to those people.

Biaggio had set a full but not frantic schedule, leaving her with plenty of time for late morning strolls and leisurely dinners at one brasserie or another. Not unlike her time in France before, though with more disposable income. And not, she realized over a glass of Bordeaux overlooking a cobblestone lane, all that unlike the life she'd managed to build in Bedlington.

Work hard, relax hard. Was that a thing? It should be.

Sy pulled out her phone to text Maddie—to see if Maddie found it funny but also to say she missed her. But she had a text from Maddie waiting, lamenting a member of her crew quitting with no notice. She settled on a few words of empathy instead and left it at that. No point gloating about her current situation. Or coming off as clingy.

Day four of the itinerary brought Sy to her old stomping grounds. When she pulled into the narrow lane leading to Le Coteau, a wave of memories washed through her. From the apprehension of her arrival to her early attempts to drive Jean's ancient truck into town, she'd never felt more out of place. But those feelings had faded, giving way not only to the best learning experience of her life, but a sense that she was finally doing the work she was meant to do. Pretty wild for a blue-collar Mexican kid from the desert.

Jean came out the moment she put the car in park, as though he'd been waiting for her. He greeted her with open arms and kisses on both cheeks. Not out of custom, but it almost felt like getting a hug from her mama.

"My petite apprentice returns as the fancy American buyer," he said, clasping his hands around both her arms.

Since he meant little novice more than literally petite, she directed her scoff at his other assessment. "Nothing fancy about me."

"But you have your own operation, yes? The Surly Sheep?"

Sy laughed. "Grumpy Goat. I get to run it, but it's not technically mine." Even with the level of free rein Clover gave her, an important distinction.

"Eh, you're but a baby yet. If you want that, you'll get it." Jean made circular motions with his hands. "Or maybe you open a shop and go around finding all the best things to put in it."

Clover's comment about being a maker rang through her mind. It struck a chord in the moment, but it had stayed with her, too. As fun as this gallivanting was, she couldn't imagine doing it all the time. She liked getting her hands dirty too much. And, she realized with a start, she liked being home. Home as in the house she'd been convinced was a money pit only a few months ago. Home as in her life there. Home as in wherever Maddie was.

"Are you seeing dreams now?" Jean asked.

She smiled at the literal translation of the French term for daydreaming. "I might be."

"Come, we'll go inside, and you'll tell me all about your Grumpy Goat and the big dreams for what you will do."

Sy followed. Just like the revelation about home, it hit her that she'd never been one for big dreams. She had dreams, obviously, and perhaps more than her fair share of ambition, but she preferred setting her sights on things that felt within her grasp. But now, with John's money, a hell of a lot more than she'd ever imagined would be feasible.

A few years ago, that would have entailed opening a restaurant of her own. She'd never rule that out entirely, but it no longer held the allure it once did. Her own cheese operation, though? That certainly did. With its own shop. One where she could sell all the cheeses her imagination could conjure, along with local products and the quirky odds and ends a visiting turophile might want to take home.

A tasting room. Part restaurant, part shop. Why hadn't she thought of that before? Had Clover? They could expand right there on the property. People could come for tours, feed the goats, and stay for cheese and charcuterie and bread she could source daily right there in town.

And there was no reason she couldn't produce her own line of cheese. Things that might prove a little too funky for the Grumpy Old Goat brand. Cheeses that would complement the GG offerings, not compete with them. Cheeses that would inspire her even if they didn't fly off the shelves. Though maybe they would fly off the shelves, too.

"Sy. You're dreaming again."

Jean's voice brought her back to the production room where she'd spent her days for the better part of a year. "Sorry."

He waved her off. "Don't be sorry for dreaming. That's where the good ideas are."

Much like Clover's comment, Jean's struck her. Made her think about things differently. What if he was right? What if she could use John's money to make her dreams a reality? And what if that dream was something that had only just crossed her mind?

CHAPTER TWENTY-EIGHT

Maddie resisted the urge to scratch where the elastic from the hairnet tickled her scalp. "It doesn't bug you that she just ran off to play...whatever it is you call people who source cheese for stores?"

"No," Clover said matter-of-factly. "Does it bother you?"

Did it? Saying yes made her feel petulant, but she couldn't shake the icky feeling that had settled in her stomach since Sy left. Even if she'd made a point of being supportive, had managed to actually feel it. At least until Sy got all distant and weird. "It just seems self-serving is all."

"So, you're saying Sy shouldn't look after her own interests, do what she wants to do?" Clover blinked at her a few times, all innocence.

She should have known better than to play that card in the first place. Clover had no patience for the shoulds of the world. She believed people got too caught up in what society—or their parents or their partners—thought and would be better served following their guts. In an ethical way, of course. "I'm saying it feels like she left you in enough of a lurch that you had to call your friend to come help you."

"One, she's entitled to time off. Even curmudgeonly you acknowledge the importance of work-life balance."

Maddie sniffed. "I'm not a curmudgeon."

"Two, I called you because the vacuum sealer scares me. Sy can't be held responsible for my fear of certain appliances." As if to prove her point, Clover opened the machine gingerly, as though it might attack her.

Maddie sniffed again.

"What's really bugging you?"

Sy's unbridled enthusiasm for this trip. The nagging feeling that, given the chance, Sy would leave Bedlington in a heartbeat and not look back. Oh, and the fact that it wouldn't be the first time she'd fallen for a woman who had her sights set on more than what she had to offer. "Nothing."

"You're even worse at lying than helping me operate this beast." Clover slapped the side of the machine.

"I'm being stupid. And hating myself for being stupid. Let me beat myself up in private and it'll be fine." She gestured to the sealer. "I'm focused now. I promise."

Clover sighed but didn't argue. They'd been friends long enough that she knew better than to try to budge Maddie when she'd dug her heels in. "Fine."

"Can't we talk about your love life instead? How was your date this weekend?"

Another sigh, this time with an eye roll. "No spark. Zero. Nada. Nil." Clover wasn't looking to settle down, at least not romantically. She took her solo poly, relationship anarchy approach to life and love very seriously. But she'd struggled lately. The people she liked wanted to get real serious, real fast. And the ones she considered suitable fuck buddies didn't seem to share the ethical half of her commitment to ethical nonmonogamy.

"I'm sorry."

Clover waved her off. "It's fine. We might be friends when it's all said and done. They seemed interested in checking out the farm and hanging out in Bedlington for a weekend."

That was the other challenge with dating. Bedlington's population was tiny and, aside from each other and the other members of Maddie's immediate family, queers were thin on the ground. "You sure there's no chemistry?"

"Ha ha. Seriously, I wish." Clover shook her head. "Honestly, seeing you and Sy in the same room together has me raising the bar, not lowering it."

The reality of what had been needling her all week landed with a thud. "Yeah, but for all that chemistry, I'm not sure how far it's going to get me."

"What's going on?" Clover asked. "Did you and Sy have a fight I don't know about? You can still tell me stuff like that, you know."

A fight would have been simpler. She'd know where each of them stood and whether the differences were irreconcilable. This vague sense that something was off? So much worse.

"Well, did you?" Clover asked again.

"No. Nothing like that."

"What then?" Clover folded her arms.

"I just get the feeling she's not telling me something. And the fact that it's coinciding with her flitting off to Europe has me feeling gross."

"Ah." Clover nodded. "So, is it your gut trying to tell you something or your general fear of falling too hard for someone you're convinced won't stick around?"

She opened her mouth to protest the fear thing, but it had a kernel of truth whether she wanted to admit it or not. "I don't know."

"Well, that's what you need to find out. Might I suggest waiting until Sy comes home and having a real conversation about it rather than stewing in her absence?"

Maddie groaned. "Do you have to be so freaking mature about it all?"

Clover nodded. "Yep."

"That was a rhetorical question." Which Clover knew, but Maddie felt the need to point it out anyway.

"Couples who are exclusive are usually terrible when it comes to taking relationship things for granted and going off assumptions rather than open communication."

She groaned again. "We had a very grown-up conversation about being exclusive, for the record."

That got her a finger to the chest. "Good for you. But you're actually proving my point. That conversation doesn't get you off the hook for having the thousand or so other ongoing grown-up conversations that should happen when you're in a relationship."

"I hate it when you're right." Or at least she did when it meant personal discomfort on her part.

"Just talk to her. For what it's worth, I think she's pretty far gone for you."

Did that make her feel better? Not really. Because they might have talked about feelings, but they hadn't talked about the future. For all she'd told herself she didn't need that—didn't want it—she did. And if Sy's future involved moving somewhere else, it was a dealbreaker, plain and simple. "I'm not sure it's worth all that much."

Clover tsked. "You are a curmudgeon."

"I'm a realist," Maddie said without missing a beat.

"I'd argue pessimist, but let's not split hairs."

"Yes. Let's not." Because what she really was was miserable.

"Let's finish up here instead and call it a day." Clover flicked her hand over the packages they'd yet to seal. "I think a girls' night is in order."

They'd done those less and less in recent years. At least by the standard of their early twenties. But the combination of junk food, facials, wine, and rom-coms still had a certain appeal. Especially when girlfriend—or boyfriend—troubles were brewing. "Your place or mine?"

Clover tipped her head back and forth. "Your couch is comfier."

"And I just picked up a case of wine. Bring snacks and pj's." Maddie grinned. "And maybe work clothes for tomorrow because you know you're going to crash by ten o'clock."

Clover, who made no pretenses about her early bedtime, laughed. "I resemble that remark."

❖

As amazing as the trip was, Sy found herself itching to be home by the end. She missed her house and the cheese room at the farm she now considered her domain. She missed Henry and, shockingly, having snow on the ground. But most of all, she missed Maddie.

It didn't help that their text conversations had been stilted and sporadic. Or that the one time they'd talked on the phone Maddie had seemed in a big hurry to get off. She'd cited a girls' night, but it was with Clover, so the need to rush or be secretive made no sense.

She'd hoped it was a function of time and distance, exacerbated perhaps by it being their first time apart. But Maddie was flat and kind of distant the day she got home, claiming a headache and heading back to her place as soon as they'd finished dinner. The next day wasn't much better. Maddie worked late and, although she stayed over, it was clear sex was off the table.

After a morning of tiptoeing around, drinking coffee at her place but both being noncommittal about cooking, eating, or doing anything else, Sy couldn't decide whether to be worried or irritated. It didn't help that she had her own questions and conundrums hanging over her head like a cloud. Should she take John's money? If she did, what should she do with it? Was she truly ready to make the sort of leap—the investment—that would keep her in Vermont long-term?

Not that Maddie asked what was on her mind.

"Why are you being weird?" Sy asked eventually, swiveling on the sofa to face her.

Maddie lifted her chin. "Why are you?"

To be fair, she'd probably started acting weird first. By rights, that meant she should be the one to talk first. Even if Maddie's weirdness came with a heavy dose of sullen and withdrawn. "My father offered me a half a million dollars."

"What?" Maddie's voice pitched high, the look on her face incredulous.

Sy shrugged. She'd sat with it long enough that the idea no longer startled her. "He says he wants to make up for not providing for me as a kid. And that I'd probably get more use out of it now than inheriting it when he dies."

Maddie stuck out both hands, clearly unimpressed with that as the whole answer. "That's bananas. Like, everything about it is bananas."

"I know." It might not startle her any more, but the assessment still fit.

"Why didn't you tell me?" Maddie asked, shock giving way to a look of confusion and hurt.

Sy blew out a breath. "Because he called me right before I left for France and I couldn't decide how I felt about it or if I was going to take it, and I didn't want that hanging over our last night together or the time I was away."

"Oh."

"Though I see now that my plan backfired colossally." Though she still couldn't see how withholding that one detail put Maddie into such a funk. She might have thought owning it would clear the air, but Maddie's expression remained serious.

"What are you going to do?" Maddie asked.

"I don't know. It feels strange to just accept it, but worse to turn it down."

"Yeah."

"It's also a life-changing amount of money." Changes she hadn't broached with her mom yet, or with Maddie.

"Yeah," Maddie said again, nodding slowly but not making eye contact, like she knew the parts Sy hadn't said aloud.

"So, anyway. Big thing, big decisions. No answers and stuck a little too much in my head. What's your excuse?"

Maddie flinched and Sy regretted her choice of words.

"Not excuse. I meant, what's bothering you?"

"That. This. Us. I don't know." Maddie glanced at her for a fraction of a second but immediately looked away again. "Nothing."

"Okay, it's definitely not nothing, so let's rule that out." She tried for a smile, but Maddie didn't budge.

"I knew you weren't telling me something."

"I'm sorry for that." And for not trusting Maddie enough to confide in her from the beginning.

"I had a gut feeling it had to do with opportunities beyond what you'd get here." Maddie lifted a shoulder. "And I was right."

"Wait, wait, wait. What?"

"You told Clover that was your dream job. Shit, it would be a lot of people's dream job. I get it."

She hated feeling dense, but the dots still weren't connecting. "So, it bothered you that I left?"

Maddie sighed, though it sounded closer to a growl. "It bothers me that you're going to leave. Like, I kind of always knew you would, but I guess I'm disappointed it's happening so fast."

The desire to offer comfort warred with the impulse to defend herself. "Maddie, I'm not going anywhere. That was a one-time thing for a friend and a really cool opportunity, not a job offer."

"You say that now, but it's only a matter of time. You'll have your fill of small town life and your small town girlfriend, and you'll hightail it out of here faster than"—Maddie stuck out her hands—"something really fast."

"Why would you think that? Going to France wasn't about getting away from here. I mean, maybe a little bit the here part. It's the middle of fucking winter. But I didn't want to get away from my work." She didn't think she should have to say it, but apparently she did. "Or you."

"But it's on the table now." Maddie's delivery was flat, almost like she'd checked out of the conversation already.

"I'm not booking it out of town tomorrow, if that's what you're implying." Quite the opposite.

"But you're not looking to stay, either. That's what you're saying. Now that you have your dad's money to play with."

"Play? Is that what you think I'm doing?" She resented the implication, and it came through loud and clear.

"I think you're swimming in a lot of possibilities that have nothing to do with Bedlington or your job at Grumpy Old Goat." Maddie lifted her chin. "Or me."

Something in Maddie's tone triggered a wave of anger and anxiety she didn't know could coexist. Her flight-or-fight response followed hot on its heels. Well, flight. She wasn't much of a fighter. "I have a lot of reasons to stay, but I also have other things to think about. Like my mother and how difficult it is to live two thousand miles away from her."

That seemed to soften Maddie. But rather than encouraged, she just looked dejected. "Of course you have to think about her. With that much money, you could start your own operation near her."

It should have made things better that Maddie had the same thought, that it was something that could be put on the table and discussed. But it felt like a kick to the gut instead. One of those things that would be getting everything she wanted while losing just as much. "I haven't even decided to take the money yet. I definitely have to discuss it with her. John hadn't talked with her about it, and I need to know how she feels. And I need to know how you feel."

Maddie shook her head. "I don't know how I feel."

"It's okay. It's a lot to take in. I'm sorry I didn't tell you about it right away. I should have, so we could talk about it."

"It's super complicated." A concession, but the kind that felt like Maddie was throwing in the towel more than looking for places to compromise.

"Yeah." She sighed.

"Do you want me to go?" Maddie asked.

"What? No. Of course not." A knot lodged in her stomach. "Do you want to go?"

"It's not a matter of wanting to. It's knowing how much you have on your plate. How much I have on mine. Maybe we should just take some time to focus on that stuff and see where the dust settles." Maddie chewed her bottom lip, looking more resolved than dejected now.

"Are you asking for a break?" What was that third reaction, again? Freeze? She didn't care what she had on her plate. Not being with Maddie would absolutely make everything worse.

Maddie's half smile was the first indication since they'd started talking that she wasn't already on the exit ramp. "Not like a break break."

But a break of some kind. The knot became more of a churn. "I don't like it, but I want to respect what you need."

"It's just to give us both a little breathing room. So we can sort things out without pressure."

She didn't see how trying to sort things out separately could possibly do that, but things felt precarious enough that she didn't want to start a fight on top of everything else. Because two out of three was bad enough. "Okay. Does that mean you're going now?"

"I think I probably should." Maddie's tone held all the definitiveness her words didn't.

"Are you sure we shouldn't be talking instead?" Not that she knew what to say.

"I'm not sure I have much to say at the moment. You?"

Of all the times to have Maddie read her mind. "No, but I'm willing to try."

"Look, I'm not mad. And I'm not ending things. I just need to think."

Was that Maddie's version of it's not you, it's me? It sure felt like it. "If you want space, I respect that. But I hope talking soon is on the table."

Maddie nodded. "Yeah. Okay."

They sat there for a minute, not looking at each other, the silence getting more awkward by the second. Sy longed to be one of those people who could whip out the perfect overture to make Maddie stay. Or the person who could simply pull Maddie into her arms and kiss her until her doubts were a distant memory.

Or maybe that sort of thing only happened in the movies.

Either way, she didn't say the right thing or pull Maddie into her arms. She followed Maddie to the door and watched rather helplessly as Maddie slid on her coat. And then she held the door and watched Maddie leave.

CHAPTER TWENTY-NINE

Jack set down his beer and climbed onto the last of the stools at the hi-top table. "I love when the four of us get together. We don't do it often enough."

Logan chuckled. "It's because none of us has needed an intervention for a while."

"Wait. Is this an intervention?" Jack raised a hand. "I didn't get the memo. Am I the one you're intervening?"

Clover gave his forearm a squeeze. "No, we just didn't get a chance to brief you ahead of time."

"It's this one." Logan hooked a thumb at Maddie.

"Me?" She feigned surprise, but indignation came naturally.

"Yes, you." Clover mirrored the indignation and then some. "You shut Sy down, don't communicate, and now she's moping around the cheese room like some emo teenager."

"I did what you told me to do. I communicated." Maddie shook her head. "A fat lot of good it did me."

Clover and Logan exchanged looks. Jack decidedly looked away. Maddie sulked and prepared to be managed.

"What exactly did you communicate?" Clover asked.

Logan cringed before Maddie could even contemplate an answer. "Whatever it was, I'm guessing it belongs on the top ten list of things never to say to a woman."

Maddie glared. "Must you?"

Logan shrugged. Jack offered a sympathetic smile. "Whatever it was, I'm sure you didn't mean it."

"Why are you all assuming I'm the one who fucked things up?" Maddie stuck out both hands, nearly knocking over Jack's beer in the process.

Clover angled her head, looking a little too much like a TV talk show host. "Did you?"

The problem with indignation was how quickly it could come back to bite one in the ass. "Sort of."

Logan groaned. Jack hung his head. Clover simply sighed. "Maddie."

"All I said was maybe we should take a break so we could sort out all the crap that had landed on our plates." Which of course sounded way worse now that she was recounting it after the fact.

"A break?" Literally all three of them spoke at once, an unsparing and unilateral statement on the absurdity of her choices.

"Not like that." Why was everyone so hell-bent on reading the worst into it?

"There's another way to read that?" Jack asked.

Logan put a hand on his arm. "No, there's not."

He looked oddly relieved, as though his understanding of how the world worked had been momentarily thrown into doubt. "Yeah, I didn't think so."

Logan jerked her head in Maddie's direction. "This one would rather make up new meaning to truths universally acknowledged than admit she stuck her foot in her mouth."

"Logan." Clover smacked Logan on the bicep. "Don't kick the poor thing while she's down."

"I'm right here," Maddie said.

"Yeah. When you should be off having welcome home sex with your girlfriend." Logan leaned out of Clover's reach, as though anticipating another swat.

Should she be off having sex with Sy? It certainly sounded more appealing than this combo of grief and pity Clover and her siblings were currently dishing out. But that would be denying reality, wouldn't it? Setting herself up for bigger heartbreak in the long run. Her current state might suck, but it would suck a lot more to pretend everything was fine and have Sy disappear after Maddie had fallen for her completely.

Who was she kidding? She already had fallen for Sy completely. Maddie let her head fall back. Fuck.

"That's I-could-be-having-sex regret," Logan said knowingly.

"Seems like I'm-an-idiot regret to me," Jack said.

Maddie rocked her head upright just in time to see Logan tip hers back and forth. "Tomato, to-mah-to."

Clover tapped her index finger against the surface. "No, definitely not the same. One means you wind up horny and alone. The other leaves you with a broken heart."

Logan cringed. "Both sound pretty shitty in my book."

Jack frowned. "Nah. A broken heart is way worse."

God bless him and his earnest self. "Thanks, Jack."

"Wait." Jack looked genuinely confused. "Are you being sarcastic right now?"

Clover shook her head. "No, I think she's admitting she screwed this one up."

"Are you?" Logan managed to look concerned rather than satisfied.

If she couldn't be honest with these three, she couldn't be with anyone. Even Sy. "Yeah."

"Well, admitting it is half the battle." Logan said.

"What's the other half?" Jack asked.

Logan and Clover made eye contact then said in unison, "Groveling."

"Do I have to?" Not that she hated admitting she was wrong, she simply hated being wrong in the first place.

"You probably won't have to grovel much," Clover said. "Sy's been miserable these last few days."

"She has?" She never wanted to be the cause of another person's misery, but it proved an odd consolation that Sy wasn't bopping along like nothing was wrong. Unfortunately, that meant she'd need to apologize for that on top of shutting down in the first place.

Clover wagged a finger. "Don't play dumb. You know she's as in love with you as you are with her."

Did she know that? They'd said as much to each other. But that was when things were easy—when they were on the same page and wanted the same things. Now, she wasn't sure that was the case.

"Obviously not." Logan rolled her eyes but then regarded Maddie with affection. "You can't be smart in all the ways all the time."

"No?" Maddie asked, already knowing the answer.

Jack shook his head, like the rest of the conversation might not make much sense, but that part did. "Not even the best of us can."

❖

Sy had never—ever—showed up on a woman's doorstep uninvited. Well, a couple of times she had, when she was confident her presence would be a welcome surprise. But this wasn't one of those times, not by a long shot. And besides, Maddie had asked for a break. Maddie should be the one showing up on her doorstep.

"I'm right on this one, aren't I?" Sy looked to Henry, who merely tipped his head one way, then the other.

"I know. I'll be waiting till the cows come home. Maybe I should go see your abuela for a while. Lick my wounds and try to decide what to do next." She stared at him more intently, willing him to give her a sign.

He flopped onto his side so he could attack his crinkle ball with all four paws instead of just two.

"Yeah, mull it over. It's a big decision."

The bundle of foil went flying and Henry darted after it.

"I'm taking that as a yes." She pulled out her phone and opened a travel app. But she'd no sooner typed ABQ into the destination box before closing it. "Here's the problem. I don't want to go anywhere. I like it here."

Henry tore back through the room, batting and pouncing and sending his prized toy under the sofa and out of reach. He looked at Sy and mewed plaintively.

"Oh, sure. Now that you want something you have time for me."

Another meow. This time with attitude and a paw swipe to her foot.

"You're worse than she is. Maybe ask nicely before you freak the fuck out." She got onto her hands and knees, but the ball of foil had worked its way just out of her reach. "Well, you've gone and done it now."

Sy got to her feet and brushed off her knees. "Now what?" The flash of headlights in the driveway caught her attention, and Henry's. "Did you order a pizza without telling me?"

She went to the front door and peered out. What she saw stopped her in her tracks. "Dude, it's her."

She turned to the small mirror that was part of the coat rack bench Maddie had helped her pick out and did a frantic finger comb of her hair before yanking open the door.

Maddie stood on the other side, hand lifted like a mime pretending to knock.

"Hi," Sy said, trying desperately to play it cool.

"Hi." Maddie's half smile gave Sy hope. "Am I interrupting you?"

She chuckled. "Only if you count my very one-sided conversation with Henry."

Maddie peered around her, smiling when her gaze landed on Henry. "He doesn't seem to mind."

"To be honest, he's not a very good listener." As if to prove the point, Henry attacked the scratching post attached to his cat tree.

"Does that mean I can come in?" Maddie asked.

Sy stepped back. "Please."

Sy closed the door. Maddie stood there, hanging her coat and taking off her boots. Like she'd just come in from a day of work, or perhaps some errand. It struck Sy how much she wanted that. Night after night after night.

She bent to move her own boots out of the way and stood just as Maddie did, and their heads bumped together. More awkward than painful, but still. "Sorry," she said, just as Maddie did.

They each chuckled uncomfortably, then went silent.

"Will you sit down, stay awhile?" Sy asked.

Maddie gave her a quizzical look. To be fair, it was kind of an absurd question. "Yeah. Sure."

They'd no sooner settled on the sofa than Henry darted over. He rubbed against Maddie's legs for a moment before jumping into her lap. "I think he missed you," Sy said.

"Did you?" Maddie scratched the spot on his neck that got him purring. "I guess I did see you every day your mama was gone."

"For what it's worth, I missed you, too." Sy cleared her throat. "While I was away but the last few days, too."

Maddie looked at her lap. Sy waited. Eventually, Maddie's gaze met hers. "I owe you an apology. I told myself I was communicating with you and really I was just communicating at you. And worse, I was letting my fear do the talking."

Sy hung her head. "I wasn't doing a great job of communicating, either."

Maddie smiled. "I didn't really give you the chance."

It had felt that way at the time, but she'd started to doubt herself. Worry that she'd been wishy-washy, unable to articulate her feelings because she didn't know what they were. "Well, I maybe didn't want to take a break, but I didn't have something better to offer."

Maddie lifted a shoulder. "I suggested a break because I didn't either."

"I'm not sure why I kept the stuff about my Dad and his money from you." Ironic, since her anxiety about what to do with it was the exact opposite of Maddie's.

"I wish you hadn't, but I'm not sure I would have responded any better than I did. You deserve better than that."

What she wanted to say was that she deserved Maddie. Or wanted her at least, and would do her best to deserve all that Maddie had to give. Instead, she looked at her feet and reminded herself to deal with one thing at a time. "I told John I'd take the money."

Maddie stiffened. "You did?"

"I'd like to invest it in your business." It had only occurred to her that morning, and she felt like an idiot for not thinking of it sooner. Even more than expanding her operation at the farm, it was the best way she could think of to convince Maddie she was in it for the long haul, whatever that looked like for them.

"I don't understand."

"You need to buy out your uncle. Or cousins. Whoever. The business is healthy, but you don't have a ton of liquid cash on hand. I do, or I will." So simple. And now that she was saying it out loud, almost glaringly obvious.

"Sy, I can't take your money."

"You aren't. It's an investment. You and Logan and Jack will pay it back. I'll even take interest. And by the time you do, I'll have an idea of what the hell I want to do with it. No point in having it just sit there in the meantime." It had made perfect sense in her mind but was starting to sound pushy and desperate. "Don't decide now. Just promise me you'll think about it."

Maddie nodded, expression serious. "Okay."

"For what it's worth, I think it's a sound business decision. I'm not just offering it to get you back."

Maddie, who'd busied her hands with petting Henry, jerked her head up. "What do you mean?"

Sy's heart dropped to the pit of her stomach. "I don't want you to feel like I'm bribing you or there's any sort of quid pro quo. But I'd be lying if I said it had nothing to do with wanting to stick around. Wanting to be with you."

"You want to be with me," Maddie said, like the very notion was a revelation.

Sy nodded. "I do."

Maddie smiled. "For what it's worth, we didn't technically break up."

She raised a brow. "No?"

"Taking a break and breaking up aren't the same thing." Maddie tipped her head. "Even if Clover, Logan, and Jack unanimously beg to differ."

Sy laughed. At the image of Maddie being outnumbered and overruled. With relief that Maddie really hadn't meant it the way every other person in the world seemed to. With hope and joy and all manner of other warm and fuzzy feelings. "So, no more break?"

"No more break."

"Does that mean you'll stay? Tonight, I mean." It might be silly, but Sy held her breath.

Maddie's smile turned sheepish. "If you'll have me."

She thought about all the ways she wanted to have Maddie. In her arms, in her bed. And, maybe someday, to have and to hold from that day forward. But one thing at a time and first things first. She stood and extended a hand. "Come upstairs with me?"

Maddie took it. "I thought you'd never ask."

Chapter Thirty

After spending way too much of the night making up for lost time, Maddie barely managed to make it out of Sy's bed in time to stop home for a change of clothes and make it to the office for the staff meeting. Logan's and Jack's worry quickly shifted gears and they were only too happy to tease her rather than console or cajole.

Despite her own reservations, she pitched Sy's proposal to the family. To their credit, everyone took it as a legitimate business proposition. But at the end of the day, they deferred to her. Because they managed to navigate mixing business and family with remarkably little conflict, but they also knew better than to take that sort of thing for granted. She spent the rest of the day mulling and, by the time Sy showed up at her place for dinner, she felt good about her answer.

Not sure how Sy would respond, Maddie didn't lead with it, taking her time warming the beef stew she'd pulled from the freezer and crisping a loaf of French bread in the oven. Sy set the table and poured wine. By the time they sat down together, everything felt so easy and cozy and perfect, she almost didn't want to.

But not talking had already gotten her into trouble once. She wasn't about to make the same mistake twice. She took a sip of wine rather than a bite of her food and squared her shoulders. "I've spent some time thinking about your offer."

"Yeah?" Sy's expression turned hopeful.

"I can't take your money." Sy opened her mouth, ostensibly to protest, but Maddie held up a hand. "Even as a loan. Or investment. Whatever."

"I don't understand. I thought you were going to talk to your family about it."

"I did. And we all came to the same conclusion." It would leave a huge gaping question in a very important part of her life, but it was the right answer for another—just as important—part.

Disappointment shone on Sy's face. "What conclusion is that?"

"That being in love with someone is a wild and wonderful and complicated thing. And it shouldn't be saddled with the burden of money stuff." She lifted a shoulder. "At least not from the get-go."

Sy frowned. "So, your family thinks I'm going to hold it over you or something?"

"No, they think you're awesome and generous. They also know I'm not going to break thirty-four years of being proud and independent overnight."

"There's nothing wrong with being independent," Sy said.

"Or proud?" She raised a brow.

"That one is trickier. I'm still working it out myself."

Maddie laughed. "One more thing we can add to the list of stuff we have in common."

"I do like having things in common." Sy shook her head. "But I'm not crazy about them, or you, feeling like this would be the death of us."

"They want us to have a fighting chance. More than a fighting chance. Hell, if you asked any one of them, I'm pretty sure they'd use the phrase happily ever after." A thought that proved equal parts lovely and terrifying. "The point is, this money business would complicate matters, even if we swore it wouldn't. And this, us, is too important for that."

Sy chewed at the inside of her lip and Maddie braced herself for a rebuttal. But eventually Sy sucked in a deep breath, then blew it out slowly. "I respect your decision."

She waited for more, but Sy didn't continue. She sucked in and blew out a breath of her own. "Thank you."

"I'm disappointed, but only because that leaves you with a big, stressful thing to deal with." Sy shrugged. "I don't like seeing you stressed."

"I've got to be honest, not knowing if we were staying together or breaking up was way more stressful than this." And now that Sy accepted her decision, she felt lighter than she had since Sy left for France.

"In the spirit of honesty, I was pretty fucking stressed about that, too," Sy said.

Maddie lifted her chin. "More stressed than when the biological father you'd never met strolled into your life and decided to sweep you and your mom off your feet?"

"Way more stressed." Sy seemed to consider for a moment. "I have to say, that whole thing has been unsettling but not terrible."

"You're going to have to decide what to do with all that money." A pretty sweet problem to have, in the grand scheme of things.

"Not to be cheesy or anything, but Valentine's Day is coming. Maybe we could do that weekend in Boston after all? Or New York?" Sy gave her the sort of eager look she could definitely get used to.

"You know, when you said cheesy, that's not the direction I thought you were going," Maddie said.

"Ha ha."

"Seriously, though. I'd love that." And if Sy did actual cheese things with the money, she'd feel pretty good about that, too.

Sy grinned. "Confession, I've never gone away with a girlfriend before."

Maddie smacked her on the arm. "Get out. I haven't either."

Sy's expression turned serious once again. Maybe too serious. "Are you a hotel sex virgin?"

She pressed her lips together. "I didn't say that."

Sy roared with laughter. "Touché. Me, neither."

"I haven't done it in a fancy hotel, though. Hell, I'm not sure I can say I've even stayed in a fancy hotel." Depended on the definition of fancy.

"Okay, let's do it."

"Do what?"

"Fancy hotel sex. Fancy dinners. Fancy fancy. You and me."

It sounded fun. And yet, so did curling up on the couch with a pizza after an afternoon of fucking in her own bed. "Not too fancy, though. Too fancy makes me self-conscious. And I'm sure you can think of something legit you want to do with that much money."

"I've got some ideas. Several that include construction projects."

"Is that so?"

"Yeah. My house needs a deck for starters. But I also think Grumpy Old Goat deserves a shop of its own. And a café. Or at least a tasting room. Will Barrow Brothers take my money if I'm a paying customer?"

She resisted the urge to dive right into the details: what Sy had in mind, her timeline, if she'd already talked to Clover. Because as exciting as all that would be—for Clover and the town and the influx of cash to Barrow Brothers—it was the underlying meaning that mattered. Sy planned to stick around. Build a life here. Correction: continue building a life here. She'd already made a pretty good start and Maddie had been a part of it every step of the way. "I think that could be arranged. Let's set up a meeting, and I'll pencil you in."

Sy grinned. "Deal."

❖

Sy didn't waste time. She put herself on Maddie's work calendar for the following Tuesday. A legit meeting at Maddie's office, complete with the ideas she'd sketched out and run by Clover. She'd even worked up some opinions on materials.

After taking copious notes and starting several lists—including the need for a site survey and zoning permits—Maddie pressed her palms to the edge of the table and blew out a breath. "At the rate you're going, you're going to need more than half a million dollars."

She could agree, cite her plans to do the construction in stages and use some of the increased revenue to fund the later phases. Or she could shrug and have fun with it. She lifted a shoulder. "I figure if I play my cards right, I can move in with you, sell my house and cash in all that sweat equity."

Maddie folded her arms. "If anyone should be cashing in equity, it's me. I actually need the money."

She'd been joking, but Maddie's rebuttal snagged her attention. "Would you want to do that? I thought you loved your house."

"I do. And it's probably a little soon to talk moving in together." Maddie tipped her head. "But it's a conversation I'd be open to eventually. Your place is technically bigger than mine."

And between Maddie's expertise and her influx of cash, they could actually do the work she'd put off with the vague hope of being able to swing it at some point in the future. "I agree about it being too soon, but I'm open. To living together. Your house, my house. A whole different house we can make our own. Pretty much anything."

"Anything, huh?" Maddie's smile was sly.

"I mean, within reason." Though it was hard to imagine denying Maddie anything that would make her happy, even if it landed outside the realm of reasonable.

"Important distinction." Maddie nodded like she was filing away a legitimate line in the sand.

"I'm not budging on Henry, though. Kira is just going to have to deal."

Maddie laughed. "If you're part of the package, I think we can wear her down."

Kira might not love other felines, but the cat did love her. Even more than Henry did, ironically. "We'll have a talk. Assure her she can be the alpha. Of Henry at least."

"Oh, she already knows that." Maddie closed her laptop and stood. "Any other t's to cross or i's to dot?"

Since they were alone in the office, Sy stood as well, closer than would pass for professionally appropriate. "Just that I love you. And I can't wait to see what adventures await us."

Maddie unfolded her arms and planted her fists on her hips. "Those are things we already agree on, not things to be sorted."

Sy laughed at the gesture as much as Maddie's words. "Then I think we're good."

Maddie moved her hands from her own hips to Sy's. "Good."

They were. More than she'd bargained for when she took a rather random job in this tiny town. More than she'd dared to hope for even when she and Maddie started sleeping together. And she had this humming sensation in her whole body that told her they were just getting started. She threaded her arms through Maddie's, pulling their bodies even closer. She took a moment simply to bask in the feeling of Maddie against her, the scent of her perfume, and the look of mischief that suited her so perfectly. And then she kissed her, long and slow. "So, so good."

About the Author

Aurora Rey is a college dean by day and award-winning lesbian romance author the rest of the time, except when she's cooking, baking, riding the tractor, or pining for goats. She grew up in a small town in south Louisiana, daydreaming about New England. She keeps a special place in her heart for the South, especially the food and the ways women are raised to be strong, even if they're taught not to show it. After a brief dalliance with biochemistry, she completed both a BA and an MA in English.

She is the author of the Cape End Romance series and several standalone contemporary lesbian romance novels and novellas. She has been a finalist for the Lambda Literary, RITA®, and Golden Crown Literary Society awards but loves reader feedback the most. She lives in Ithaca, New York, with her dog and whatever wildlife has taken up residence in the pond.

Books Available from Bold Strokes Books

Hands of the Morri by Heather K O'Malley. Discovering she is a Lost Sister and growing acquainted with her new body, Asche learns how to be a warrior and commune with the Goddess the Hands serve, the Morri. (978-1-63679-465-5)

I Know About You by Erin Kaste. With her stalker inching closer to the truth, Cary Smith is forced to face the past she's tried desperately to forget. (978-1-63679-513-3)

Mate of Her Own by Elena Abbott. When Heather McKenna finally confronts the family who cursed her, her werewolf is shocked to discover her one true mate, and that's only the beginning. (978-1-63679-481-5)

Pumpkin Spice by Tagan Shepard. For Nicki, new love is making this pumpkin spice season sweeter than expected. (978-1-63679-388-7)

Rivals for Love by Ali Vali. Brooks Boseman's brother Curtis is getting married, and Brooks needs to be at the engagement party. Only she can't possibly go, not with Curtis set to marry the secret love of her youth, Fallon Goodwin. (978-1-63679-384-9)

Sweat Equity by Aurora Rey. When cheesemaker Sy Travino takes a job in rural Vermont and hires contractor Maddie Barrow to rehab a house she buys sight unseen, they both wind up with a lot more than they bargained for. (978-1-63679-487-7)

Taking the Plunge by Amanda Radley. When Regina Avery meets model Grace Holland—the most beautiful woman she's ever seen—she doesn't have a clue how to flirt, date, or hold on to a relationship. But Regina must take the plunge with Grace and hope she manages to swim. (978-1-63679-400-6)

We Met in a Bar by Claire Forsythe. Wealthy nightclub owner Erica turns undercover bartender on a mission to catch a thief where she meets no-strings, no-commitments Charlie, who couldn't be further from Erica's type. Right? (978-1-63679-521-8)

Western Blue by Suzie Clarke. Step back in time to this historic western filled with heroism, loyalty, friendship, and love. The odds are against this unlikely group—but never underestimate women who have nothing to lose. (978-1-63679-095-4)

Windswept by Patricia Evans. The windswept shores of the Scottish Highlands weave magic for two people convinced they'd never fall in love again. (978-1-63679-382-5)

An Independent Woman by Kit Meredith. Alex and Rebecca's attraction won't stop smoldering, despite their reluctance to act on it and incompatible poly relationship styles. (978-1-63679-553-9)

Cherish by Kris Bryant. Josie and Olivia cherish the time spent together, but when the summer ends and their temporary romance melts into the real deal, reality gets complicated. (978-1-63679-567-6)

Cold Case Heat by Mary P. Burns. Sydney Hansen receives a threat in a very cold murder case that sends her to the police for help where she finds more than justice with Detective Gale Sterling. (978-1-63679-374-0)

Proximity by Jordan Meadows. Joan really likes Ellie, but being alone with her could turn deadly unless she can keep her dangerous powers under control. (978-1-63679-476-1)

Sweet Spot by Kimberly Cooper Griffin. Pro surfer Shia Turning will have to take a chance if she wants to find the sweet spot. (978-1-63679-418-1)

The Haunting of Oak Springs by Crin Claxton. Ghosts and the past haunt the supernatural detective in a race to save the lesbians of Oak Springs farm. (978-1-63679-432-7)

Transitory by J.M. Redmann. The cops blow it off as a customer surprised by what was under the dress, but PI Micky Knight knows they're wrong—she either makes it her case or lets a murderer go free to kill again. (978-1-63679-251-4)

Unexpectedly Yours by Toni Logan. A private resort on a tropical island, a feisty old chief, and a kleptomaniac pet pig bring Suzanne and Allie together for unexpected love. (978-1-63679-160-9)

Bones of Boothbay Harbor by Michelle Larkin. Small-town police chief Frankie Stone and FBI Special Agent Eve Huxley must set aside their differences and combine their skills to find a killer after a burial site is discovered in Boothbay Harbor, Maine. (978-1-63679-267-5)

Crush by Ana Hartnett Reichardt. Josie Sanchez worked for years for the opportunity to create her own wine label, and nothing will stand in her way. Not even Mac, the owner's annoyingly beautiful niece Josie's forced to hire as her harvest intern. (978-1-63679-330-6)

Decadence by Ronica Black, Renee Roman, and Piper Jordan. You are cordially invited to Decadence, Las Vegas's most talked about invitation-only Masquerade Ball. Come for the entertainment and stay for the erotic indulgence. We guarantee it'll be a party that lives up to its name. (978-1-63679-361-0)

Gimmicks and Glamour by Lauren Melissa Ellzey. Ashly has learned to hide her Sight, but as she speeds toward high school graduation she must protect the classmates she claims to hate from an evil that no one else sees. (978-1-63679-401-3)

Heart of Stone by Sam Ledel. Princess Keeva Glantor meets Maeve, a gorgon forced to live alone thanks to a decades-old lie, and together the two women battle forces they formerly thought to be good in the hopes of leading lives they can finally call their own. (978-1-63679-407-5)

Murder at the Oasis by David S. Pederson. Palm trees, sunshine, and murder await Mason Adler and his friend Walter as they travel from Phoenix to Palm Springs for what was supposed to be a relaxing vacation but ends up being a trip of mystery and intrigue. (978-1-63679-416-7)

Peaches and Cream by Georgia Beers. Adley Purcell is living her dreams owning Get the Scoop ice cream shop until national dessert chain Sweet Heaven opens less than two blocks away and Adley has to compete with the far too heavenly Sabrina James. (978-1-63679-412-9)

The Only Fish in the Sea by Angie Williams. Will love overcome years of bitter rivalry for the daughters of two crab fishing families in this queer modern-day spin on Romeo and Juliet? (978-1-63679-444-0)

Wildflower by Cathleen Collins. When a plane crash leaves eleven-year-old Lily Andrews stranded in the vast wilderness of Arkansas, will she be able to overcome the odds and make it back to civilization and the one person who holds the key to her future? (978-1-63679-621-5)

Witch Finder by Sheri Lewis Wohl. Tamsin, the Keeper of the Book of Darkness, is in terrible danger, and as a Witch Finder, Morrigan must protect her and the secrets she guards even if it costs Morrigan her life. (978-1-63679-335-1)

A Second Chance at Life by Genevieve McCluer. Vampires Dinah and Rachel reconnect, but a string of vampire killings begin and evidence seems to be pointing at Dinah. They must prove her innocence while finding out if the two of them are still compatible after all these years. (978-1-63679-459-4)

Digging for Heaven by Jenna Jarvis. Litz lives for dragons. Kella lives to kill them. The last thing they expect is to find each other attractive. (978-1-63679-453-2)

Forever's Promise by Missouri Vaun. Wesley Holden migrated west disguised as a man for the hope of a better life and with no designs to take a wife, but Charlotte Rose has other ideas. (978-1-63679-221-7)

Here For You by D. Jackson Leigh. A horse trainer must make a difficult business decision that could save her father's ranch from foreclosure but destroy her chance to win the heart of a feisty barrel racer vying for a spot in the National Rodeo Finals. (978-1-63679-299-6)

I Do, I Don't by Joy Argento. Creator of the romance algorithm, Nicole Hart doesn't expect to be starring in her own reality TV dating show, and falling for the show's executive producer Annie Jackson could ruin everything. (978-1-63679-420-4)

It's All in the Details by Dena Blake. Makeup artist Lane Donnelly and wedding planner Helen Trent can't stand each other, but they must set aside their differences to ensure Darcy gets the wedding of her dreams, and make a few of their own dreams come true. (978-1-63679-430-3)

Marigold by Melissa Brayden. Marigold Lavender vows to take down Alexis Wakefield, the harsh food critic who blasts her younger sister's restaurant. If only she wasn't as sexy as she is mean. (978-1-63679-436-5)

The Town that Built Us by Jesse J. Thoma. When her father dies, Grace Cook returns to her hometown and tries to avoid Bonnie Whitlock, the woman who pulverized her heart, only to discover her father's estate has been left to them jointly. (978-1-63679-439-6)